BIRD IN A
CAGE

PREVIOUS MYSTERIES BY LEE MARTIN

Inherited Murder
The Day That Dusty Died
Hacker
The Mensa Murders
Deficit Ending
Hal's Own Murder Case
Death Warmed Over
Murder at the Blue Owl
A Conspiracy of Strangers
Too Sane a Murder

BIRD IN A CAGE

A DEB RALSTON MYSTERY

Lee Martin

ST. MARTIN'S PRESS ✠ NEW YORK

Library of Congress Cataloging-in-Publication Data

Martin, Lee.
  Bird in a cage / Lee Martin.
    p.   cm.
  ISBN 0-312-13028-7
  1. Ralston, Deb (Fictitious character)—Fiction.   2. Policewomen—
Texas—Fort Worth—Fiction.   3. Fort Worth (Tex.)—Fiction.
I. Title.
PS3563.A7249B57   1995
813'.54—dc20   95-14723
                                                                  CIP

First Edition: August 1995

10 9 8 7 6 5 4 3 2 1

This one is for all my friends who hang out on the CFS Bulletin Board on Prodigy. Hi, y'all!

Author's Note

All characters and incidents in this book are totally fictitious, as are the Bird Cage and the circus families mentioned.

Deb Ralston's situation and opinions do not necessarily reflect those of the author or her family. In fact I, not my husband, am the computer nut of the family; all of my offspring love computers also, though only one is still living with me and playing with my computer. The bishop did indeed ask my husband and me to take over the ward newsletter because we had a nice new computer, but we were delighted with the call.

Bird in a
Cage

Prologue
. . . .

West Berlin——1957

ON TELEVISION THE circus will be nothing. On television the circus will become sequential—a lion tamer here, a clown there, an acrobat after the station break.

But this was not television. This was the circus itself, a great, golden, glowing, glittering gestalt with all of its sights and smells and sounds assaulting the senses at once, and everything happening at once—a lion tamer in ring one surrounded by lions and tigers; fourteen clowns in ring two, climbing out of a half-size Volkswagen painted gaudy red and sprinkled with glitter, rushing about with fire-rescue nets and fire extinguishers that sprayed multicolored water; elephants in red and gold headpieces in ring three gravely sitting on stools reading newspapers as bears in green vests rode bicycles around them; and in the top of the tent, tightrope walkers above the lion tamer; gorgeous aerialists, the young woman in a yellow sequined leotard, the young man in a sequined parody of a tuxedo, above the clowns and the elephants and bears.

The crowd gasped as the man leaped into space, making a triple somersault in the air and catching the arms of the girl, who hung by her heels on the trapeze above the neighboring ring. They swung that way for a moment, his hands on her wrists, her hands on his wrists, before he sprang up to stand beside her, their eyes fixed on each other in unmistakable pride and tenderness. They bowed to the crowd, waved, threw kisses.

. . . . .

He poised there for a moment longer, keenly watching the empty trapeze swing back and forth. Then, as the trapeze swung in their direction, he fairly flew back to it, this time a straight leap with no somersaults.

She held on by her teeth to a cord and spun dizzyingly in the air forty feet up, her arms crossed in front of her, each hand on the opposite shoulder, her left knee making a perfect square with the toes of her left foot pressed to her right knee.

Then she leaped back onto the bar and swung back and forth, back and forth, back and forth, leaning backward and forward as she pumped, before leaping as he had done, only with a quadruple backward somersault, leaping toward him with her hands confidently reaching toward his.

He swung toward her, hanging by his knees, his back arched up as he reached out for her hands.

Their hands almost touched, not two inches separating her fingers from his.

And then the entire crowd was on its feet, screaming; nothing else happened in the ring, as even the performers turned in alarm at a sound that was not the usual sound of the crowd enjoying the circus.

And the girl catapulted down, down, down, past where a net should have been, down—

Still twisting in the air, never ceasing to try to find a way to land safely—

The clowns ran toward her, holding up a fireman's net that had been part of their act—

But she missed it, and landed hard, on her back.

$O n \varepsilon$
. . . .

It didn't work last time I tried it, either.

It was about fifteen years ago, when I was temporarily assigned to Ident. I'd been there only a couple of days, and was just starting to get interested in fingerprints when no less a person than the chief of police walked in and handed me the old Speed Graphic we were still using then—that's that huge box camera you see reporters carrying in the old black-and-white movies, the one that's so tough you can hit somebody in the head with it and turn around and go right on taking pictures. I was used to an Instamatic. That Speed Graphic had more numbers and meters on it than I had ever seen—things like f-stops and shutter speeds that I knew nothing whatever about. I looked at it and said feebly, "Me? That?"

"You. That." The chief turned around and walked away, leaving me staring aghast at a camera I very soon fell in love with, to the extent that when it was finally retired because the film packs for it had become prohibitively expensive and we were switching to color film anyway, I felt I'd lost an old friend—an elderly, unfashionably dressed one, perhaps, but still very dear. It took wonderful pictures, using a four-by-five negative you could enlarge to practically any size at all with no appreciable grain, and if you'd used only three pictures from a pack and needed them right then you could go to the darkroom, extract and develop those three sheets of film, and put the rest of the pack right back in the camera box to use next time.

. . . . .

Maybe someday I'd feel the same way about the computer my husband, Harry, had bought me three months ago, the computer that we'd hauled all the way from Salt Lake City, where he bought it, slightly used, back to Fort Worth, Texas, where it had been assembled.

So far I had figured out that you could play a mean game of solitaire on it without the risk I run when I play solitaire on my bed, namely that of discovering after losing ten games in a row that I'm sitting on two cards. And most important to me, it had a multimedia CD drive, which meant I could check CDs out of the library and play them without having to figure out where we were going to squeeze a CD player into our seriously overcrowded house. The house had become somewhat more crowded when Harry jammed into the one remaining semi-empty corner of our bedroom the computer desk he bought at Kmart, without which there would have been nowhere to put the new computer, let alone the cheap color printer he had bought me because, he explained ingenuously, he had an expensive monochrome printer, and if we did it this way we'd have access to both.

After maneuvering desk, chair, and computer, et cetera, into the corner, which was more work than it may sound like in view of the fact that he had to move the bed (queen size), his dresser, and my dresser to make room, he proceeded to call friends to help him fish the walls as he (probably illegally, but I'm not a building inspector) rewired both electricity and telephone to put outlets exactly where I—or rather, the computer—needed them. It was July, of course, and the attic is hot at the best of times. All the men emerged some time later, dirty, sweaty, and obviously pleased with themselves. I believe Harry likes to fish walls; it makes him feel like the mighty caveman hunter bringing home the biggest mastodon to Mrs. Caveman. When I told him that the next day, he laughed and didn't answer, which confirmed my opinion.

After he got all the equipment assembled and hooked up to his satisfaction, he warned me that unless I wanted to fry the entire sys-

. . . . .

tem, everything had to be unplugged and otherwise detached from the wall wiring in the case of thunderstorms, which are not uncommon in this part of Texas. He showed me how he had considerately arranged everything so that all I had to do to reach either the electric socket—yes, singular; a breaker strip was plugged into it, and all the computer paraphernalia was plugged into the breaker strip—and the telephone outlet into which the modem was plugged was to reach over all the computer paraphernalia. This was easy for him. He is about a foot taller than my five feet two inches. But all the same, I could reach it, if only barely, and I was grateful for the warning. Not that I was in love with the computer, but I like to feel that I am thrifty, and thrifty people don't fry a multi-thousand-dollar computer system no matter how cheaply they bought it used.

He then downloaded—I believe that is the correct term—my computerized grocery order form from his computer to mine, so that I could fill it out and fax it to the store and have the groceries delivered. Content that he had done his duty, he departed whistling to spend the rest of Saturday fishing with his friends, which was fine with me because it gave me time to clean up after the wall-fishing job, which had left Sheetrock dust all over the new desk, the new computer, et cetera, and the bedroom carpet.

But three months later I was still going out to the grocery store most of the time, and I still hadn't learned to do anything much on the computer except fax grocery lists and play solitaire and CDs. Harry had begun saying, at first plaintively and then more and more insistently, "That isn't what I bought you the computer for." What, I wondered, *did* he buy me the computer for, except to assuage his own conscience?

I should have expected it.

Somebody—it could have been Lori, but I really think it was Harry—snitched to the bishop.

Now that I had such an excellent computer, I wouldn't mind doing the ward newsletter, would I?

. . . . .

Mormons do not say no when the bishop tells them they wouldn't mind doing something.

So I went home, looked at the Microsoft Word the computer came with and the WordPerfect Harry had added to it, and said, "Me? That?" I didn't bother to say it feebly, as nobody was in earshot and if they were they probably wouldn't have been sympathetic anyway.

I really should have known better than to complain. There was no help for it. As I said, the phrase didn't work. I was going to have to learn to use the computer.

Then everybody started getting into the act. The following week Captain Millner dropped in to the Major Case office and said that since all any of us (us being the Major Case Squad) knew about computers was how to enter or call up reports from the department mainframe, and more and more cases seemed to involve computers, it sure would be nice to have at least one person in the squad who was really knowledgeable about the small ones. Now that I had a good computer of my own I was the ideal person. "So," he went on, "since you don't have anything pending right now"—that was quite true; I had put Julian Blythe in jail the day before on an unusually ingenious con game, which had taken approximately a quarter of a million dollars from elderly Tarrant County residents in about six weeks, and the case was now in the DA's hands; in the Major Case Unit officially it's one person, one case, and sometimes it really works that way—"I think tomorrow"—tomorrow was Thursday—"you should wind up everything you've got pending and plan to spend the next week working at home, learning all about personal computers."

Stop laughing. Of course I knew it was impossible. But that's one of the few problems about Captain Millner: he's sixty-three, and although he uses and appreciates such modern conveniences as microwave ovens, VCRs, and computers, he doesn't program them himself, so he has no idea how complicated even the simplest home computer is. I tried to tell him, and he said complacently, "Well, you can get started in a week, can't you?"

. . . . .

6

A *week?* I thought dismally. Even *beginning* to learn "all about computers" was likely to take ten years, particularly with my son around. When I said that to Harry, he pointed out that I have no son around during the day these days. Our nineteen-year-old, Hal, is on his mission, trying with a notable lack of success to convert the entire state of Nevada to a religion that forbids smoking, drinking, gambling, and even coffee and tea. Our four-year-old, Cameron, is in play school in the morning and day care in the afternoon, now that Harry and I are once again both working all day.

I was defeated. With my husband, my bishop, and my captain all ganged up against me, what could I say or do?

Thursday afternoon, after dutifully winding up everything I could, I told Captain Millner I was going over to the city computer system to set up an Internet account. I hoped he would yell about that; there has been recent publicity about Internet, "flaming," and drive crashes. No such luck.

I got an Internet account, in my name, and billed it to the police department. Now if I could just figure out how to use it—oh well, if I couldn't Harry would love to, using my E-mail address.

Then I told Captain Millner I had to get some computer manuals. These are not cheap. I hoped he'd say the department couldn't afford them. Again, no such luck. He asked how much they would cost, gave me two hundred dollars, and told me to bring him the receipts and tell him if I needed more.

So I spent all day Friday buying computer manuals and mouching around computer stores asking stupid questions. I spent all day Saturday cleaning up the house, so I could get to the computer without feeling guilty. I spent all day Sunday going to church, feeding self and family breakfast and lunch, and lying in bed self-righteously reading my scriptures and my Sunday school lesson for next week, except of course for the time spent checking on and playing with my four-year-old, until it was time for dinner, which we were having at a daughter's house. Need I add that I was still in a snit at Captain Millner?

. . . . .

Then I spent all day Monday reading computer manuals, gingerly pushing keys, and calling help lines. Most of them were 800 numbers. Many of them were not. Harry was going to scream bloody murder when he saw the long-distance bill. On second thought, no he wasn't. I was going to dump it on Captain Millner's desk. After all, this was his idea.

I spent all day Tuesday reading computer manuals and pushing keys a little less gingerly. I would learn how to word process. I would learn how to make notices. I would even get a copy of that book from Elsevier that has the BASIC program in it for figuring out the trajectory of blood spatters, so I could start using it even if figuring blood trajectories *was* actually Irene Loukas's job.

But none of that was going to make me a hacker, and clearly a hacker was what Captain Millner wanted. I dashed out to the library to check out books and wound up spending Tuesday night after everybody was in bed except Harry, who was in the living room shooting down Martians, in bed reading paperback historical novels with buxom damsels (usually with red hair) and gorgeous male hunks on the cover, which was fun but got me nowhere.

Wednesday morning I pushed the keys that I thought would get me out of Windows into DOS, so I could load my blood-spatter program. (As it comes on paper, not on disk, load in this case meant type it in. I am not the world's most accurate typist. Computers do *exactly* what you tell them to, whether or not that's what you mean.) Once into DOS I started pushing buttons and keys. The computer froze and sneered at me. I turned it off and right back on and it went right on sneering at me. I tried again. This time, it forgot it had a mouse.

Defeated, I went to the reference books on DOS and found out that if you turn off the computer because it has frozen and is sneering at you, you have to wait at least thirty seconds to turn it back on; otherwise sometimes it doesn't notice you turned it off. The book did not tell me it also forgets it has a mouse, but I had figured that out for myself.

. . . . .

I turned it off, went and made myself a cup of Pero—that's a German coffee substitute made of wheat and rye and preferred by such Mormons as do not like Postum, of whom I am one—and went and turned the computer back on. It made triumphant music at me and gave me my normal Windows screen. I went back into DOS, tried to start typing in my blood-spatter trajectory program, and it froze and sneered at me again.

The heck with that. I'd spent about fourteen hours a day the last two days glued to this screen, and I was only paid for eight hours a day. I owed myself some free time. And besides that it was my anniversary and Harry would probably remember it somewhat past the last minute (though he might do a little better this time because we'd had a large ' family celebration Sunday evening, at our oldest daughter's house, and even Harry can't forget that fast) and expect me to be ready to go out to dinner the moment he remembered, so I'd better go bathe and wash my hair and put on something decent instead of the grungies I'd worn to argue with the computer.

"Are you sure we can afford this?" I asked Harry, staring uneasily at the menu the waiter had given me, which had discreetly omitted the right-hand line. I tried to look at Harry's menu, which of course did include the right-hand line, but he moved it out of my reach.

"It isn't our twenty-fifth anniversary every day," he pointed out. "We can afford it. Quit worrying."

Never mind how it could be our twenty-fifth anniversary when we have children older than twenty-five. These things relate to the ages children are at adoption. I have a friend who can pull out a birth certificate proving that she and her husband entirely legitimately co-produced a child in Galveston, Texas, at a time when both of them were in fact married to other people and living in other towns and had not even met one another yet.

Of course I did not quit worrying, except to wonder where I was going to find room to put whatever meal I wound up ordering. The

. . . . .

waiter had already brought us huge baskets of fresh hot breads and a slab of cheese that looked to weigh about ten pounds, and Harry and I were both nibbling on bread and cheese.

I finally ordered steak and lobster, reasoning that I always have room for lobster and if necessary I could take the steak home and eat it tomorrow for lunch. That might even make arguing with a computer at least acceptable if not pleasant.

The salad had greens in it I'd never even seen and so of course couldn't identify. The house dressing was just tart enough, just spicy enough. *I do like interesting food,* I first thought, and then said to Harry, who replied, "I've noticed that." I wasn't sure I liked his tone of voice, which was amused and—what?

Lobster and melted butter . . . I was glad I wasn't going to have my cholesterol checked in the next day or two.

A huge potato, so flaky it must have been baked on a bed of rock salt.

By now I was eating almost absentmindedly, watching the floor show, which in fact was more like a rafters show. A woman in glittering yellow tights studded with yellow sequins and yellow-dyed ostrich feathers, complete with a huge yellow bird tail made mostly of more yellow-dyed ostrich feathers and a helmet of the feathers sleeked down on her head, had climbed a purple velvet rope ladder, entered a gold (presumably imitation gold, considering the weight and value of real gold) cage high above the diners' heads, closed the door behind her, and had parked herself on a perch inside the birdcage. As I watched, she did something that caused the birdcage, perch, and the rest of the paraphernalia, to move out into the center of the room, and began swinging herself, and the entire cage, back and forth. Meanwhile, on the stage with the small orchestra, a man had begun to sing through a megaphone, in a Tiny Tim–style falsetto voice, "I'm Only a Bird in a Gilded Cage."

"How did you find out about this place?" I asked Harry. Normally fish-and-chips is his idea of haute cuisine.

"We came here on a company meeting a couple of months ago," he answered, "and I decided then it would be a good place to bring you for our anniversary."

"It's terrific," I said, and he patted my hand and we both returned our attention to the show.

The "bird" strutted, danced, and stood on her hands in the cage, which by now was swinging so far it covered half the enormous and well-filled dining room. I was so entranced I hardly noticed the waiter flambéing my cherries jubilee.

And then, quite suddenly, quite without warning, people were screaming, trying to run, running into each other and knocking each other over, as the left cable supporting the entire cage apparatus snapped about twelve feet from the cage; the cage first canted over at a crazy angle and then pulled entirely free from the right rope; the acrobat, clearly trying to twist herself around so that she could land on her feet, was thrown clear of the cage; and cage, trapeze, and acrobat tumbled forty feet onto the concrete floor. Before I even knew I was going to, and while the cage was still falling, I had snatched up my purse, stuck my hand in it, and begun to stand, knocking over my chair in the process. This rout had to be stopped fast, or people were going to be trampled to death.

The cage, which to my surprise was flexible, came to rest, draped partly across the table beside ours where the acrobat had fallen and partly across our own table—I barely avoided having it land on me by stepping hastily back a couple of feet, and Harry, standing, knocked that part of it onto the floor.

By this time I had snatched out the London police whistle I keep in my purse and blown three shrill, loud blasts on it.

Near-silence fell over the room, as people stopped in their tracks looking around, but then the rush for exits resumed only slightly more slowly. In my opinion most of the people running hadn't the slightest idea why they were running, as any person with any sense whatever could have seen there was no further reason to run. But in a crisis—

. . . . .

and outside of one, for that matter—people often have a herd mentality. *If three or four people are running,* they seem to nonreason, *maybe I should run too.*) Several people had already been shoved down in the crowd pushing toward the exits, and one of them was screaming. And all this happened in far less time than it takes to tell it.

I blew my whistle again. "I'm a police officer!" I shouted. "Please return to your seats." But my voice was almost lost in the vastness of the room.

The singer, dashing through the space cleared in the middle of the room by people rushing to the exits, appeared suddenly beside me and put his megaphone in my hand.

"I'm a police officer!" I shouted through it. "The danger is over. Please return to your seats. Ambulances are en route"—I could say that confidently because I had noticed someone on the stage grabbing a telephone and punching only three numbers into it, three numbers that had to be 911—"and there is no more need for panic. Please return to your seats. You'll be able to leave quite soon, but please return to your seats now."

As I spoke, Harry was elbowing his way through the crowd to stand at the main exit door and send back inside everyone attempting to leave, and several obviously levelheaded people I didn't know were blocking the other exits. Almost certainly this was an accident, but all the same we'd need names and addresses of all witnesses. For someone who is not himself a cop, Harry has long since developed good police instincts, and at a time like this—not that there had ever before been a moment in our lives exactly like this—he always knows what to do to back me up.

With most of the crowd returning to their seats reluctantly or otherwise, I was finally able to turn my attention to the acrobat.

She was dead.

So, apparently, were two of the four diners who had been seated at the table the cage had landed on; at least if they weren't dead yet they were clearly beyond any help I could give them. Judging from their

. . . . .

12

suits and mobile phones, I expected they were businessmen. Their dinner companions, looking dazed and horrified, had obediently re-seated themselves after the table flipped away from them to lie on its side with its feet toward them. "I don't know anything about it," one of them gabbled at me.

"Stay here," I told her, and took off.

There were other injuries at tables nearby, mostly caused by panic, though a few people had been hit by flying ice or cutlery; scattered around the room were at least six people who had fallen or been shoved to the floor, and possibly trampled, during the panic. *Triage,* I reminded myself. I went first to the person who was screaming and seemed most seriously injured, and by the time I had him halfway stabilized the building was swarming with EMTs and uniformed police officers, who took over security and first aid.

I stood in the middle of the room and thought.

Then I returned to the table where the two dead businessmen, and their dates, had been enjoying the evening. There seemed to be more blood in the vicinity of the table than I remembered, but I probably remembered wrong. Despite being a cop, I am as susceptible to shock as the next person. "Rainbow Escort Service?" I inquired, fairly sure I recognized at least one of the damsels, the one who had so loudly proclaimed her ignorance.

"Yeah. But we're legit, you know?" she added hastily. "Just—decoration, you know?"

Which was probably, though not certainly, true. "You know either of them?" I asked, gesturing toward the dead men. "I mean, really know them?"

Both girls—I couldn't call them women; they looked to me like unfledged chicks, which come to think of it was an unpleasant comparison at this time—shook their heads hastily. "I mean we know their names," the apparent spokeswoman added. "But—you know. They were just here for a couple of days. They didn't want to be lonesome. That's all."

. . . . .

Whether that was all or not, it was beyond possibility that anybody had deliberately stationed the two men at this table and thrown an acrobat and a birdcage at them. These women were witnesses, no more. "I'll get your names later," I said. "Why don't you move on over to my table? At least it'll be more pleasant than sitting here."

Not much more pleasant, to be sure, as my table was within sight of the bodies, but maybe a little better, I thought, seeing them seated.

What to do next? I revolved slowly and looked about, and then headed back toward the resting place of the cage.

Although officers were now visibly on the scene, the situation to my mind remained extremely risky. It wouldn't take much to spook these people all over again, sending them stampeding once more toward the exits. The building had originally been a large warehouse, before being remodeled into Fort Worth's most popular new restaurant-nightclub combination. It would, I estimated, easily seat eight hundred, and right now it wasn't far short of full. The double-wide main entry-exit doors had been flung back against the wall of the lobby in the position they presumably occupied all evening; the requisite number of fire doors were lit with the red EXIT sign. But those were far from sufficient for eight hundred terrified people to rush through.

The fact remained, however, that the only danger now was from people stampeding like wild horses, not even knowing quite what spooked them. The cage would move no farther; its bars, reaching from our table to the fatal one, were draped over one body, which lay partially across the table that had been flung over on its side. About six feet of the twelve-strand nylon cable, now bereft of its purple velvet jacket, which had remained in the rafters with the other end of the cable, had fallen across scattered plates, hunks of cheese and bread, salad and steak and lobster. A bottle of champagne had been thrown twenty feet, with its ice bucket about midway between it and the table and the ice flung along its entire route. The bottle must have narrowly

· · · · ·

14

missed hitting me as it flew through the air, but I had absolutely no memory of seeing it go by.

If I could correctly piece together what I saw—all right. I am trained to remember details. So remember already.

When the fall started the trapeze had been just past the top of its swing, had just started back down. The acrobat had been standing upright on the trapeze, which was in the middle of the cage, strutting in an exaggerated hips-forward, back-leaning-back prance with her hands on the back of her hips. The first jerk when the cable broke had catapulted her off the bar and she fell head-downward right through the bars, which spread to the size of her body.

Ever since experiments involving things dropped off, I believe, the Leaning Tower of Pisa, it has been known that no matter what they weigh, in our gravity objects in a vacuum fall at the same speed—thirty-six feet per second, about fifty miles an hour, which is too high a speed with which to hit a concrete floor.

But this wasn't a vacuum. The cage, actually made of cloth-of-gold, had acted somewhat as a parachute.

So the athlete, unattached to the parachute, came down first, landing feetfirst on the table and knocking it over. One side of the table hit the floor and instantly bounced back up, catapulting her back up and swinging her around into another position, so that her head and the head of one of the men came into violent contact. She fell from there to the floor of the restaurant, which was concrete with sawdust, in keeping with its circus theme, scattered over it.

Some of this I had seen; some of it I was mentally reconstructing as I looked at the woman's body. I could easily see, on both her head and the first man's head, evidence of the collision. As far as I could see without moving bodies, further injury to the acrobat included both legs broken below the knee (I could tell from the way they were bending) and a compound fracture of the right arm; splintered bones were protruding from the flesh.

· · · · ·

On the first man, the only visible injury was obvious severe skull damage. He was sprawled on his back, still entangled with his chair, which also was sprawled on its back.

That explained the deaths of the acrobat and the first businessman. But how had the second man died?

On closer examination, I had seen that the cage was not intended to bear any weight. The trapeze was in it, but not attached to it except where its cables were threaded through the top. I could only assume those small areas of contact were enough to make the cage swing as the trapeze swung. The cage bars were made of cloth-of-gold sewn into a tube and stuffed with fleece; I could tell that because one of them had burst along the seam and the stuffing was protruding. They were attached at the top to a gold-metallic ring, which in turn was attached to a purple velvet-jacketed secondary cable that came down between the main cables and held nothing but the weight of the cloth cage, which retained its birdcage shape only because of two light wooden hoops sewn inside, one at that point of the top where the bars, gathered at the top and gradually spreading out, finally reached full circle, and one at the bottom to keep the floor of the cage stretched out. That cable had snapped when the main one did. The floor of the cage, also of cloth-of-gold, was two-ply, lightly quilted together. Both hoops had splintered when they struck the floor, and the birdcage shape was no longer apparent.

I could see, now, the cause of the second man's death, the man who was lying partly under the cage: one splintered portion of the wooden hoop, released suddenly by the breakage from the circular shape it had been forced into, had speared him in the groin at the level of the femoral artery and then, perhaps as the springy wood continued to react to the release of the circle, had yanked itself back out. He'd bled to death, probably while I, assuming he was already dead, had been off checking the man who had been trampled. *But I couldn't have done anything anyway,* I assured myself uneasily. *It takes only about five minutes, if that, to bleed to death from a severed femoral artery.*

I went into the kitchen, then, to wash my hands and to get as much of the blood as I could off my brand-new dress. I knew better than to try to get into the women's rest room; the line was twenty feet long *outside* the rest-room door. When I went back to our table, Harry, who had been relieved of guard duty and seemed somewhat underwhelmed at having been joined by two employees of Rainbow Escort Service, looked gloomily at me and said, "Shit."

That was as good a comment as any. I love my job, but I do wish I could escape murder and mayhem for a year or two at least. That's not what the Major Case Squad is supposed to deal with.

I sat down, introduced myself, and asked the first Rainbow Escort her name. "Jeannette Dunning," she said, and spelled Jeannette for me. Once again she added hastily, "But we don't know anything."

"I'll try just to ask things you do know," I said. "Can you tell me, from your point of view, what happened?"

She'd seen less than I saw.

The other escort's name was Bobbie Crow, and Bobbie was short for Barbara, not Roberta. She also had seen less than I had seen. She added wistfully, "That guy I was with, his name is Jack Putnam and he's real nice. You think he's gonna make it? I saw he had that big ol' piece of wood stuck in his leg and I pulled it out to help him breathe."

"To help him *breathe?*" I repeated, somewhat puzzled as to what a piece of wood stuck in somebody's leg had to do with his breathing.

"Yeah, he fell over hard on his back, you know, when that girl kicked him—"

"Was he sitting or standing at that time?" I interrupted.

"Oh, he was standing. He started standing up, I guess he was trying to get out of the way, and then the girl kicked him, you know, when she was falling down, and then he fell down on his back real hard. And then that cage thingie fell down, you know, and that wood thingie broke and stuck in his leg and then I saw he was having trouble breathing so I pulled the wood out."

"When did you do that?"

"Oh, right after it happened. I saw that big ol' piece of wood stuck in his leg—pulled it right out. It seemed like he was having trouble breathing and the wood must've been in the way. He started bleeding like crazy soon's I pulled it out, but he stopped bleeding just before you got to our table the first time. If he stopped bleeding he's going to be okay, right?"

"Stay here," I said, and moved back toward the death zone, noticing as I did so that panic still hung on the air almost palpably.

I looked down at that body. This time I imagined the scenario Bobbie had described. He had started to stand, to dodge the falling acrobat and cage. But the acrobat's foot had struck him before he had time to run, and he'd fallen on his back hard, the fall temporarily knocking the wind out of him. The cage landed partially atop him, and the hoop splintered when it struck the table. The broken hoop end jammed into his groin—severed and blocked the femoral artery (and I was sure it was an artery, not a vein, from the distance the blood had spurted). Bobbie helpfully pulled out the wood, whereupon the bleeding previously semicontrolled by the blocked artery began—but not for long.

But a severed femoral artery is going to be fatal anyway, unlike a severed carotid artery, which might let the person live as long as eight to ten minutes, maybe long enough to get help. Bobbie whatever-her-name-was had been stupid, but she hadn't caused anything that wouldn't have happened anyway.

A camera strobe went off and I looked around, startled and angry, wondering who had let the press in. But it wasn't the press. It was Irene Loukas, head of the Identification and Crime Scene Unit. She works days; she had to have been at home when this happened. I had no idea whether Dispatch had called her or whether she had heard the news on her scanner and called Dispatch to say she was en route. But I should have known she wouldn't miss the chance to have a look at anything this odd.

"What happened?" she asked me, very quietly, cognizant of many listeners nearby who, though they might have seen the same thing I saw, would have been unlikely to have seen them in the same way.

I told her.

"Accident?" she asked then.

"I don't know how it could have been," I said, only now voicing what must have been in my head from the start. "But I don't know how it couldn't have been, either."

The two of us scrambled through cage debris, food litter, and fallen chairs to where the end of the cable lay. We examined it together. Irene photographed it.

We'd have to check the other end of the cable, the one almost invisible in the beamed ceiling. And we would have to send it to the lab for official analysis. But we'd seen enough. We knew, now.

I went to find the manager. Irene went to be sure Dispatch had telephoned Captain Millner. He likes crazy stuff as much as she does.

". . . Is *impossible*," Jan—pronounced *Yahn*—Pender was saying vigorously. He was a small, slender man with graying hair, very dark eyes, and a pronounced Eastern European accent overlaid with Texanisms. "It had to have been an accident—there is no possibility—"

"Who is it that arranges all the cables and stuff?" I asked. We were standing in the kitchen, where a disgruntled cleaning crew was putting away food that would normally have been cooked and served as the evening progressed.

"The fly work," Pender said, almost absently. "That's Arlo Gluck. But if you think Arlo—"

"I think I want to talk with Arlo," I said. "That's all I'm saying. I want to talk with him. That's all."

"For now," he said gloomily. "For now. That's all for now. But later—"

"We'll take care of later when we get to it," I said. "For now, I just want to talk with Arlo."

Arlo was summoned. Arlo arrived, a slim young man in sequin-spangled white leotard and tights, red-eyed as I would have expected. "I'm Detective Ralston with the Fort Worth Police Department," I told him. "Could you tell me how to get up to that platform?"

"Just climb the ladder," he said dully.

"And can I get what's left of the trapeze and cage ropes back to the platform?"

"Just pull the ropes."

"Which ropes?"

After a couple of fruitless minutes spent trying to explain to me what ropes he meant, he said, "I'd better go up and show you."

About ten minutes later, Irene, Arlo, and I were standing—extremely uneasily, at least as far as I was concerned; in fact, to be honest, I could feel myself shaking and was afraid I was going to throw up—on a small platform forty feet above the concrete floor. Arlo manipulated ropes and brought what was left of the trapeze assembly back to us.

It was Irene who clambered out far enough to catch the loose purple velvet dangling from the shorter trapeze rope and pull on it until she had brought the end of the rope itself into grasp. Then, rather than try to push the velvet up the rope like pushing cloth around an elastic waistband one is trying to install, she simply severed the seam around the end of the rope and pulled the rope end through.

We both looked at it.

Not to our amazement, we saw the same thing we had seen on the ground.

Two strands of rope end were very badly frayed and ripped.

Twelve strands of rope end were cut clean.

It was murder.

I held the cable while Irene photographed it, and then Irene, leaning at a much more precarious angle than I felt comfortable even watching much less doing, severed the rope a foot above the original cut.

. . . . .

On the ground, on the way back to the kitchen where I had, at least for now, set up command headquarters, I finally thought to ask, "What was her name?"

"Julia Gluck," Arlo said dully. "She was my wife."

. . . . .

Two
. . . .

CAPTAIN MILLNER WAS in the kitchen by the time I got back in there. I could have anticipated his words—in fact I *had* anticipated his words—and he said exactly what I expected. At least, that was the second thing he said. The first thing he said was, "I got here just about the time you and Irene turned into mountain climbers. What have you got?"

"Murder," I said succinctly, after glancing around to be certain Arlo Gluck was out of earshot. If he hadn't figured that out yet, I'd just as soon he not figure it out for a little while longer.

"You're on it," Millner said, which as I have mentioned was no surprise to me.

"Okay," I said. I did not argue. I did not say, "What about the computer?"

He probably thought I was about to, though, because he added, "You can get back to the computers later. And I've got patrol officers taking names and addresses and letting people go. So you don't have to do that."

He turned and strode back to the dining area, leaving Mr. Gluck and me effectively alone in the kitchen. Not really alone—people all around us were cleaning and putting things away, big shiny copper bowls and steel pans and skillets that hung from hooks, wooden and metal spoons, ladles with bowls that could hold a pint—but effectively alone, because the kitchen crew flowed around us with as little obvi-

. . . . .
22

ous interest as fish in a stream might have in a swimmer.

I turned my attention back to Mr. Gluck, who was standing in a doorway looking lost. He seemed so young, I thought, glancing at him. His black hair was tousled; his dark eyes looked shocked, hurt, bewildered; his very fair skin looked bruised under the eyes, where he had been rubbing it. I felt momentarily ashamed of myself: I should have found out who the woman was, who the man was, before I started asking questions and going—as Captain Millner put it— mountain climbing. But that feeling was only momentary, for I reminded myself that he'd have had to take us up on the platform whoever he was, whoever she was, because there was no one else who could.

I went back to the doorway to join him. "I'm so sorry about your wife," I told him.

He nodded. "So am I," he said dully. "It—happens. Things like this. My dad, he fell from a trapeze when he was forty. Didn't kill him. But he sure wished he was dead, there for a long time."

"Then what happened?" I found myself asking.

"Then he took all the pain pills that was in the bottle, the day my mom refilled the prescription. So then he was dead." He turned away from me long enough to get a stained earthenware mug with *Arlo* painted on it in red script, to walk toward the huge stainless steel percolator and get a mug of coffee. Methodically, as if it could take away the pain, he poured three spoons of sugar into it, opened one of the massive stainless steel refrigerators and took out a half-pint of milk, and added some of it to the coffee. He returned the milk to the refrigerator shelf beside a forty-pound bag of carrots. Then, holding the mug in both hands, he turned back toward me. "But we're all dying, these days. That's what's wrong. We're all dying."

I waited as he took a gulp of coffee. Clearly, he wasn't through talking.

And I was right, because after a moment he went on. "The big circus families, I mean. It's like—you know how old circuses are?

· · · · ·

23

You know how far they go back?" he asked, his words rather more passionate than his tone, as though he had said this same thing so many times the audible passion had burned off through repetition. "Thousands of years. Thousands of years. The Romans—their bread and circuses—we think of lions that ate Christians, and gladiators killing each other for the emperors' pleasure, but they had real circuses, too. Acrobats. Clown acts. Animal trainers. And in the Middle Ages—carts traveling from village to village. Not whole circuses, then, nobody could afford to put a company together and feed it, but single acts going through villages. Maybe a dancing bear, maybe a tightrope walker, a juggler or two, that kind of thing. Two hundred years ago, that's when circuses really got going, what we think of as circuses, that is. And—two hundred years ago there were Saranas and Glucks in those circuses. Before that, I don't know, but my guess is before that we—they—still were acrobats. My guess is there were Saranas and Glucks performing in front of Julius Caesar. Well, Saranas anyway, maybe not Glucks; we'd have been in the lands Caesar couldn't conquer. The lost eagles, you know."

I nodded as if I knew what he was talking about. Actually I hadn't the slightest idea.

"So maybe we'd have been performing for Germanic chieftains, maybe when they were celebrating chewing up a legion." (That, I supposed, must be how the lost eagles he was talking about got lost—I did remember that legions had standards with gold eagles on them.) "But we're all interbred anyway, the circus families. Julia, she was a Sarana before I married her. The Soaring Saranas and the Gliding Glucks, well, we aren't as famous as the Flying Wallendas, sure, but even so—two hundred years. Two hundred years of Saranas and Glucks. Two hundred years my people and hers have been flying through the air. Flying, we call it, you know, when somebody leaps from one trapeze to another, when one person is caught by another in midair. And—it's dying now. Two hundred years, maybe two thousand years, and it's dying. The circuses combine and combine and

. . . . .

combine and every time they combine they really get smaller, because there's only one circus where there used to be two, or eight, or twelve. And after they combine they only need one wild animal trainer, one tightrope act, one acrobatic act, and—where is everybody supposed to go? What do you do, when all that your family has done for that long is going or gone? Some of us have moved to other lines of work—but who wants to do that? Any of us, we'd be just another whatever, just another mail carrier, just another grocer, but—in this, we're tops. We take pride in what we're doing. And—sure, people get hurt, people get killed even sometimes, but—you just accept it as part of the risk.

"So—if you can't find a circus anymore—you go where you can go. Maybe you go to Las Vegas and work in that nightclub hotel casino place, Circus Circus. Maybe you try to put together a little traveling carny of your own, hit the small towns real circuses don't go to now, travel with the fair midways, but—that's a heck of a way to make a living." He half sobbed, half laughed, got in somebody's way long enough to grab a paper towel and wipe his face with it.

Then he went on, "I remember one time, I went to look at one of those little shows, they'd invited Julia and me to travel with them, and—they had this bear act. Bears riding bicycles. Bears reading newspapers. And it looked okay till you looked close. Then you saw the bears were so scared they were pooping and sitting in the poop and getting it all over their fur. Bears don't *do* that. They just don't. Somebody had brutalized those bears. So—Julia and I—we decided that wasn't for us. But what was? What was anybody—any of us—going to do? Maybe you put together something, you hit the small-town high schools. We tried that for a while, on our own. But you can't make a living that way."

He sobbed out loud for a couple of minutes, as I remembered the time a ballet troupe came to our   school. From the seats in the auditorium, they looked gorgeou   ent backstage after the show, to ask for autographs. The lead danc   , who from where I was sitting had

· · · ·

25

looked like the most knockout blonde I ever saw, whose costume had glittered with sequins, seen up close had brassy hair with dark brown roots, had incredibly coarse pores that had been filled up with grease-paint that didn't conceal them, had a mouthful of teeth that were rotten from untreated tooth decay and black along the gum line, had a dingy costume from which whole strings of sequins hung loose, coming unsewn.

No, you wouldn't want to try to make a living taking the circus to the small-town high schools, I thought. Fifty dollars honorarium per assembly if you were lucky, and you might not get two assemblies a week.

He threw his paper towel in the general direction of the trash can, snatched another, and looked back at me. "So we took this. Pender offered it, we took it. It wasn't what we wanted. But it was something. It was better than nothing. It paid the bills; Pender—he's got a lot of faults, but he's not cheap. It kept at least one of us performing. It wasn't what we wanted, but it was what we could get. Right now—this week, when the circus is in town—times like this are the worst. You don't know whether to go, and feel so homesick you could die, or not go, and feel like you've turned your back on the real world. Julia—she'd been fretting about that. Whether to go to the circus or not go. Not just the show. I mean visit. Friends, relatives. I don't know. I think—she—I think we would have gone. And the way she was feeling, fretting, if she had fallen I could have sort of understood it, but not—not something like this. I check those ropes all the time. None of them were frayed—I don't understand how this could—"

He stopped.

His voice had sounded emotionless the whole time, despite the impassioned nature of his words, but I was guessing shock rather than complicity. In fact, although Irene and I had stood on that dizzying midair platform and hauled the rope in right beside him, right past him, I doubt he had ever realized exactly what we were doing except

· · · · ·

that after a fatal accident people always want to—or have to—take pictures and look at things.

I turned and glanced at Irene, who was standing a few feet away from me with the cut rope end, now in a labeled plastic evidence bag, still in her hand. I didn't say anything; Gluck was sobbing again, and I wanted to give him time. After a moment, Irene said, "Deb, initial this. I've still got work to do out front."

I added my initials beside hers on the *Collected by* line, and she turned and went back into the dining area.

"Mr. Gluck," I began.

He shook his head. "Arlo. That's my proper name. Arlo. Not Mr. Gluck."

"Arlo, then," I said. "As I said earlier, I'm Detective Deb Ralston, with the Fort Worth Police Department."

"I figured that," he said. "I mean, that you were a cop. Not your name. But—when Dad fell, there were cops all over the place for a couple of days. Kept trying to say he hadn't fallen by accident. But he had. And he wasn't drunk or anything like that—you don't drink and get on a trapeze, not unless you're a heck of a lot crazier than anybody in my family is, or her family either for that matter. He just—lost his footing for a split second. Lost his footing and fell."

"Didn't he have a safety net?" I asked.

Arlo shook his head again. "We don't use safety nets. Well, when we're training, when we're developing new routines, of course, because you can work it out on paper all you want to but you never know quite how it works, even *whether* it works, until you've tried it out a few times in the air. Then you use a safety net, of course, and even a mechanical—that's a safety rope that somebody on the ground controls—because if you thought it would work and it doesn't work all of a sudden you're falling—" He stopped, his face grim. "Falling like Julia did," he said then, his voice tremulous. He took a deep breath and went on. "If you have a safety net and hit right you're fine, and that's the first thing we learn, all of us, how to hit right. But no matter how much you know, if you fall wrong sometimes you can't manage to hit right, and if you have a safety net and hit wrong you might as well not have one. It takes a lot of presence of mind, midair contortions, to hit right. You might as well use that presence of mind to keep from falling to start with. So I don't think nets are worth using; they can make you feel secure when you're not secure, make you feel like it's okay to fall, and it's never okay to fall. Not to me, anyway, or my family, or her family. I know some people, even some other flyers, don't agree with me, but that's just how I feel. Oh, of course a few places the law says you have to have safety nets to perform, so of course you do there. But a routine you already know, where the law doesn't say you have to—it's a matter of pride, you see. Other people use safety nets. But the Wallendas don't use safety nets. The Saranas don't use safety nets. We—the Glucks—don't use safety nets."

I barely heard the end of his sentence, because near my ear somebody—actually several somebodies—had begun clashing pots and pans together with a mighty clamor. "Is there somewhere quieter than this, maybe a private place, where we can talk?"

He shrugged. "Yeah. I guess."

The private place turned out to be a small anteroom with a couple of chairs; a counter the right height for a seated person, with cosmetics, cold cream, and cleansing tissue on it; a sink; a lot of lights. Street clothes, men's and women's, were hanging on a rack behind the door. "It's Julia's dressing room," he said, and sat down on one of the chairs, the coffee he set on the counter beside him sloshing wildly over the edge of the mug. "It's Julia's dressing room," he repeated, and then he started to cry again. This time he didn't even try to stop for a while.

I shoved the tissue box toward him and waited for what must have been five minutes, before he blew his nose, wiped his eyes, and said, "Okay. I'm okay now."

Of course he wasn't. Of course he wasn't going to be. Not soon, anyway.

"What do you think happened?" I asked him.

"I know damn well what happened," he said, and burst into tears again.

After a while he said, "What you're saying—I heard what you told that other guy—it didn't happen. It *couldn't* happen. Not murder. Not Julia. So—what did happen? We were—she was—we were going to have a baby. We want—wanted—that baby. Both of us. So Julia was pregnant. About seven weeks. And—sure, she wasn't showing yet, and we hadn't told anybody yet, but even five extra pounds in the wrong place can throw you off balance, something that ticky. It's your center of balance, you see. If your center of balance changes any at all—I told her—she should have already stopped performing. But she said she felt just fine, and a lot of women perform when they're pregnant, heck, my mother was flying until she was five months gone with me, so as far as I could see there was no reason—until *she* felt off balance—"

"Arlo," I asked, "how could changes in Julia's balance take down the entire cage assembly?"

"I don't know," he said, "but—what else could it have been? And—I don't know, maybe I should have leaned on her a little harder about stopping performing, but I figured she ought to know whether her balance felt right or not."

"How long had you and Julia been married?" I asked.

"Eight years."

That was a little bit of a surprise; they both looked so young.

He half chuckled, half sobbed again, and added, "We'd have got married when we was thirteen if they'd've let us. But they wouldn't. I mean we knew they wouldn't, so we didn't bother to ask. We just— we met where we could, when we could. Of course Sarasota in the winter, we were mostly together there, but even then not always. As soon as we were both eighteen we didn't have to have anybody sign. Then we took off downtown, got the clerk of courts to marry us, and got right back to practice three hours later. You do. That's just how it is. We had a nice reception later, of course."

"Arlo," I asked, "was there anybody jealous of you and Julia? Or of you *or* Julia?"

"In the past, you mean? Oh, sure," he said, "there's always people jealous. They sneak around, watch you, maybe try to steal your act. But lately? No, ma'am. We—you could say, we dropped out. Dropped out of our world. So jealous now? I wouldn't say so. People in our world, more likely they'd scorn us. Pity us too, probably, but still scorn us."

"Then what about people from outside your world?"

He shook his head. "People from outside our world, they look at Julia and they see just a nightclub performer, they look at me and see a man living on his wife's income. That's all there is to see. And away from work, people in the neighborhood—they just see a couple in a rented apartment living quiet and not making waves. Recently her sister moved in with us, so she could go to college in Arlington, but that was no problem. I mean, I've known her sister since she was born. It's not like she was a stranger. We all get along okay. So—what's to be jealous of?"

That was a good question, and one which I couldn't answer. "Is there anybody who dislikes you or Julia?"

He shook his head dully. "People like us, we don't make enemies. We're just—outside of performing, we're just ordinary. We don't bother people; they don't bother us."

What to ask next? Maybe a walk-through, a fishing trip. Very often, on something like this, police officers go on a lot of fishing trips. Usually there aren't any bites. But finally somebody will ask just the right question, of just the right person, at just the right time, and there's a little bit of a nibble. Then we know where to concentrate more questions.

· · · · ·

"You said you check the ropes all the time, but that's a pretty vague statement. How often, exactly, do you check them?"

"I check the knots every day, before Julia gets on the trapeze," he said. "That's why I'm in tights too, so I won't look like some working stiff up there on the platform. The ropes themselves—I don't know, every week or so. Those are strong ropes. They don't fray in two." He stopped, apparently replaying in his mind what he'd just said. "It was cut, wasn't it?" he asked then. "That's why you and that other lady cut off part of it. Because it was cut. Under the velvet, it was cut." His eyes were fixed intently on me.

I nodded. "It was cut most of the way through. It frayed the rest of the way."

"Damn!" He slammed his fist down, hard, on the counter. "So if I'd checked tonight before she got on the trapeze—"

"It probably wouldn't have helped," I said. "Delayed things a little, maybe."

"But at least then we'd have known," he argued. "That someone was trying to kill her, I mean."

"That's true," I agreed. "But try not to feel guilty. You had no reason to check the ropes more often than you did. And a determined murderer will usually succeed eventually."

He nodded, muttered, "But *why?*" and picked the coffee mug back up and held it in both hands again, as if it could warm the shock out of his body. And he was shocky; I could tell that, and getting worse, beginning to shiver just a little. The EMTs had already tried twice to take him to the hospital and he'd refused each time. Well, maybe talking—sometimes talking will delay or even reverse shock. So I went on asking the necessary questions that otherwise would seem merciless.

"When you check the ropes themselves, what do you do?" I asked. "And I don't know what kind of jargon your profession might have, so please try to put it into words I'll understand."

"I push the velvet up as high as it will go and feel the rope. I look, too, but sometimes just looking you miss something. So I feel as well as look. Then I climb the safety rope up to the top where it's anchored and I push the velvet down as far as it will go and check it the same way. The middle part, I just feel the whole length of it through the velvet. But really, when it starts to fray, it's near the knots, because that's where you get the most flexion. The middle part sort of moves as a unit, so it hardly frays at all. I've changed ropes a lot of times. I've changed ropes just about all my life, and I've never seen one frayed in the middle, unless it was rubbing against something all the time."

"And last time you checked it—"

"This Monday," he said, and then paused, his eyes taking on that faraway thinking look. "This is Tuesday, isn't it?" I nodded and glanced at my watch. It was getting pretty close to being Wednesday. "Yeah," he said, "it was yesterday I checked it. Sunday and Monday, those are—were—Julia's days off, so usually Monday was the day I checked the ropes."

"What about rehearsals?" I asked. "Do you rehearse during the day?"

"You mean, does Julia rehearse during the day? Uh-uh." He shook his head emphatically. "What for? What she does a four-year-old could do. Hell, she *did* it when she was four years old. No flying at all. Just swinging. It looks scary to the audience because it's so high up in the air, but there's nothing to it. I could probably teach you to do it in two hours."

"No, thank you," I said emphatically, and he half grinned at me. "Okay," I said then, "talk me through a show, the way it's supposed to be."

"The way it's supposed to be," he said musingly and shivered again, but his voice picked up speed and strength, and his shivering let up again, as he recounted the familiar. "All right, usually Julia will do three shows a night, each one half an hour long. She starts off by climbing up that rope ladder I showed you, the one you climbed up. The first time she goes up I go with her, to check the knots once more. Then I use a rope on a pully—like a block and tackle, you know—to pull the trapeze toward her, and she steps from the platform inside the cage. I give her a good shove, and she starts to swing. Once she's got it swinging good, she dances a little, struts around, tries to make it look dangerous. After about half an hour she comes down. That's really the riskiest part.''

"Oh?''

"Yeah, you sort of slide down this rope, looking glamorous and smiling and waving all the way, and most people when they do it they land on a net but we don't use a net. So, if you're not careful, you land pretty hard. She twisted her ankle a couple of weeks ago, and Luisa had to go up for her a couple of days.''

"Luisa?''

"Her sister,'' he clarified. "I told you about her. She's nineteen, just started to college.''

"Okay,'' I said, "can you think of anything else that might help us find out who would have wanted your wife dead?''

He shook his head. "Ma'am, if I knew who it was, you wouldn't have to find them, not if I found them first. But—no, I guess I wouldn't really, because I wouldn't want to sully Julia's memory that way. If I think of anything else I'll tell you.''

I gave him my card, with my home and business phone numbers on it, and stood up. "Thank you,'' I said. "I may need to talk with you again later, but—''

He stood too. "Ma'am?'' he said. "What do you think happened? I mean—isn't there some way the rope could have gotten cut accidentally?''

"What do you think?'' I countered.

He shook his head. "I can't think of anything. But what I'm hearing, what you said to me, what I heard you say to that big guy, you're calling it murder, you're thinking somebody did it on purpose, and ma'am, I'm telling you again, people like Julia and me, we don't have that kind of enemies.'' He looked at me, large, deep brown puppy-

. . . . .

33

dog eyes begging me to tell him it didn't happen, begging me to tell him Julia wasn't really dead, begging me to tell him Julia would be okay, begging me to tell him nobody really murdered Julia.

But I couldn't tell him that. It did happen. Julia was dead. Julia wasn't going to be okay. Somebody did murder her.

"Then you think of another way it could have happened," I challenged him.

He shook his head. "Ma'am, I can't."

So I thanked him again, urged again that he go to the hospital—he, of course, refused again—and I went back into the main part of the restaurant, leaving him alone in the dressing room.

Captain Millner was over talking with Harry, and I noticed at once that our Rainbow Escort girls were gone. "I asked Harry if he wanted to stick around till you're ready to leave," Millner said, "or if he'd rather go on home now and let me bring you home later. He said he'd stay."

"It is our anniversary," Harry said remotely, with only the slightest emphasis on *is*.

"You find out anything about the owner of this place?" Captain Millner asked me.

"Gluck said it's somebody named Pender," I said, "but that's as far as I got."

We—Millner and I—found Jan—pronounced *Yahn*—Pender in his office, maudlin drunk and crying. "You want a drink?" he asked, and shoved a bourbon bottle and a couple of clean glasses at us.

We both declined. He poured more for himself, gulped it down, then peered at us owlishly. "Who're you?" he asked, as if Captain Millner hadn't just told him.

I told him again.

He started crying again. "You're here about Julia. Trying to find out who murdered Julia. Somebody murdered Julia in my restaurant, my own restaurant. How'd they do it?" he demanded. "And *why* did they do it?"

. . . . .

"We're still trying to find out," I said, "and we'd like some help from you."

"Nobody ought to hurt Julia. She's—she was—the sweetest little girl in the world," he told us, the effect somewhat spoiled by a hiccup. "Nobody oughta hurt sweet little girls like that. And Jerry, he's telling me murder—ain't nobody would want to hurt that sweet little girl—"

"Who's Jerry?" I interrupted.

He peered at me through red-rimmed eyes. "My lead singer. Jerry. You know, sings through a megaphone? Sounds like ever-what's-his-name, that Tiny Tim feller—got married on Johnny Carson or something like that, you know, married some girl named Miss Vicki—you look old enough you ought to know that Tiny Tim feller—"

I was, but I didn't appreciate having that brought to my attention right now. Rather briskly, I asked Jerry's last name. It was Anson. I'd talk to Jerry Anson later. Right now I was still trying to get something approaching sense out of Jan Pender, and Captain Millner was still watching me do it.

"What's this going to do to the restaurant?" Pender asked then. "Mister detective feller, you tell me that. What's this going to do to my restaurant?"

"Why should it do anything to it?" Captain Millner answered remotely, his eyes telling me—though probably not Pender—that he was feeling pretty disgusted.

"Well, you know, people might not want to celebrate where that sweet little girl died. An'—I got everything tied up in this restaurant. Everything I own. So I gotta—even if Julia's dead—I gotta think of my investment."

"I doubt you'll need to worry about your investment," Millner said. "I predict you'll be full every night for a month."

My prediction, if he had asked me, would have been the same. In some ways people can be ghouls.

. . . . .

35

"You said you wanted my help," Pender said to me. "What kind of help?"

"We'd just like to ask you about enemies she might have had, enemies you might have had. That kind of thing."

He hiccuped. "I'm pretty drunk right now."

I agreed. He was pretty drunk right now.

"I think maybe I ought to wait to talk to you till tomorrow," he said. "I'll get my lawyer, have him here. Is that okay?"

"That's your right," Millner said, sounding even more remote.

We—I, that is, as Captain Millner had to be in court—made an appointment for nine o'clock tomorrow morning, in the office of the restaurant. Pender said he'd be sure the back door was open for me to get in.

Considering Pender's present condition, I wasn't at all sure he'd remember either the appointment or the door. But all I could do was agree. I certainly couldn't force him to talk to me.

I went then to try to find Jerry Anson.

By now the restaurant was pretty well empty, but Jerry Anson was sitting on the little bit of stage, looking out at the emptying room. I recognized him at once; he was, of course, the man who'd given me the megaphone, which, come to think of it, I had never returned. Apparently someone had, though, or else he'd retrieved it himself, as it was sitting on the floor beside him.

I introduced myself, and he nodded. "Thanks for the loan," I said, gesturing at the megaphone.

He nodded again. "That scared me," he said. "When everybody started running, I mean. I heard one time about this nightclub, I think it was in California or Florida or somewhere like that, the Coconut Grove or the Orange Grove or something like that, where they had a fire, and a whole bunch of people were trampled to death trying to get out. I think it was my grandmother told me about it; I think it happened when she was a kid. I was afraid something like that was going to happen here. With a lot less cause. Fire, like in that nightclub, can kill anybody in the room, so it's worth running a risk to get out. This—you were right. The danger was over before anybody started running. So what in the hell were they running for?"

"When panic starts, nobody stops to think."

" 'The sky is falling,' said Chicken Little?"

"Something like that," I agreed. Unlike Pender, Jerry Anson wasn't waiting to talk until he had his lawyer; in fact, there might be a slight problem with shutting him up.

"So, Detective Deb Ralston," he said, stretching and grinning at me, "what do you want to ask me?"

"Tell me a little about yourself, to start with," I suggested. "Who is Jerry Anson?"

"Jerry Anson," he said, "is a fellow who's working for a degree in mathematics, and trying to support himself and wife and two and two-thirds kids at the same time. Eventually I want to teach high school math. Right now I just want to keep a roof over our head and food on the table without running up the biggest student loan in human history. I'm twenty-six, I'm Catholic, and I used to be in my high school glee club. Pender advertised for a singer. I applied and I got the job. I've had it about eight months. Pender pays well, and I study backstage between shows. Anything else?"

"That's pretty comprehensive," I said. "Now tell me about Julia."

He stretched again. "I've got a calculus exam in the morning, you know that? Okay, okay, death takes precedence. Julia and Arlo. You can't think of either of them alone. It's always both of them. Julia-and-Arlo. Arlo-and-Julia. Like a pair of Siamese twins. They—what do you want me to say? I mean, you've already talked with him. I saw you in the kitchen with him. They both grew up in circuses. They've been married, I don't know, quite a while. They're—they were— Julia was nice and Arlo is nice. You're asking me why somebody would do this, lady, I don't know. I wish I did know. I absolutely, literally, cannot imagine a soul on this earth that wouldn't take to Julia on sight. Arlo, I don't know, till you get to know him sometimes he seems a little distant, but—"

Why go on?

Everybody I talked with that night agreed. Either Julia and Arlo were both paragons of virtue whom nobody would ever want to kill, or everybody was lying—and I have a pretty good feel for when people are lying, and I didn't think there was much, if any, lying going on.

So I had a murder there was no reason for.

And I don't care who the victim is, murder doesn't happen without reason. That doesn't mean the reason would make sense to anybody else. I've seen murder done because somebody accidentally shoved somebody else going out a door; I've seen murder done because two twenty-year-olds were quarreling over a pool score; I've seen murder done because two retired men wanted to use the same outdoor water faucet at the same time to water their neighboring gardens. I've seen the aftermath after an eighty-two-year-old woman shot her fifteen-year-old granddaughter six times in the back with a bolt-action rifle for stealing five dollars from her purse. I've seen murder done because two people wanted to use the same pay phone at the same time, or because one person thought another person was wearing the wrong color shirt. But for no reason at all?

No.

So all that meant was that I hadn't found the reason.

It was nearly 1 A.M. by the time we got home.

I didn't think the entire evening could have been appreciably disimproved from what it already was.

I was wrong.

Cameron had an earache. Cameron was howling. Unable to reach us by phone (because I was up on a trapeze platform when the earache developed, and Harry was returning Jerry's megaphone, so of course he was not where the restaurant's reservation seating chart said he was), Lori had called Sister May Rector, who had dashed right over.

Now, I think the world of May Rector. She's a neighbor—not just someone who lives near me, but a real neighbor. She's the second counselor in Relief Society—to non-Mormons, that means she's an officer in the church women's group—and she insisted on baby-sitting Cameron free until I put him into preschool.

But Sister Rector's ideas of child care and mine do not always jibe.

This time Sister Rector was trying to soothe Cameron's earache by putting warmed olive oil into his ear with a medicine dropper—which is exactly what his pediatrician told me *not* to do for his earaches. "I couldn't find your aspirin, dear," she told me, "so I couldn't give him any."

Since the time Sister Rector's children were small, pediatricians have decided that aspirin is not supposed to be given to people under eighteen. His baby-sized acetaminophen tablets, grape flavored, were in my medicine cabinet rather than the one in the bathroom the architect (whom I frequently suspect had no children and never cleaned a kitchen or bathroom in his life, or he wouldn't have designed our house the way he did) had intended for the use of children and guests.

And Sister Rector went on talking. "I suppose you heard about the Walkers and the Denisons and the Richardses?"

"No," I said wearily, "I didn't. What happened?" I could easily guess, and I could certainly find out in the morning at work, but why deprive her of the pleasure of telling me about the latest attack of the highly elusive daylight burglars who were eating our neighborhood alive?

"They were all robbed today!" She clearly relished the news; she also clearly did not know the difference between burglary (stealth theft from a residence or business) and robbery (theft from a person no matter where that person is, with the element of violence or threat of violence included). When I get too tired I have an unfortunate tendency to nitpick.

I reminded myself that if I nitpick only inside my head at least I

· · · · ·

don't offend anyone else. "What did they get?" I asked. "Have you heard?"

Slightly incoherently, she recited a litany of guns, medicine, jewelry. I found the news distinctly disturbing, because now that Harry's back at work there's nobody home during the day. Oh, of course, our half pit bull, Pat, would be a considerable deterrent, except for one thing: the mail carrier refuses to deliver the mail if Pat is in the front yard, so we have had to devise a system of interconnecting fences and gates that keeps Pat in the backyard all day but gives him the entire yard at night. So, of course, any intelligent burglar—in a neighborhood in which both adults working outside the home is a given— would just enter through the front door.

I did not kid myself that our dead-bolt lock would keep out a determined burglar. I used to be on the Burglary/Robbery Squad.

I thanked Sister Rector profusely, for the news and the first aid. Harry walked her out to her car. I got some acetaminophen down Cameron, cleaned out his ear the best I could, which wasn't very well—olive oil within the ear is extremely clinging, and the pediatrician had firmly told me never to stick anything inside a child's ear that is smaller than one's elbow, meaning, of course, don't stick anything inside a child's ear no matter how dirty the ear looks—and finally got him settled down before I crawled into bed at 2 A.M., knowing I had to be back up at 6:30.

And, of course, I spent the entire night seeing, over and over and over again, Julia Sarana Gluck toppling to her death, and the glazing eyes of the man who'd bled to death and the man who'd died of concussion.

Three

. . . . .

"No, I can't take Cameron to the pediatrician," I told Harry for what was actually only the second time, though it felt like the tenth time because I had been mentally rehearsing the argument in my head the whole time I made breakfast. "You know perfectly well that I've got an—"

"At nine o'clock. You've got an appointment at nine o'clock."

"And just how long do you think it would take me to take Cameron to the pediatrician?" I inquired as sweetly as possible, clinging to the fraying edges of my patience as I slammed the butter dish down in front of him. "I'm sorry, Harry, but I haven't yet learned to be in two places at one time."

"What about Lori?" Harry demanded, also for what felt like the tenth time. After a bite of scrambled egg, he answered his own question: "All right, all right, I know, she's already left for seminary—in *my* truck—and after she gets back she's got to go straight to high school."

"She will go to high school on the school bus," I pointed out, "a schedule which will return your truck to you in plenty of time for you to get to work *or* the pediatrician. It always does. Harry, for cryin' out loud, Hal has been using your truck to go to seminary for the last three years."

"I wasn't working then."

"Part of the time you were."

. . . . .

"Anyway we weren't talking about my truck, we were talking about Lori taking Cameron to the doctor."

"*You* were. *I* wasn't. And besides she—"

"She hasn't got the legal authority. I know. Isn't there some kind of piece of paper we could give her—"

Indeed there was some kind of piece of paper we could give Lori that would legally authorize her to get Cameron medical care. It's called a limited power of attorney and Harry was right, we should have thought to give her something like that a long time ago. If she'd had one last night she could, if she'd thought of it, have taken Cameron to the emergency room. But all the same, she was already graduating high school a year late—even though she'd actually be in high school only four and a half months before entering Tarrant County Community College—because of being struck by a car last year, and it would be in no way reasonable for us to expect her to miss more school. Letting her occasionally baby-sit in the evening, especially when she had offered to do so, was one thing; keeping her out of school to take Cameron to the doctor was another thing entirely.

Neither Harry nor I mentioned Sister May Rector. Letting her take Cameron to the doctor, as delighted as she would be to do it, was totally out of the question. We both knew her well enough to know that her report to us of what the doctor had said would be very strongly mixed with her ideas of what the doctor *should* have said. Not that she was at all untruthful; she just seemed to interpret things— almost all things, actually—through a smoke screen of her own knowledge and misknowledge.

"Look," Harry went on wrathfully, having finished his eggs and toast, "this kind of thing was just fine when I was home all the time, but now—"

"Now you are in management," I pointed out, "and you're not punching a time clock. You already told me you didn't have any meetings or anything else scheduled this morning. So you can call your secretary, tell her you've got to take the baby to the doctor, do so, go by the pharmacy if necessary, take the baby and his prescriptions to the day-care center, and then go on to work, just the same way you always expected me to do with the other kids. I'm sure your in-basket will be waiting patiently for you."

Cameron was semifollowing this discussion, but because he did not by that time consider himself a baby he wasn't relating it to himself, and Harry and I were both working at keeping our voices calm enough that Cameron would not interpret the discussion as a quarrel and start howling.

"I wish I hadn't told you anything about my schedule," Harry muttered, pushing his chair back so suddenly he narrowly missed a cat's tail—which cat I couldn't tell, because all that reached my senses was a yowl followed by a streak of retreating fur. At that speed, a short-haired calico (Margaret Scratcher) is hard to distinguish from a long-haired tabby (Rags).

About that time Lori came in, said a brief "Hi," and headed straight for the front bathroom. I assumed she had headed there to do the additional primping necessary before gobbling her bowl of Cheerios—she does not like scrambled egg—and dashing out to catch the bus to school. Preseminary primping, it seems, is adequate for seminary but not for the regular classroom.

Harry pushed his chair the rest of the way back from the table, picked up Cameron, who looked surprised—as well he should, having not yet finished his breakfast—and marched him toward our bathroom. "Harry," I called after him.

"Later," he said irritably, and I could hear assorted splashings as he washed Cameron's hands and face.

At four, Cameron was no longer making quite as complicated messes as he used to make, but I doubt he will ever be a tidy child, at least not until he reaches the age at which adolescent males gaze admiringly into the mirror and say things like "Hello, you handsome devil."

"Harry, I'm trying to tell you—"

· · · · ·

"Tell me later," he snarled over his shoulder, dashing out the front door still carrying Cameron, who was perfectly capable of walking—or even running—by himself.

"But—"

"Later!" he roared.

The front door slammed, the gate squeaked open, the dog whined in the front yard, the gate clashed shut, the pickup truck's doors slammed, the engine roared almost as loudly as Harry, and Harry and Cameron were gone.

If he'd listened, I'd have been able to tell him that the pediatrician's office didn't open until ten, and furthermore that it is best to call the pediatrician at ten and find out when Cameron can be worked in, rather than simply arriving unannounced. He was going to have a very long wait, which would not improve his disposition in the slightest.

Of course in his bad-tempered rush he had left the interior gate open, so that Pat had access to the entire yard and presently was in the front yard whining and probably working up to howling. Pat, our half Doberman, half pit bull, adores Cameron. He worships Cameron. The departure of Cameron breaks his heart all over again every morning.

Oh, of course I *could* have taken the extra time to try to lure Pat into the backyard long enough to lock the gate. But I didn't have time to bother. So we wouldn't get any mail today. Oh well—if we didn't get any mail, we also wouldn't get a burglar. A pit bull with one corner of his lip curled up to show his teeth, saying "Rrrr-rrrrr-rrrr," is a strong deterrent.

So I left Pat, very proud of himself, sitting in the front yard when I departed to rush in to the police station just long enough to sign in, to very briefly check the Bird Cage and Jan Pender to see if any previous crimes involved him in any way, to get a radio and the keys to a police car, to sign out on the whiteboard, and to depart, hoping pessimistically that Jan Pender had remembered his appointment.

Surprise, surprise. He had. The back door to the restaurant was

. . . . .

44

standing open, and somebody who was working in the kitchen—judging from my last investigation involving a restaurant, I supposed he was probably a pastry cook—led me straight to Jan Pender's office, which was occupied by Jan Pender, three red vinyl-over-steel chairs with the vinyl torn and the stuffing protruding, a red vinyl couch in similar condition, a beat-up metal desk (probably military surplus), three four-drawer file cabinets (ditto), one of those ubiquitous computers that are now turning up everywhere including my own bedroom, and several dozen large stacks of badly sorted papers spread about on the desk, the tops of the file cabinets, and the floors. Clearly he had chosen to spend his money on the parts of the restaurant that showed, which was probably good thinking. As he had promised, he even had his attorney, one Ted Siebenborn, with him.

Pender looked hungover: his skin was pasty, and there were bags under his bloodshot brown eyes that didn't look likely to go away anytime soon. He'd been sweating, not just because of the heat as his office was practically icy, and his straight dark hair was tousled. Siebenborn did not look hungover; he was a heavyset blond who seemed altogether too perky for anybody to have a right to look at nine o'clock in the morning, at least not after I had a very late night. He shook my hand vigorously, invited me to call him Ted, invited me to have a seat either beside him on the couch or in an adjacent chair (which he quickly swept free of papers), invited me to have a cup of coffee, and started looking around to see what else he could offer me. I accepted the adjacent chair, politely declined the coffee, and asked Pender how he felt.

"Like shit," he said, wiping his forehead with a huge white handkerchief. The Eastern European accent was virtually gone this morning; apparently its strength related to how drunk he was, which I suppose makes a little bit of sense. "Y'know, all night long I kept trying to tell myself I'd dreamed it. I was drunk and I dreamed it. It didn't really happen. Stuff like this don't—doesn't happen. Nobody murders sweet little girls like Julia. I got up this morning and I called

· · · · ·

Ted and I told him I had this hell of a dream, about Julia and the whole damn cage falling onto a table and killing Julia and two guys, and Ted said—tell her what you said."

"I had the newspaper open in front of me," Siebenborn said. "And I told him he didn't dream it."

"So I told him he better come up here with me this morning to meet with you," Pender added. He fidgeted for a minute, and then added, "I—it really was kind of like a dream. It was just—like it had to be a dream, you know? It had this like surreal quality to it, like a fish swimming in sand, like a bird flying in the sea. Not like a thing that happened."

He looked down at his hands, then back up at me. "It was like that. I thought—nobody would really murder that sweet little girl. So—it had to be a dream I had. Only it wasn't."

"No," I agreed, "it wasn't." I hoped he would not go on referring to Julia Gluck as "that sweet little girl." I had a hunch he was going to go right on doing it.

"She sewed that velvet tube, you know, the one that covered all the ropes. I guess I should say those velvet tubes, there was more than one of them. She sewed them herself. You know that?"

"No, I didn't."

"She brought her sewing machine up here to do it. I remember— her and Arlo laughing, her sewing the velvet and him making sure the rope would fit through the tubes, and then the two of them up there in the rafters bouncing around like seals, like sea otters, like it was water up there instead of air, bouncing around and laughing fit to kill—" His voice trailed off; he shuddered visibly. "Laughing fit to kill," he repeated.

"Mr. Pender—"

"I know. You've got to ask me questions. But—damn! You don't think I could have had anything to do with it. I'm sick over the whole thing, anybody killing that sweet little girl—"

"Mr. Pender," I interrupted, driven slightly beyond endurance,

· · · · ·
46

"she wasn't a sweet little girl. She was a grown woman. She was twenty-six. If a female doesn't get to be a woman when she's twenty-six, when does she get to be a woman?"

He stared at me—rightfully, I suppose, because I had interrupted a witness with my own irrelevant feelings. "Okay, she was a woman," he said finally, "but to me she was this sweet little—she was sweet," he amended carefully. "I mean, there was just no reason for anybody to want to, you know, do what you said. But you got to understand, I've sunk everything I own and everything I ever hope to own into making this place work. If it fails, man, I might just as well go down to the river and stick my head in the water like that song says, you know, stick my head under three times and bring it out twice, 'cause there's nothing left for me to do except go to work as a street sweeper, and last time I looked, they weren't hiring street sweepers. Man, I can't stand any problems now."

"I don't know quite how to get this across to you, Mr. Pender," I said, "but you've got problems already."

"Yeah, I know. Somebody could sue me. The survivors of those two guys that were killed, they could sue me, couldn't they?"

Siebenborn moved restlessly and started to answer.

"Never mind, I know, I know," Pender said. "They can, and they probably will. But—if I can prove, if the city can prove, that it was a crime directed at me and they just got caught in it, then maybe they can't sue me so bad, right?"

"Maybe," Siebenborn said. "And maybe not. And I tried to tell you, you've got other problems. I'm not even sure the city's going to let the place stay open. They could close it down, couldn't they?" He was directing that question at me.

"I suppose they could," I admitted. "Nobody that I know of wants to do it, but yes, I suppose the city could close your business down right now, at least until the crime has been more thoroughly investigated."

"Yeah, but they won't, will they?" Pender's question was so repetitious I was beginning to wonder whether he was still drunk.

Siebenborn must have been wondering the same thing, because he stood up briskly, headed to the door, and yelled, "Rio, bring Jan another cup of coffee."

Rio—the pastry cook I had noticed earlier—obliged, but I wasn't sure Pender even noticed. At least he didn't pick up the cup after Rio handed it to Siebenborn and Siebenborn slammed it down on the desk in front of him. His eyes fixed on me, he repeated, "They won't close me down, will they?"

"Not unless I recommend it. And before you ask, no, I'm not recommending it. I don't see any reason to. I don't think you had anything to do with what happened—not just because of what you say, but because of what I'm seeing in you. But—there's a chance you might know something."

"But I don't—" he started to protest.

"Mr. Pender," I interrupted, "you might not know you know something. This is something that often happens in relation to planned crimes—somebody has seen, or heard, or otherwise noticed, something that looked perfectly innocent at the time and probably still does. So that's what I'm thinking now—that you could know something that might look perfectly innocent to you but not to me. I've got to try to get things out of you that you might not even know you know. I'm glad you've got your attorney here, because he'll be able to advise you on some of the questions."

Ted Siebenborn again stirred restlessly. That seemed to be one of his habits. "I've got some advice to give him right now." He looked directly at Pender. "Jan, you pay me to give you advice, but you don't take the advice very well. Now, I want you to give me permission right now to tell these people what's going on, or I want you to hire another attorney."

Pender slumped dejectedly over his cluttered desk. "I guess you might as well. I guess it could be related."

"Right," Siebenborn said, "and I guess Noah's Ark was built to

· · · · ·

48

float on a slight rise in the river. Detective Ralston," he said to me, and for once I didn't offer my first name instead, "let me tell you what's going on. Let's see, it's September fifth now, the restaurant opened up in April—of course it took about three months before that to get all the paperwork done, especially the liquor license, you wouldn't believe how complicated that is, and the Glucks had been getting things ready, getting the equipment up and practicing and rehearsing and everything, since January to be sure everything was down pat by opening. We actually got the lease on the building about, I guess, November or October, end of October I think it was. Anyhow, so—" He came to a halt, staring at me. "Are you wired?" he demanded abruptly.

"Wired?" I repeated in some bewilderment, before realizing what he meant. "Oh. No, I don't ever use tape recorders. Except on an undercover job, I'd never use one without the knowledge of everybody I was talking with."

"Well, I kind of wish you were," he said. "Okay, anyway, we opened up April third, and the first letter came April sixth."

"Okay," I said cautiously.

"Aren't you going to write this down?" He was glaring at me almost as forcefully as he had glared when he realized I wasn't wearing a concealed tape recorder.

"Some people get nervous when I start writing," I said, "and I've got a pretty good memory. But if you don't mind—" I pulled a yellow legal pad out of the leather briefcase-purse combination I'd recently taken to carrying and made a few notes—unnecessary, because everything I had been told so far was fixed in my memory well enough that it would stay there until I made my regular notes after I got outside. But if it reassured them for me to make the notes now, then I would make them now. "You opened up April third and the first letter came April sixth—"

"Yeah," Pender said heavily.

"What letter?" I asked.

. . . . .

Pender and Siebenborn both started to speak at once, and then each tried to defer to the other. "You tell her," Pender said.

"You better tell her about the first letter," Siebenborn said, "because that's the one you didn't show to me."

"Okay, okay," Pender said. "Okay, like he said, the first letter came April sixth. Well, actually it wasn't the first letter."

"What did you say?" Siebenborn demanded, with the righteous wrath of an attorney who's just learned his client has been lying to him. "You told me——"

"I told you about the letter that came April sixth," Pender said. "But it wasn't the first letter. It was just the first like——like that. There were letters before. While the place was still being remodeled. I just threw them away. They were all about the same thing——monotonous. Stuff like telling me, you know, there was a real big problem with theft of construction equipment and supplies, if I wanted to open on time I better hire a guard agency for protection."

"Did the letters suggest a specific guard agency?" I inquired.

"That was what was weird. They did. But it was a different one each time. Like whoever was writing the letters wanted me to hire some guard agency or other but they didn't really care which one. They were even——" He looked surprised. "I had forgotten this and I just now remembered. They were in alphabetical order, like the first letter might have mentioned something like Ajax Guard Service and the second something like Bentley Detective Agency——those weren't the names, I don't remember the names, it was just the sequence. Like somebody was going down the Yellow Pages listing each guard service shown and telling me to hire it."

"So did you?" I asked.

"Hire a guard agency? No, I didn't have to. The contractor had a guard at the site every night. He told me it was perfectly true that there's a lot of theft of construction supplies and he'd found it cheaper to pay a guard than to worry about replacing stuff over and over."

· · · · ·

"Well, whether that's true usually depends on how exposed and isolated the site is," I said, "but it makes pretty good sense to me, providing it was a guard from a good agency."

"Yeah, well, I guess this guard was from a good agency," Pender said, "because he always had this dog with him, a German shepherd it was, and it was always sniffing around and acting like it would eat the head off anybody in the wrong place. And nothing ever did go missing. Then. But then we opened. And this letter came April sixth. It looked to me like it was from the same person, you know, but the others were handwritten and this one was typed, this little bitty type, real worn, like it was from one of those cheap portable typewriters."

"If you had saved one of the earlier letters, we could compare the two," I said.

"Well, I didn't so that's that." He was avoiding both my eyes and Siebenborn's. *He didn't get rid of them,* I thought. *He did save them.* But we'd get to that later. "Anyway, this new letter, it said something like 'Congratulations on your opening. But you're not safe yet. Restaurants are highly subject to burglaries, robberies, and vandalism. For protection, leave a thousand dollars in twenties in a paper bag marked *lunch* on your back steps when you close Friday night.' I mean those aren't the exact words, but that's the gist of what it said. So I did."

"And as soon as I heard about it I told you it was a dumb-ass thing to do," Siebenborn said.

"All right, it was a dumb-ass thing to do," Pender said. "I mean, yeah, sure I know stuff like that's illegal. It's extortion. And it's a racket. It's even got a name. The protection racket." He seemed rather proud of himself for that knowledge. "But I thought, well, okay, it's illegal, but say I reported it to the police, how long would it take them to find out who was doing it? And what would happen to my restaurant in the meantime?"

That was a legitimate point. And now I was highly interested, because it had been a long time since I'd heard of a protection racket opening in Fort Worth. This was going to have to go to both our Intelligence Squad and the Metro Intelligence Squad, as soon as possible.

"And I was figuring," Pender went on, "that—look, guys like that, they don't make a profit if I don't make a profit. I figured they'd know probably better than I do how much money I take out of this place, how much I owe, how much I could afford to give them without going out of business. And you don't kill the goose that lays the golden eggs. You feed it lots of corn so it will go right on laying. Isn't that right? Isn't that how they play it?"

"Usually," I admitted. "Though sometimes their idea of what a business can afford to lose and the business's idea of what the business can afford to lose don't jibe."

"Well, yeah, I see that. But still—I figured they'd up the ante a little bit, but they wouldn't keep on and keep on and keep on."

"But they did?"

"They damn sure did," he said. "I mean, I left the thousand dollars where he told me to, and the next day—not the next week, the damn fu—the damn *next day,*" he interrupted and corrected himself, with a sheepish look at me, "they asked me for another thousand. Well, look, this business does good, but it doesn't do that good. I have employees to pay, I have suppliers, I have bank loans, I have taxes—I managed to get that thousand, though Ted told me not to, but I left a note in with the bag, I couldn't do this every day. Every week, yeah, sure, if I had to, though it would be pushing it. But not every day."

"So then what happened?

"So then there was another note the next day. It asked for two thousand dollars. That night."

"And what did you do?"

"I didn't have it. I just—flat—didn't have it. So I called Ted and asked him if I should report it and he said call the FBI. So I did, and the FBI said they couldn't do anything about it. So, look, what do I pay taxes for if the FBI can't do anything about it?"

. . . . .

"There's a thing called primary jurisdiction," I tried to explain. "The FBI wouldn't have primary jurisdiction in this case. If it became reasonably clear that it was interstate racketeering going on, then we could ask them to get involved, but from what you're telling me there's no real evidence of that. Did you ever report it to the Fort Worth Police Department?"

I was sure he hadn't, because if he had something would have come up on the computer about the Bird Cage or Jan Pender when I checked it this morning.

Not to my surprise, he shook his head. "No," he said then. "They said in the note—they knew I'd called the FBI. I don't know how they knew, but they knew. And they said if I called the police they'd burn the building."

"I told him to report it anyway," Siebenborn said. "But he wouldn't. And I couldn't. Not legally. Not if my client had ordered me not to."

"So then what happened?"

"Well, they kept on with the letters and the threats. Sometimes I paid them. Sometimes I couldn't. Sometimes I could give them something but not all they wanted. I—I did what I could."

"Was there ever anything other than threats?"

He nodded. "Yeah, a couple of times. Once—it was during the day, nobody here but the pastry cooks, that was how early it was, and Julia out rehearsing a little, trying out something new, and Arlo was up on the platform some of the time and other times he was down on the ground holding this rope like so she couldn't fall, that was the only time I knew them to have a safety net up, and Arlo told me it was 'cause it was a new thing she was trying—she wound up not doing it because my insurance company said it was too dangerous, and she had to just go back to doing what she did, you know, sort of a bump and grind on a swing—and anyhow, I was out watching them rehearse and I heard this commotion in the kitchen and ran in there and Rio and Sarah, you know, they were grabbing for fire extinguishers and

· · · · ·

53

Billy, he'd run to the phone to call nine-one-one, but by the time the fire trucks got there he'd already got the fire out."

"Where was the fire?" I asked, rather surprised that a fire could be set under the noses of three pastry cooks with nobody noticing anything.

"It was—okay, it's like this." He began gesturing with his arms. "We've got this, like, well, all our ovens and ranges, they're gas, you know." I nodded, though in fact I didn't know at all. "And one of the ovens, somebody had crawled under it and slit one of the gas hoses with a knife, right where it passed under one oven going to another one. As long as everything was turned off there wasn't even much of a leak, 'cause they'd slit it where the weight of the hose kind of kept the slit closed. But then, in the morning, when they turned on the ovens, it started leaking a little more and then the flame, like, leaped from the top burner onto the hose and then the hose sort of started to melt and the leak kept getting bigger. Well, so Rio, he was aiming the fire extinguisher onto the flame itself, and Sarah, she crawled under the range and turned the gas off at the wall. And then of course that stopped it. Didn't do any real damage, except we had to shut that range and oven down until somebody could come and fix it. And the guy from the gas company, when he came and fixed it, he told me he thought somebody'd cut the hose on purpose."

"What else?"

"Well, that was all, we just got the gas hose fixed and went on working."

"But you said there'd been another incident."

"Oh, that one, yeah. Well, what happened was this: I refused to pay them one more time and they slit my tires. All four of them. There I was outside the door at two A.M. in the morning, ready to go home and get some sleep, and all four tires flatter'n pancakes."

"Were there any other incidents?"

Jan sighed and shook his head. "No," he said, "no, there weren't. Just—I kept paying them. Probably I've paid them sixty thousand

· · · · ·

dollars since April, and if you think I can afford that, well, guess again.''

"And you never reported it?'' I asked when he paused.

He'd been staring out into space. Now he looked back at me, seeming startled as his eyes focused on me. Nearby, Siebenborn wriggled a bit, loud-sounding in the silence that was otherwise broken only by occasional sounds from the kitchen. "What?'' he said to me.

"You paid out *sixty thousand dollars* and never reported the extortion to the police?''

He shook his head. "I—couldn't see what good it would do. When I had guards here they—he—whoever—got past the guards. I figured, the police send somebody, he'll get past them just like he got past the guards. You keep a whole squad of cops here—which you aren't going to do—and he'll either get past them or he'll just wait till they're gone. Anyway—places I've lived—cops were on the take. Maybe they're not here. I've heard they're not. But I don't know. So—report it? I didn't see the use. I just asked them to wait a little, let me get the money together. But—it wasn't worth Julia's life. I'd have paid them. I'd have paid them whatever they wanted, or I'd have shut down the place even if I did lose everything. But they never told me they wanted to hurt anybody, Julia or anybody else, they were threatening the kitchens and that sort of thing, except for that one time after I called the FBI. I'd have—if I'd known they wanted to hurt Julia I'd have found the money somehow. I don't know how, but I'd have found it.''

"Jan,'' I said gently, "no matter how much money you gave them, they'd just go right on upping the ante again. They already proved that to you. So it wasn't your fault.''

He wasn't hearing that; he was crying again, and he muttered something under his breath, something about "Julia and the baby, dammit, why'd they have to—''

"Baby?'' I asked. Because I knew Julia had been pregnant; Arlo had told me. But Arlo had also told me they hadn't told anybody else.

· · · · ·

55

"Oh, you might as well know," Jan said. "You too, Ted. Not that it matters now, I guess. Julia, well, she was going to have a baby with me. Now, don't go thinking things. Arlo, he thought it was his baby, and Julia and I neither one were going to tell him different. She didn't want anything from me for it. All she wanted was the baby. That's what she told me."

That might or might not be what Julia had told him.

It might or might not be true, even if it was what Julia had told him.

All of a sudden, the case that was looking semiclosed was wide open again.

Four
· · · · ·

"WHICH MIGHT OR might not be true," Captain Millner agreed, leaning back in his chair behind his huge desk, which he very rarely actually used. "Any of it, I mean. Except that the baby is his. I doubt anybody, given the situation, would say that if it weren't true. Come to think of it, I'm surprised that anybody, given the situation, would say that even if it was true. What did his lawyer, this Siebenborn fellow, do when he said it?"

"Last time I saw somebody with that look on his face," I answered, "was about ten years ago when we picked up that guy for shotgunning his friend."

I didn't have to explain any further; Captain Millner would remember the case as well as I did. We'd picked up the fellow for a murder that even we knew would turn legally into what it was really, negligent manslaughter. A public defender was called right away, and said lawyer, right in front of about six of us, asked the defendant what happened to his four front teeth—you could tell she was hoping some of us had knocked them out so she'd have a great big federal case—and he said, "The back of the shotgun hit them, you know when the gun went off and hit Buddy."

"Remember that?" I said. "Remember how horrified and resigned she looked at the same time?"

"Very well. But Siebenborn didn't actually say anything? To you or to Pender?"

· · · · ·

"What was there to say?"

"True, true," Millner said.

"It's not that the protection racket is new," I mused, reverting to the case at hand, "but neither is adultery resulting in a baby of uncertain parentage. And I'd say that the latter results in a lot more murders than the former."

"It always has. And I don't know of any protection rackets, or any other professional-style extortion rings, operating in the Metroplex right now." Hastily Millner added, "Obviously that doesn't mean there aren't any."

"And Pender was right," I went on, "that most times, the protection racketeers don't kill." As a member of the Major Case Squad, I had encountered the protection racket before, and Millner knew I had, to say nothing of the fact that he'd probably been coping with protection rackets when I was still in junior high. "Of course how much they think can be taken out of the business without killing the business, and how much the owner thinks can be taken out of the business, often aren't the same—I told Pender that, but I'm not sure he understood it—so I figure they've driven quite a few businesses into bankruptcy. But they don't usually kill."

"Bear in mind that there's always the possibility that they're just starting up," Millner pointed out. "In that case, they might have picked Pender as the Horrible Example they can point to if any of their other victims show signs of getting out of line. But even so—I don't know. Given the timing—you said Pender might have gotten the first note as early as October, even though it was April before he told Siebenborn about it—"

"He never told Siebenborn about it; Siebenborn found out when Pender told me," I interrupted.

"Okay, but I mean he didn't tell Siebenborn about any of the notes until April. What I'm getting at is, I figure if they started in October, or even in April for that matter, they'd have picked a lot more than one victim by now. The fire in the kitchen, maybe. That feels right for this sort of thing. But murder? Especially this kind of murder? I agree with you. It doesn't feel right to me—but if that wasn't the motive, then from all you've learned so far the motive just about had to be the baby, which would make either the husband or the boyfriend the perp. How do you feel about that?"

That wasn't as much of a loaded question as it might sound like. I do get hunches. And although my hunches turn out to be wrong about as often as they turn out to be right, still they're good enough, often enough, that Captain Millner considers them reasonable investigative leads. That being the case, I chose my words carefully.

"My gut feeling at this time," I said, "is that both Arlo Gluck and Jan Pender—and he's not what I'd call her boyfriend anyway—were totally surprised and stunned by the woman's death, and neither of them has any real idea what is going on."

"Then we'll look first at the protection thing," Millner said, "without putting the whole thing about the baby totally out of mind."

"The motive doesn't have to be the protection or the baby," I pointed out. "There could be all kinds of things we haven't figured out yet."

"There always could," Millner replied. "And guess whose job it is to find that out?" He stood purposefully. "Where did you stash Pender and Siebenborn? And did you bring them in, or just have them follow you?"

They had followed me to the police station in Ted Siebenborn's car, which was rather a relief to me because I had a hunch Pender wasn't fit to drive, and now they were stashed in the third interview room down the hall, the nicest one, the one we usually don't use for suspects unless there's a real big game of good cop/bad cop going on, and that game is a lot harder to play if there's an attorney sitting in. Which means in general it's been a lot harder to play for the last thirty-odd years, which goes back well before I started policing.

Jan Pender wasn't—quite—a suspect. And he did have his attorney sitting in.

. . . . .

I reintroduced Captain Millner to Jan Pender, introduced him to Ted Siebenborn and explained what he was doing there, and he and I both sat down at the conference table across from Pender and Siebenborn, who both were polite but not effusive. "Mr. Pender," I asked then, "when did you get the most recent letter?"

"This morning," he said.

"This morning?" I repeated incredulously. "After I left last night, you mean? Surely you didn't get your mail before nine——"

"It wasn't in the mail," he interrupted. "It never is."

Rule number one of police work: Never make assumptions. I have violated that rule many times. I had just violated it again. "Then how do you get them?" I asked.

"Different ways," he said. "Sometimes they're on my office desk when I get to work. Sometimes they're taped to the back door."

Captain Millner and I did not exchange glances. There was no need to do so. I knew that he, as well as I, had instantly spotted what Jan Pender apparently had not spotted at all: The fact that for an extortion letter to be left on his desk, the extortionist had to have access not only to the inside of the restaurant but even to Pender's office, which presumably—but I wasn't going to jump to conclusions again—was kept locked. I asked. He said it was—for what that was worth.

"Open?" I asked then. "Just the letter, lying out flat?"

"Envelopes," he said. "The dime store kind. With my name written on it. Oh, if it was on my desk sometimes there was no envelope, and in that case yeah, it would be laying out flat—I mean, look, you saw my desk; anything that wasn't laying out flat on top of everything else I never would notice. But it was in an envelope anytime it was where anybody else could see it, and sometimes it was in an envelope when it was on my desk. Today it was."

That probably meant it was somebody who often had access to his office but couldn't always count on it, and so had prepared the letters so they could be left in any of several places. "The one today," I said after he stopped. "How did you get it?"

. . . . .

"When I got out to my car this morning, at my apartment, it was taped to my windshield. In an envelope."

Captain Millner uttered under his breath something I didn't quite guess, but it was safe to assume that it was scatological, profane, blasphemous, or all of the above. But he didn't say anything audible. This was still my case, and he was officially just an observer.

"Did you by any chance bring the letters with you?" I asked.

"I gave them to Ted," he answered. "I don't know—" He glanced at Siebenborn, who was already opening his suitcase-sized briefcase on the table in front of all of us. After rummaging briefly through what looked like the contents of one entire file drawer, he handed over to me a manila folder.

I opened the folder, laid it out on the table so that Millner and I could both see it. "This is the most recent letter?" I asked.

"Yes," Siebenborn said. "I've kept them in order." His tone of voice seemed to add, *and you better do the same.*

Today's letter was hand-printed (and hadn't he told me they were usually typed now?) on a torn-off sheet of green-line computer print-out paper, in pencil. Although I was sure it would already contain the fingerprints of both Pender and Siebenborn whether or not it also contained the prints of whoever wrote it, I was careful to weight it down with the barrel of a ballpoint pen rather than with my own hand, and when I was ready to turn it I would turn it with the barrel of a ballpoint pen.

This one read:

It's a shame about the axcident, isn't it? To prevent more axcidents, leave you're insurance premium in a suitcase outside you're kitshen door when you leave the restorant tonite. But becuse you've already had one fatal axcident the preimum has gone up now it's $20,000 in twenty-dollar bills. Thatll keep you covered for a month.

You're Insurance Agent

I turned this page over to look at the back, hoping whatever the printout had been would tell me something. It didn't; the back was blank. "Do you use this kind of paper?" I asked Pender.

"Yeah, sure," he said.

"What for?"

"Mostly accounting, that sort of thing. Some supply tracking, but I mostly do that just on-screen."

"Where would you store the paper?"

"Before or after it's used? Well, actually that doesn't matter," he said. "Either way, it's going to be either in my office or in the storage room."

"Thanks." That told me nothing at all, so I went on to the next—well, actually the previous one—which unlike the other was typed on a pulpy-feeling sheet of blue-lined paper approximately half the size of standard typing paper, call it 8 ½ by 5 ¼ inches. Probably torn from a writing tablet, the adult kind rather than the student kind. Probably a type of paper available at just about every drugstore, discount store, and dollar store in the Metroplex. The ink was black, and it had smeared enough on the porous paper to suggest that the perp had run sweaty hands over it before the ink dried.

You're restorant is in danger of an axcident. You better be careful. You're insurance preimum is due now. Leave $10,000 in twenty-dollar bills in a brown paper bag outside the restorant door when you leave tonite.

You're Insurance Agent

Millner, who had leaned over to read the first letter, was still reading the second. "This doesn't feel right," he muttered.

It didn't feel right to me either. The complexity of the sentence structure, along with the consistency with which misspelled words were misspelled, suggested to me that somebody quite literate had meant to sound semiliterate—something that often happens in situations involving ransom notes, protection demands, and anonymous letters of all kinds. But I could be wrong. A person could be quite well educated in the oral culture without having ever learned to spell. And consistency is not found only in highly literate people any more than inconsistency is found only in less literate people. Shakespeare, for cryin' out loud, spelled his own name at least three different ways.

"When did this one come?" I asked.

"About the end of August."

"When exactly?" *The end of August,* depending on who is talking about it and what the context is, can mean anything from August 15 to August 31.

"Last Friday," Pender said. "The thirtieth. I guess it was the thirtieth. And I gave it to Ted, I guess, Monday. Wasn't Monday September second?"

"Wednesday was the fourth—yes, Monday was the second." I'm not always that sure about dates. But Wednesday had been, after all, my twenty-fifth wedding anniversary. "Did you leave them the money?"

"I didn't have it," Pender said. "I left the paper bag. I left a note in it saying that I needed more time to raise the money, I needed to talk with the bank and it was closed Saturday. I asked him to give me four days, until September third, and then tell me when and where to leave it. I had it—damn it, I had it yesterday, I had it ready the day before that, but he didn't ask for it again—damn it—"

Pender was crying again. I slid him a box of Kleenex tissues; we keep them just about everywhere, because you never know when anybody—victim, suspect, or witness—will suddenly need them.

In the name of common decency, we all waited till he was through crying. Meanwhile I leafed through the rest of the letters, finding most of them, as Pender had said, typed in a very small typeface, worn ribbon, worn keys, on the same kind of tablet paper the penultimate letter was on. With the advent of daisy wheels, laser printers, and jet printers, typewriter identification had become almost a useless skill. But it just might prove useful here.

Then we all went on waiting until Pender finished crying. Finally, after he had gulped a couple of times and wiped his eyes and face thoroughly and begun to stare fixedly at the battered tabletop, Millner said, "And then you got another letter this morning asking for twice as much money. We'll put stakeout units at the Bird Cage tonight, and every night this week, if that's all right with you—"

"Yeah—" Then Pender looked up. "No, it's not all right. I'll just leave the money. I'm not going to risk anybody else's life—if they'd told me they'd do something to Julia I'd have gotten the money Friday somehow, I don't know how but I'd have done it. I won't let them hurt anybody else. I'll find the other ten grand somewhere. I'll leave the money."

"Do that," Millner said, his voice a trifle remote, "and he'll raise the ante again. He's already proven that. You paid him and he raised the ante. Your words, what you told Detective Ralston. You paid him and he raised the ante. You paid him again and he raised the ante again. Next time he'll want twenty-five thousand. Or thirty thousand. How long can you keep on paying?"

"If he bleeds me too dry then I'll close the restaurant. I don't want anybody else to get hurt—"

"Jan," Siebenborn said, "you going to take my advice this time? Because if you'd taken my advice and gone to the cops to start with this might not have happened at all. The killing, I mean. Sure, it might have taken a while to catch him. But he might have been caught and nothing would ever have happened to Julia."

"You're saying I ought to let them put stakeouts?"

"That's what I'm saying."

Pender shrugged. "Okay, so do it. You want me to leave the money like he said?" When he said that he was looking somewhere between Millner and me.

. . . . .

"No," Siebenborn said bluntly, "I didn't want you to leave the money to start with."

"I wasn't asking you," Pender said. "I was asking the cops."

"Use your own judgment on that," Millner said. "What we're going to try to do is pick him up when he picks up the bag. So unless something goes wrong you'll get your money right back, if you do leave money. But you might just as well leave a lot of cut-up newspaper, because we don't intend him ever to get the bag open. And in the meantime, we need to keep this file."

"What for?" Pender demanded. He turned to Siebenborn. "Can they do that?"

"Not without your permission," Siebenborn said, closing his briefcase without reinserting the file and lifting it, with some effort, back off the table to set it on the floor. He straightened back up. "At least not without getting a court order, which I assure you they could get quite easily. But I strongly recommend you give permission."

"What do you want them for?" Pender asked Millner. "The letters. What do you want them for?"

"We're going to fingerprint them," Millner said. "And because we know, from what you've told us, that both you and Mr. Siebenborn handled them, we'll need to get your prints for elimination."

"What does that mean?"

"It means," Siebenborn said, "that they have to figure out which prints are ours, and then the ones that are left after that might belong to the criminal." He sounded extremely exasperated. I couldn't blame him. If I had to cope with Jan Pender in his present mood for as long as Siebenborn had to cope with him, I'd be extremely exasperated too.

But maybe—probably—when he wasn't in his present condition of semishock, when he wasn't in the state of panic and guilt that had hit him when he began to blame his own response to those letters for Julia Gluck's death, his thought processes were a little more normal.

A slight surprise—Millner himself decided to escort Pender and

Siebenborn down to Ident for them to be fingerprinted.

As soon as they were gone, I grabbed Millner's phone and called the Metro Intelligence Squad, getting one Lieutenant Hollenbeck. As Millner and I had thought, there was no known protection racket operating in the Metroplex at this time. "And if one's moved in," Hollenbeck said, sounding highly unamused, "I want to know about it yesterday. You mind if one of my crew comes over to work with you?"

"Not at all," I said more cordially than I felt, although I really should have expected this. "If Captain Millner has any problem with that, I'll call you back and let you know. But you'd better know that Millner and I both think there's a real good chance this is an inside job."

"And there's also a real good chance that it isn't," Hollenbeck said, "or that if it is, they've got somebody on the inside in some other restaurants. That's not real hard to do."

Which of course was true, and I knew that as well as he did. A lot of protection rackets have somebody on the inside in just about every place they hit. It's easy enough to do; turnover in restaurant help is high. A cook, a server, a busboy—it doesn't have to be anybody high up, just somebody who can be bought for an extra ten, or twenty, or hundred dollars a week. Or, even, controlled by threats.

I wasn't far enough along to know, yet, who in Pender's organization might be that broke or that vulnerable. Right now at least I was provisionally ruling out Ted Siebenborn because he'd tried to talk Pender into reporting the crime, out of leaving the money. But the cooks? The maître d'? The servers? The cleaning crew? I hadn't talked with any of them. I made a few more notes, reminding myself whom to talk with, what to ask.

Then I called the medical examiner's office, getting—as I had hoped I would—Andrew Habib. "Have you already done the post-mortem on Julia Gluck?" I asked, carefully avoiding the word *autopsy,* which Habib insists—incorrectly—means surgery on oneself.

. . . . .

"Just finished it," he said cheerfully. "Cause of death, in your language, massive skull fracture and brain trauma. If she'd lived she'd have been not much more than a vegetable. Other injuries—"

"Never mind other injuries," I interrupted. "I saw her fall."

He whistled between his teeth, a sound that is at least ten times as annoying over the telephone than it is in person, and it is bad enough in person. "Glad I didn't. Looks like it must have been one hell of an accident," he said, "but what are you doing on it?"

"I'm on it because it wasn't an accident."

"She fell however far it was—"

"Forty-odd feet," I interposed.

"—and it wasn't an accident? Somebody must have had it in for that girl. *Woman,*" he amended quickly, leaving me to deduce that someone recently had taken him to task for calling women girls.

"Was she pregnant?" I asked.

"Oh, yeah, about seven weeks. Is that why?"

"Not that I know of. But I don't know that it's not, either. Is it possible to collect genetic material from the fetus and determine which of two men was the father?"

"Oh, yeah, sure," he said, "provided you can get both the men to agree to providing genetic material, or you can get a court order. And even then a DNA fingerprint takes about two weeks."

"I know that," I said, "and I'll have to think about what I can do about the men. In the meantime, can you collect the maternal genetic material and the fetal genetic material and store it?"

"I'm way ahead of you," he said. "I—it looked like an accident. But when I looked at the lab request form and it said to send the reports to you, I figured something hincky was going on. And anytime you've got a pregnant woman murdered, unless it's a hundred percent certain it's stranger on stranger, you've got to wonder, at least a little bit. So I've frozen some genetic material on both mother and fetus, and I've started DNA testing on more material. So when you get the go-ahead, just send the men over here—or I can go where they are, if you'd rather. I won't need much. A little blood, maybe a hair root—"

"Let me see what I can do," I said. "And thanks, Andy."

"Never let it be said that you caught me napping. TTYL."

TTYL is computer-bulletin-boardese. It means "Talk to You Later." Habib, I gathered as I hung up the phone, must have fallen prey to the information octopus I had so far avoided except when summoned by my husband to look at something funny so-and-so had said on whatever bulletin board he was currently reading, although it—the information octopus—was eating my husband, who had almost totally abandoned his ham and CB radios on the grounds that the computer nets were more interesting. This did not, of course, mean that he had decided to sell the ham and CB radios. No such luck. He didn't want them right now, but he might want them again later. So they were all taking up room in the maze of small cubicles our former garage had been transformed into, and a monstrous antenna, big enough to serve a small-town commercial radio station, still towered over our house.

Millner came back without Pender and Siebenborn. "I sent them back to the restaurant," he told me. "I told them you might come back." He sat down and reached for his telephone.

"If you're getting ready to call Metro Intelligence," I said, "I already did."

He replaced the receiver. "Who did you get? And what did they say?"

"Hollenbeck. He says he has no information about any protection racket operating in the Metroplex right now and he wants to send somebody over to work with me."

"Did you tell him we thought it was probably inside?"

"I did," I told him, "and he said it might not be. And that even if it was—well, you know how protection rackets work. I told him I'd call, or you'd call, if you had any problem with somebody coming over."

. . . . .

"No problem at all," he said, and grinned at me. He knows quite well I prefer to work alone. "Now go make reports."

Theoretically computers—I seem to be hung up on computers these days, and I don't know how to get loose—were supposed to create a paperless society. What they've actually done is create an endless use of more and more and more paper. When Harry was still in school getting his MBA, he would often go through five drafts of a paper I knew quite well he'd have turned in the first draft of in pre-computer days. And those were only the drafts he printed out. He probably went through about forty drafts on the screen.

And computers haven't reduced the number of reports police officers have to write. But now, instead of dictating them into a little tape recorder and handing them over to Millie to be typed, we're back where we started, usually typing them ourselves, only now instead of using manual or electric typewriters we're typing them straight into the computer, on our own little terminals that hook into the city mainframe.

Which means that we can't just make the reports and forget about them, not (to be truthful) that very many of us ever did that to start with.

No, we have to fiddle with them endlessly, wondering whether we should say this before or after we say that. And then after that we get printouts for our own paper files if we want them, which almost always we do, and we get printouts for the official detective-bureau paper files. And Records gets printouts. And—oh, never mind. The ultimate result is that we're using a lot more paper, rather than a lot less paper, than we used to.

I went and made reports.

About an hour later Mark Brody from Metro Intelligence showed up. He's a tall brown-eyed blond who refuses to dress like intelligence officers usually do, namely scuzzy, and he was wearing tan corduroy trousers, a white shirt and tie, and black socks and tan Hush Puppies. Considering the way some of the men around here dress, I consider his attire a treat. I've worked with him before and he and I got along together pretty well—in fact, if he and I both weren't happily and faithfully married there might be the possibility that something could have developed between us—which (the fact that we get along, as Hollenbeck certainly didn't know anything beyond that) is probably why Hollenbeck, who knows me well enough to know that I don't like to work with just anybody, chose him to send over. He's a sergeant in the Arlington Police Department, Arlington being between Dallas and Fort Worth. He sat down in front of me, sideways in a chair the way he usually does, and said, "Hi." He then lifted one eyebrow. Like several others of my friends, he can do the Spock bit to perfection, and once at a science fiction convention Harry and I attended we'd encountered Mark and his wife, Mark dressed as a Vulcan and Marguerite, complete with bikini top, slit skirt, and green body paint, as an Orion dancing girl.

I'm not into that stuff, really. Although Harry was disguised as Harry Mudd complete with tribbles and both Hal and Lori were running around somewhere in Spock ears, I was just dressed as me. Mark had expressed considerable disappointment in that fact.

"Hi yourself," I said.

"We've got a lot of restaurants in Arlington," he told me.

Trying to keep from bursting out laughing at his put-on air of secretiveness, I said, "I've noticed."

"Yeah, you've eaten at some of them, haven't you?"

"It was in Arlington," I said, "that I first learned to like guacamole."

"Yeah?"

"At Pancho Villa's."

"Yeah, I like that place. All those pictures of Pancho Villa all over the place—but none of them without his shirt."

We both burst out laughing then. It had been Mark himself who took me to Pancho Villa's, at the close of a very exasperating case involving the protection racket, blackmail, and other unsavory crimes, and all the way from Fort Worth to Arlington after we got the warrants signed he kept singing all the verses he knew of Pancho Villa's marching song *"La Cucaracha"* because I was sulking because I wanted to go home, not back to Arlington for the third time that day, and I was pretending not to listen. I had finally given up and started laughing when he reached what has remained my favorite verse:

> *Una cosa me da risa,*
> *Pancho Villa sin camisa.*
> *Ya se van los Carrancistas*
> *Porque vienen los Villistas.*

That means "One thing makes me laugh: Pancho Villa without his shirt. Now the followers of Carranza are running away because the followers of Villa are coming." But all the same Carranza had remained president of Mexico and Villa had wound up dead with or without Ambrose Bierce, whose disappearance was a case I was devoutly thankful had preceded my birth by a sufficient number of years that I didn't have to get involved with it in any way.

"There's another verse of it I used to like," I told Mark now. "The one about the baker."

"Which, *un hornero fué a misa?*"

"That one. I think."

"I don't remember it in Spanish any longer. In English it's 'A baker went to Mass; he did not go to pray. He went to ask the Holy Virgin for some money to spend.' There's another version that says it was money to gamble with."

"You're no help," I said. "I already knew it in English." Despite his highly Anglo name, Mark is half Hispanic. His mother came from somewhere in the Mexican state of Coahuila, and he speaks Spanish as well as he does English if not better. And I knew him well enough to know that he would not settle down to business until the amenities—lots of chatter and laughter—had been satisfied. I'd told him at the convention that he'd never have made a decent emotionless Vulcan.

"I never did figure out why you suddenly decided you like guacamole," he said.

"It tasted green."

"That's what you said then. And I still don't know how anything can taste green."

"Well, it did, that's all."

Apparently that was enough of the amenities, because he leaned back—since his right side was to the back of the chair, he could lean a long way back—and stretched, then straightened and said, "We figure if they're hitting in Fort Worth they're probably hitting in Arlington too."

"You're probably right," I said. "Unless it's a personal thing, and I told Hollenbeck it might be."

"So we're going back to look at this Bird Cage place first, right?"

"Right," I said.

"So what are we waiting for?"

"The stakeout squad."

We went on waiting, while I explained to him what we had and hadn't learned so far, and after a while Captain Millner came back in with Trish Warner and Dennis Nelson. Both were properly dressed for looking inconspicuous in the absolutely worst part of town, which is to say that both looked pretty scroungy: Trish, who has a bachelor's degree in criminal justice, was in glossy purple leather short-shorts, a lavender crop top, and plastic thong sandals, with her hair cornrowed with lavender, purple, and violet beads. The cornrowing itself might have looked elegant, were it not for the fact that to my definite knowledge she had left it that way for the last six weeks, and more and more tendrils were escaping the beads. She also had on purple lipstick and purple fingernail polish. I hadn't the slightest idea where she was hiding her pistol in that getup, but I knew quite well she had one despite the seeming impossibility. I had asked her once how she would chase somebody if she ever had to, with those thong sandals that were practically her trademark, and she answered, "I run a mile barefoot every day."

"What about broken glass?" I asked.

"I avoid it," she said, and then grinned impishly. "But the general idea is, I try to avoid having to run on duty."

Dennis was dressed a lot like my husband on a bad day: paint-stained high-water khaki trousers, a very faded military shirt with darker patches where rank insignia (private first class, it looked like) had been ripped off, visibly stained white socks, and brogans that looked too heavy to walk in. He had completed the ensemble with a tan canvas web belt and a tarnished brass Cub Scout belt buckle.

"I hope neither of you expects to hide *inside* the Bird Cage," I told them both.

"I'll be outside," Dennis said, "sleeping in the Dumpster."

"Gross," I said, remembering the time I'd had to go Dumpster diving trying to find a murder weapon.

"Nobody messes with me when I come out," Dennis said.

"I can well believe it."

"And I'll be at the bar until it closes," Trish said.

"Or until you get thrown out," I said, "which I estimate will happen about thirty seconds after you go in. The Bird Cage is a classy place."

"Don't worry, I'll be dressed up," Trish said. "Hey, look, I was out till four A.M. hunting a pimp."

"It took you that long to find one?"

"It took me that long to find the right one," she said, her voice a little grim, and I remembered then that we'd had several "working girls" very severely beaten up by a pimp they refused to name. "And then two more hours to make reports and take out warrants and so forth. So I got to bed about six, by which time the son-of-a-bitch was probably already out on bond, and when Millner called me I just threw on what I had on last night. I'll have a look around this morning. Then I'll go home and get some rest, and then go get my hair

redone and go back out there tonight looking decent. Or at least looking like a call girl instead of a five-dollar whore."

"How long does it take you to get your hair done like that?" Mark
asked, obviously fascinated. "Or do you do it yourself?" I knew the
answer, having asked once before, but Trish was quite capable of answering for herself.

"Myself? You've got to be kidding," she said. "I'm not that much
of a contortionist and I don't know anybody who is. It takes about
four hours of sitting very still, which explains why Whoopi Goldberg
on *Star Trek* wore that great big hat. It was to cover her hair so she
didn't have to get it redone before and after each day's filming, since
we can't assume cornrowing will still be in style three hundred or so
years from now." Trish actually looked quite a lot like Whoopi Goldberg herself, except for her height of less than five feet.

"And before you ask," she added, "no, I don't have to redo it every
day. When you have your hair cornrowed you sort of wash around it
for a week or two." She felt her head. "In my case, it's been longer
than that. But I was working at looking nappy."

We went to the Bird Cage in two cars, Mark and I in his and Trish
and Dennis in Trish's, as most likely they would want to leave a long
time before we were ready to go. That was fine with me except that if
they'd been in the same car with Mark and me, Mark might not have
felt compelled to sing *"La Cucaracha"* all the way to the restaurant,
sometimes expurgating the chorus so that instead of the cockroach not
being able to travel very far because he didn't have any marijuana, the
student *ya no puede estudiar*—could not study—because he had no
chicle para masticar—gum to chew.

After about forty-nine verses of *"La Cucaracha,"* Mark looked over
at me and asked, "Are you still married?"

"What? And would you please look at the road."

"I asked if you were still married. And I *am* looking at the road."

"Yes, I'm still married. What brought that on?"

. . . . .

"Oh, Marguerite pulled the plug on me last year. So I just thought I'd ask."

"I'm still married," I repeated, "and I intend to stay this way. But—uh—it was friendly of you to ask."

He glanced over at me again, his eyes twinkling with laughter. "You have the most interesting way of telling me to go jump in the lake."

"Was that what I said?" My eyes were probably twinkling too, and my tone of voice had been deliberately arch. But he got the message just the same, which is what I meant him to do.

"Sounded that way to me. Is this where we want to turn?"

"Yes," I said, "and there's the restaurant over that way."

Not unexpectedly, both Pender and Siebenborn—but Pender especially—looked utterly appalled at the sight of Trish and Dennis, and it took me a little while to calm him adequately and assure him that if either of them was where they could be seen when his customers were present they wouldn't look the way they did now. But finally I succeeded, and Trish and Dennis took the master keys, reluctantly handed over by Pender, and went wandering around, talking to each other in a sort of half-code I'd forgotten what I knew of, familiarizing themselves with the layout of the place.

Siebenborn left, then, and Mark and I, with Pender tagging along behind us, stepped into the dining area, so that I could show him where the killing happened, and to my utter astonishment I saw Arlo Gluck, an older man, and a young woman up restringing cables. I turned to Pender, my mouth open.

Before I could say anything, he said, "The girl is Julia's sister Luisa Sarana. I know Arlo told you about her. She's substituted for Julia two or three times before, for one reason or another, and she told me this morning she'd take over the position full time, to work her way through school. Well, actually, we'd talked about it before, because of

. . . . .

Julia being pregnant and all that, and Luisa was going to take over when Julia started showing too much—"

"Wait a minute," I said. "Julia hasn't even been buried yet."

"What does that have to do with anything?" Pender asked, sounding completely puzzled.

"What do you mean, what does that have to do with anything?" I said, just managing not to scream it. "There are just a few little minor factors like safety—not to mention decency—"

"That's Beppo Sarana up there with them," Pender said patiently. "Beppo may be past seventy, but he's still got all his marbles. If Beppo says the ropes are safe they're safe. He—when Julia was doing the show, most of the time Beppo helped Arlo check the cables, and he did a lot of the planning and stuff when we were getting it all set up. Look, I've known Beppo over half my life; he worked with me when I was flying."

"When you were what?" I asked involuntarily, before remembering Arlo Gluck's explanation of terms the night before.

"Flying," Pender said. "I used to do it. I can't now, of course." I made a mental note to find out what he meant by that *of course,* as he went on, "Beppo won't let Luisa go up if it isn't safe. He wouldn't have let Julia, if he'd checked the cables, but from now on we're going to check them every evening before the first show. And decency? I don't know what you mean, decency. The show has to go on. It always has. That's just the way it is."

Five

. . . .

I WAS RIGHT. Pender had saved the earlier letters and even their envelopes, and with Siebenborn now gone, he was willing—though definitely not eager—to produce them. "I just, you know, didn't want Ted to know how stupid I was," he told me, carefully avoiding Mark's eye. I suppose I must have seemed less threatening. "I mean, if I'd known then what I know now, I'd have done everything they told me to from the start. They say hindsight's always better than foresight—sure it is, if you're thinking about how right it is, but the problem is you can't do anything with it. If I'd had enough foresight—"

He stopped, sitting quite still and swallowing hard, and finally Mark said, "If frogs had wings they wouldn't bump their tails when they hop. Human beings have to act on what they know then, not what they might know six months later."

"Yeah, I realize that," Pender said, "but the results aren't always this bad. It's just—I thought—you know, to start with I just thought it was some kind of kook. Writing the letters, I mean."

The file he handed over in bits and pieces wasn't nearly as organized as the file Siebenborn had left at the police station; in fact, it wasn't organized at all. Pender, in the course of considerable search and thought, had brought out fourteen letters, some with their envelopes paper-clipped to them, from several different cubbyholes in, on, and around his desk, sticking them all into a manila folder as he did so. "I think there were more," he said apologetically, handing the folder over to me, "but I disremember where I put them. You know how that goes."

"I know how that goes," I agreed, looking with some dismay at the folder full of letters and envelopes he had crunched every which way in his hands before he dumped it all on the debris-laden desk in front of me. But then I reminded myself that I wasn't responsible for the way he handled them, no matter how much we needed any evidence for this case, including the letters themselves; at this late date warning him how to handle them would do no good. After all, he'd surely had his hands all over them as he put them all into the assorted cubbyholes from which he extracted them. All I could do now was handle them correctly myself: with tweezers, maneuvering each letter and each envelope into a heavy plastic sleeve so that it could be read and the handwriting compared to the other letters without adding more fingerprints and palm prints.

"Why are you doing that?" he demanded, watching me intently as I moved another of his binders so I could use a corner of it to hold the file open.

I explained. With luck, at least those few fingerprints and palm prints of the perp that might, by any conceivable stretch of the imagination, still be usable would be preserved. It's not that they would be wiped off by careless handling; unless the paper is extremely highly glazed the prints aren't on the paper so much as they are in it, sunk into the very fibers so thoroughly that in experiments fingerprints have been found on ancient Egyptian papyri more than three thousand years old. No, the problem was that if other prints are superimposed they also will sink into the fibers of the paper, so that the original prints will be so overwritten as to be illegible.

"You mean I did that wrong too?" The look on Pender's face as he watched was so gloomy it would have been comical if the situation were not so serious.

"I'm afraid so," I said, "but don't worry about it now. Just, if you get another one don't touch it at all. Call one of us." By now I had slid the last check into its plastic sleeve, and I began numbering the pieces of evidence, initialing and dating the write-on label on each bag, and handing them over to Mark so he could do the same. Mark added his initials, inside a neat end–barred oval almost like an ancient Egyptian cartouche, and stacked them insecurely between the two of us.

That completed, I picked up one at random, still inside its plastic sleeve, to read.

On second thought, I gathered all the plastic sleeves in my hands and started looking around for somewhere to lay them all out flat. This, in Pender's office, was a joke. Fortunately he realized what I was looking for and said, "You might want to take that out into the dining room."

I took them out into the dining room, with Mark Brody following, right hand in his pocket and left hand carrying his briefcase, glancing up occasionally at the acrobats working above our heads.

After settling down at a double table and spreading out the letters so that I could glance quickly at all of them, I began examining what seemed to be the first letter as Mark reopened his briefcase and took out the small red notebook he'd just put in it in the other room. Unlike the few of the later letters I had examined, this one was, surprisingly, dated. December 6. A quick look over the rest of the plastic sleeves told me that all these letters were dated. "When did he stop putting dates on them?" I asked Pender.

"After the fire."

"What fire?" Brody asked quickly, looking up from his notebook where he was listing the items of evidence collected and describing each one in case it got separated from its plastic sleeve.

"The fire in the kitchen. Didn't Detective Ralston tell you about the fire?"

"Not yet," I muttered, not wishing to tell Jan Pender that the only way I could have told Mark Brody about the fire would have been to shout it over repeated choruses of *"La Cucaracha,"* which included such important items as the story of a spotted cockroach who said to a red cockroach, "Let's go to my town to spend the summer"; an explanation of the best places in Mexico to find *serapes,* shoes, pretty girls, and love (*par amar toditos lados*—"any little place at all"); and a loud and semicoherent insistence that all girls have two stars in their eyes but Mexican girls are the prettiest. If I didn't know Mark as well as I did, I'd have sworn he was drunk on duty in the middle of the day.

And Mark Brody didn't even look embarrassed. He just put the notebook back in his briefcase and sat back down beside me, a little closer to me than I was comfortable with, to read over my shoulder.

I would just about have sworn these fourteen additional letters were written by the same hand that wrote the ones I'd seen in the police department, which didn't make much sense considering the wording was so wildly different. But I'm no handwriting examiner, and there were differences as well as similarities.

Like the others, these were all written on blue-lined paper, but these were written on the kind of blue-lined paper children use in school, wide-ruled and three-hole punched. Like the others, these displayed problems with spelling, grammar, and mechanics, but when I had looked at the other letters I'd had the feeling that somebody quite used to writing was pretending not to be, while these gave me the feeling the writer really was that ignorant. That puzzled me, until I realized I was reacting not to the actual writing but to the pencil and cheap paper.

Like the others, some of these had been enclosed in cheap business-size envelopes, but unlike the envelopes that had been with the others, these had either Pender's name and address or the name and address of the Bird Cage written on them in pencil. Some of them had been stamped, with perfectly ordinary postage stamps of the type you can get from vending machines, and had gone through the mail system.

This difference suggested a little something to my mind. Could the treatment given the earlier letters mean that the letters written before the restaurant opened had been written by someone who didn't—or didn't always—have access to the inside of the restaurant, while the different treatment, the different delivery system, of the later letters—written, probably, by the same person—indicated that person now did have access to the inside of the restaurant? Because we—Millner and I—had agreed whoever it was certainly had access now, whether or not he or she did earlier.

Well, maybe. Or maybe it was just somebody who wanted us to think that. Or maybe it was somebody who didn't know, or care, what anybody would think.

Unlike the others, these—including the envelope addresses—were written in pencil. Unlike the others, both the threats and the demands were extremely vague.

I sat back, still looking at the letters, letting my subconscious process data until, like an intricate organic computer inside my skull, it spat out whatever else it wanted to spit out. Then I realized what was bothering me.

The later letters—the ones now in our Ident office being finger-printed—had felt to me as if they meant business. These didn't.

These felt to me like somebody new to the protection racket, maybe somebody who thought he had invented the idea himself. Or maybe—put together with the fact that the real crimes seemingly aimed at the Bird Cage ranged from fairly mild (although the gas leak in the kitchen could have caused an explosion rather than a small fire, so the fact that it led to nothing in particular might not mean much) to very serious indeed—they were planned and written to distract attention from a real crime to be committed later.

In that case, was the murder of Julia Gluck and, incidentally, of the businessmen on whom her birdcage fell (because not even my some-times-weird mind could believe that anybody could manage to station the businessmen in such a place that they would be killed by a falling birdcage), the real crime, or was the real crime yet to come?

Were these letters even relevant to this murder? Maybe not, but until I knew for sure I had to assume they were.

Whichever was the case, I couldn't blame Pender for not taking these letters seriously. And now I had to start all over, because now I had to figure out what the real crime, the crime everything else was intended to cover, was, and who the real crime was aimed at. Julia Gluck? Arlo Gluck? Jan Pender? Or somebody who either wasn't on the stage at all yet, or somebody I'd never have thought of? Because another thing I absolutely did not believe was that the real crime was protection, whether or not the same person was aiming the protection racket at other restaurants and nightclubs at the same time.

I left Mark Brody talking with Pender, and I went over to the ladder leading up to the suspended platform. "Arlo!" I yelled.

"Yo?" he yelled back.

"Can the three of you come down and talk with me?"

"In a minute, we're in the middle of something."

I stood and watched them climbing around doing things with ropes and cables, and after a while Arlo came down, the girl and the older man following him. Arlo introduced Beppo, who said nothing, and then, defensively, Arlo said, "I guess you think this is pretty heartless, with Julia not even buried, but you've got to understand: this is the way we were raised. If somebody falls, gets hurt or worse, you cry by yourself, but the show goes on. Understand? That's how it is. That's how it's been for hundreds of years. That's how it's got to be."

Not wishing to let myself in for another lecture on circus history, I hastily admitted that although I didn't understand it myself, I could see that he did and that was how it ought to be. But then I thought, *Maybe I do understand it without realizing it, because what I understand is the same in quality even if it is different in kind.*

When Carlos Amado was shot to death at Clean Harry's Used Automobiles, we did our crying and we went on about our business, which was to identify and stop the bank-robbery team that shot Carlos Amado and Clean Harry and several women bank tellers taken hostage. And none of us stopped policing because of it.

I told Arlo that, and he said, "Yeah, that's the way of it. And I guess

. . . . .

82

to most people circus performers don't matter the way cops do—but to us we do."

That, too, I could understand.

"Arlo," I said, "I really need to talk to each of you separately, starting with you again. Could we use the dressing room again?"

"Yeah, sure."

Directing my attention to Luisa and Beppo Sarana, I added, "I'll need to talk with the two of you also, so I'd appreciate it if you'd stay available. Maybe get some rest, have a cup of coffee or something?"

"We'll wait here," Luisa said, and now that she was on the ground I could see that her eyes were red-rimmed and bloodshot. She'd been crying about her sister, but she was still planning, this very night, to go and do the stunt that had cost her sister's life, even if the props weren't all finished—the ropes were not covered with velvet, the birdcage was a little sketchy—and even if she was worn out from working on props all day and grieving for her sister.

Beppo Sarana didn't say anything at first; he just looked at me, wrinkle-rimmed bloodshot anthracite eyes burning with antagonism. Then, as I refused to look away ("Don't stare, it's not polite to stare," mothers teach their children, but cops learn to stare even as they learn why they were first taught not to, even as they learn that staring is a weapon), he shifted position, looked at the floor, and said, "Yeah."

"You guys wait in here," Arlo said. "I'll talk with the detective first." He turned to follow me, rather than lead, as I knew the way now.

Inside the dressing room, I said, "Do you understand that when we're investigating a crime, we have to ask a lot of questions that might sound like they're not our business? Might even sound insulting?"

"Yeah," he said, fidgeting a little.

"Well—somebody, I'd rather not say who, told me that you weren't the actual father of Julia's baby, that somebody else was. Is

· · · · ·

83

there any possibility at all that there's any truth to that?"

He looked toward some point beyond me on the left, maybe in the corner of the room, and slowly turned deep red. "Yeah," he finally answered. "Yeah, that's right. But I don't know who would have told you." He went dead silent, and I waited for him to resume speaking. Finally he did. "I just didn't see any reason to tell you that. I—um— I had mumps when I was sixteen. I don't know if that's the reason— the doctor told me a lot of doctors say now mumps doesn't really make any difference—but that or something else left me, well, you know, I can do it but it's like firing blanks. For the first few years after Julia and I were married, we couldn't figure out why we weren't getting a baby. And then—we went to a doctor. She went, first, to see if it was something wrong with her."

I was listening to this with pity and identification. For the first three years of our marriage Harry and I had gone through the same thing. Then a doctor told me, as gently as he could, that it was highly unlikely I'd ever be able to conceive. We'd adopted, then. The first was Vicky, who'd come to us as a six-year-old from a reservation in Oklahoma, where she had been considered unadoptable because of health problems she'd gradually over the next ten years grown out of; they didn't want to let her go out of the tribe but they finally decided the fact that Harry's about one-eighth Cherokee, even if he's not registered with the tribe, was enough. Next was Becky, who was only three weeks old and was genetically my sister's child; then Hal, six months old, from a Korean orphanage that took in abandoned children who were mixed Korean and Occidental. And Hal was fifteen when I unaccountably turned up pregnant with Cameron.

"So then," Arlo went on, "the doctor said he'd have to see us both. And he checked us both, I mean some really funny stuff you wouldn't think was medical at all but he explained the reasons for it. And then he told us that it was me. Julia was okay. But I wasn't."

"That must have been very distressing for you," I said.

"Yeah," he said briefly. "And—we talked about adopting—but

adoption agencies, they look at people like us pretty funny. You have to be stable and dependable and all that, and they don't think circus folks are. Now that's not true, I think we're as stable as anybody else and you couldn't make it in this kind of world if you weren't dependable, but you know, the way we look to other people."

"Their perception of circus people?" I suggested when he paused again.

He nodded. "Yeah. That. I don't know, maybe we could have done a private adoption, but that's risky, you hear about these people who sign all the papers and hand over the baby and then turn around months or even years later and say somebody made them do it and now they want the baby back, and you hear about these people who promise the same baby to a bunch of different people and rip them off for a lot of money and then keep the baby. Or even just women who change their minds in the delivery room, and hell, you can't blame 'em for that. And even where there's nothing goes wrong it can get real expensive. And besides that—physical stuff, flying, athletics in general, that's our life, that's the life of the whole family on both sides, and if we got a kid with two left feet, well, we could live with it, we'd love the kid anyway, but how would the kid feel?"

"But you—well, Julia—could have given birth to a kid with two left feet," I pointed out, "despite all the athletes in the family. It's like the Osmonds, that singing family from Utah. One of their sons is deaf and couldn't learn to sing. And from all I hear, he's having just as decent a life as the rest of the family."

"Yeah," Arlo said, "but he's not having to cuss out the rest of the family for *deliberately* bringing him where he wouldn't fit in."

He had a point, and I told him so.

"So—we talked to one of those artificial-insemination places. They said they could try to match us up with a father enough like me nobody would tell the difference, at least in looks, and they said they'd try to find an athlete but they couldn't promise anything beyond that. And hell, I mean, to them a football player is an athlete and you sure as hell can't turn a fullback into a flyer. You could a gymnast, sure, but how many Olympic-class gymnasts are sperm donors? And they wanted like two thousand dollars even to try and even then they couldn't guarantee it would work. They'd try again if it didn't but that'd be another two thousand dollars. And so on. And they told us some people caught the first time, but others, they came back five, ten times before they caught and some people never did. And we don't have that kind of money. Not even the first two thousand dollars."

"That sounds very difficult."

"So—we talked it over, and we talked it over, and finally we agreed she'd—just go find the baby a temporary daddy. Only temporary, you see, because I was the permanent daddy. She was—I asked her not to tell me who it was. I didn't want to know. I'd rather he was an athlete—gymnast, maybe, or tennis player; she knew as well as I did what we wanted—but if not, at least somebody pretty small, lean, strong, and agile, keep good genes in the family—but—she promised me she'd tell him he wouldn't have any claim on the baby. She'd tell him before they ever did it, so he'd know from the start what the score was. And she did. She did tell him. When she told me she was pregnant, she told me she'd told—him—that I was going to raise the baby as mine and he better not ever tell anybody different, not me, not his friends, not our friends, not the baby as he—well, he or she—grew up. She'd picked him to father our baby and that was a compliment to him, but he wasn't involved anymore. That's all. So—if you were wondering if I knew—yes. I knew. And that's not why anybody killed her."

About 100 percent certain, that was true, though I couldn't imagine why she would have selected Jan Pender as the father. Or could I? Jan was small and lean, and he had said something to me about "when I was flying" as though I ought to know about it. Maybe, once, he had been good. Maybe he did have the kind of genes the Saranas and Glucks wanted to keep in the family. And if he did, most likely Julia would have known it.

. . . . .

86

But I'd need to talk with Jan Pender again, too, and see just how much of this story he confirmed—without telling the story myself to give him a hint.

Arlo left, then, telling me he'd send Luisa in to talk with me.

Never mind the conversation; it was painful for both of us and added nothing to my store of knowledge. Summed up, Luisa said that everybody loved Julia and nobody had any reason to want to kill her, and she and Arlo had a wonderful marriage, and no, there certainly was not anything between Luisa and Arlo and I had no right to ask.

"I'm afraid," I said patiently, as I have said so many times before, "that cops have to ask offensive questions sometimes."

"Well, that one was pretty darn offensive." Her dark eyes continued to scowl at me. "The very idea—I'm engaged." She saw me glance at her bare left hand. Covering it defensively with her right hand, she said, "You don't wear rings when you're flying. Not unless you want your finger torn off. And I don't. He's in the Marines. We'll get married when he gets out. He went on this program that helps people save up college money, and we figure I'll have my degree by the time he gets out of the Marines, and then I can have a job while he's getting his degree—he's trying to finish up his first two years by correspondence, you know those correspondence colleges aimed at military people." (I did indeed; Harry had also gotten two years of college that way.) "So then I'll work while he finishes college and gets his MBA."

"My husband just got his," I said. "What do the two of you plan to do then?"

"Circus," she said. Involuntarily, she sobbed a moment after that. "Arlo convinced himself and even Julia that it was finished, no matter what he tried to keep going, no matter what anybody tried to keep going with nightclubs or carnivals. I'll bet he told you that, too, didn't he? The circus is finished. The last circus train, the last big tent show, was before I was born. This is the end of it." She gestured, presumably

· · · · ·

87

in the direction of the trapeze that wasn't in the room. "A restaurant floor show!"

I could barely remember going to a three-ring circus in a tent; it was sad that this girl, whose life was the circus, couldn't remember the tent shows at all. The hot smell of sawdust and peanuts and cotton candy; the dazzling spectacle of the clowns in ring one, the big cats in the center ring, the elephants and dancing bears in ring three, the flyers and aerialists overhead, all going on simultaneously so that no one knew where to look and everyone tried to take it all in at once; the grand parade with each elephant balancing its trunk on the previous elephant's tail and every elephant caparisoned in scarlet and gold with gorgeous women posing on them and gaily dressed trainers marching beside them, and glittering men and women standing caped and bareback on white horses, and clowns in toy cars and the ringmaster in his top hat and tailcoat; all of us walking outside before the show to see the lions and tigers snarling in their cages, the peaceful elephants using their trunks to shovel hay into their mouths and then, with the same trunk, daintily accepting a single peanut out of a person's hand— but Luisa was right and Arlo was right. It was gone. The circus that's left performs in an amphitheater or on television.

"He convinced himself, and he convinced Julia," Luisa added. "But it's not dead at all!"

"Oh?" I murmured in surprise.

"That's what Terry—my fiancé—says, and he's right, not Arlo, no matter what he got Julia to believe. I'm just doing this"—another sweeping gesture—"for Arlo, and just until I can get through college—it's better than waiting tables. And maybe I'll be able to convince Arlo, where Julia couldn't and really wouldn't even try, because she believed everything he said. I'll stop this—floor show—when Terry gets home. I'll probably stop a long time before that."

"Unless you're stopped before you get around to stopping," I said softly.

She looked at me, her eyes wide.

. . . . .

88

"Luisa," I said, "you're going up tonight to perform exactly the same act your sister died last night performing. Doesn't that make you feel nervous?"

"Of course I'm nervous," she said, "but—that's the family. That's what you do. You just do, that's all. You just do."

"Arlo sure convinced *me* the circus is dead," I said, half to myself.

"Ringling Brothers and Barnum and Bailey just added a fourth unit," she said softly. "Yes, it used to be two companies, and before that it was three, and now it's one. But that's only top management. They do shows all over the world. Every unit is a whole circus by itself. They need everything—clowns, animal acts, flyers—everything. I don't know why Arlo and Julia didn't try to get on; they're—they were—certainly good enough; but Arlo—and I really think he got it from his dad—convinced himself it was dead or dying just because it wasn't the same shape it was when his dad was young. But it's not dead; it changed, that's all, changed with the times, just like it always did, and it'll go right on doing it. When oxcarts were all that was available, the circuses, and they were little then, traveled in oxcarts. When railroads were built the circus traveled on trains and carried tents along because most places didn't have any building big enough to hold it. Then when the tents were no longer needed the tents were discarded. That's what Terry's dad says—the circus is adaptable; it always changes whenever it needs to, but it'll never stop. When it finally happens that people go into space in large number, to settle other worlds, the circus will go right along. Terry thinks he might get into management—they need MBAs, too, just like they need clowns and flyers and bareback riders and veterinarians and cooks and costume designers and—oh, and everything. Terry and I, we won't leave the circus. He just doesn't want to perform. But he doesn't have any problem with me going on flying, with one of my brothers or cousins as catcher." She took a deep breath. "You don't need to hear this. You're trying to find out about Julia. Do you need to ask me anything else?"

"I guess not," I said. "You've been very helpful. Thank you for talking to me. If you think of anything later—"

"I'll tell you. But I won't. Think of anything else, I mean. Do you imagine I've been thinking about anything else since it happened? There's just not anything. There—is—no—reason, can you understand that?"

"Yes," I said, "but there has to be a reason, even if it's one that wouldn't make any sense at all to anybody else."

"If there's a reason I don't know what it is." She stood, decisively. "Do you want Beppo now?"

"Yes, if you can send him in," I said.

Trying to question Beppo Sarana was futile; his European accent was enough to make Henry Kissinger sound like Walter Cronkite, and about all he said—and this he repeated often—went something like this: "Julia was a good girl. The Holy Virgin welcomed her into heaven. And Luisa is a good girl."

"I understand all that," I said, "but the Holy Virgin didn't make Julia fall. I'm trying to find out who did."

"She fell because she fell. She fell because Arlo didn't take care of her. He won't take care of Luisa, either. Those Gluck men, they never know how take care of women."

"What do you mean by that?" I asked.

"I mean what I say. Those Gluck men, none of them know how take care of women."

"What would a man have to do, to be taking care of a woman?" I asked.

"He takes care of her. That's all. But the Gluck men, they don't know how."

It didn't get any better, or any more coherent, than that.

I did ask what relation he was to Julia. "My niece," he told me sullenly. "Daughter of my sainted brother." He crossed himself, which I took to mean that his brother was dead. But of course I had to ask.

. . . . .

After having been informed about six times that his wife, his brother, his sister-in-law, and his niece were with the Holy Virgin, I thanked him for his help and he departed. I shook my head. In the South—and Texas is as much the South as it is the West—you get used to fundamentalist Protestant religious fanatics. Unless I missed my guess, I'd just encountered the first Catholic religious fanatic of my career.

I wanted to get Arlo, Beppo, and Luisa together and see if the trio could think of anything one of them alone couldn't, but when I went back to the dining room—Beppo had refused to carry a message for me—Arlo and Luisa were back up in the rafters. "I want to see all three of you again before I go," I yelled.

"Okay," Arlo yelled back. "Give us ten minutes."

Ten minutes was probably long enough for the other thing I had to do. I hadn't the slightest idea where Mark Brody was—he clearly was not where I left him—so I headed back toward Jan Pender's office off the hall at the back of the kitchen. On the way I found Mark; he was lying on his back under one of the large kitchen ranges, studying the gas pipe. "Where you going, Deb?" he asked me.

"How did you know it was me?"

"I recognized your ankles. Nice ones."

"Such gallantry I can do very well without," I told him sweetly.

After slithering partway out from under the range, he tried to sit up a little too soon and rapped his head sharply on the edge of the oven. "Ow!" he yelled, and scooted farther out, still on his back, and then sat up and began to rub his forehead.

"That'll teach you to look at women's ankles instead of your work," I said. "If you'd been watching what you were doing—"

"But the view there was less interesting. Is there no mercy in you? Is there no balm in Gilead? Come kiss it and make it well."

"You have rocks in your head," I told him, briskly checking the rising lump to make sure he hadn't broken the skin. "What did you do with the letters?"

"I don't know about rocks in my head," he said, "but I've sure got a knot on my head." He rubbed it ruefully. "The letters are in the car, o best-belovéd. Where are you headed?"

"To talk to Jan Pender. And I am *not* your best-belovéd."

"Again?"

"What do you mean, again? I never was your—"

"Only in my dreams . . . but that's not why I said 'again.' " Suddenly he abandoned the flirtatious mode, which I was having increasing difficulty responding to gracefully, and slid back into cop mode. "I mean why are you going to talk with Jan Pender again. You've already asked him everything you can think of."

"I thought of something else," I said. "Never mind, you might as well crawl back under the stove."

You know what? He actually did. On his back. I still didn't know what he was looking at.

"I don't remember exactly what it was she said," Jan told me. "Why do you want to know?"

"I'd rather not say," I told him. "Let's just say I want to know more than I do right now about Julia Sarana Gluck's love life."

"Love life." He snorted. "I don't know what it was, but it wasn't that." I waited a moment for him to go on. "Well, actually I do know, but—It was like she wanted it but she didn't want it. I mean—it was the damnedest thing. She came in to the kitchen one night after the last show was over, I remember Arlo was out sick that day and Beppo covered for him, and Julia and me, we started, I don't know how it got started, but we were talking about when I was with the circus, when I was flying. I guess I was drinking—well, hell, I *was* drinking— and I told her a lot of stuff, damn, I don't know what-all. I'm a lot older than she is, you know, I knew her when she was a baby, they had her up on a trapeze when she was two. And then she said she wanted to have sex with me. I mean, just like that, clinical. I didn't hardly know what to say, guess I just sat there with my mouth open till

· · · · ·

92

I managed to say okay or something like that. She said she'd tell me when and where, and then she got up and walked off like it was some sort of business deal. Well, hell. I was flattered, you know. And there were only two days one month and two days the next month, both times she got this motel room and told me where and when to be there. And then she didn't want anything to do with me anymore, I mean not just that way, in fact for a couple of weeks she was treating me like a stranger who'd just hired her for a floor show, and dammit, I never was a stranger to her, not since the day she was born. I asked her why she'd started ignoring me—look, she was no treat, she was like a zombie in bed even if she did thank me real nice each time, but she was a good kid and she works—worked—for me, and I didn't want her to be mad at me, especially for doing what she said she wanted. So she told me she was real sorry she'd been rude, she didn't mean to be—like that was all that mattered—and she said I'd been real sweet to help her, and she hoped she hadn't hurt my feelings. And she said now she was pregnant and that was what she wanted. And then she said she told me that to start with."

He rubbed his chin. "Well, maybe she did, I don't remember but sometimes when I'm drunk I don't remember everything real well. But I'm telling you, the whole thing didn't make sense. She wanted a baby, sure, most women want babies, but she had a husband. I thought, what the *hell?* And I—it was like I just about went into shock. Thought Arlo was going to kill me. These Gluck men, damn, you don't want to mess around with their womenfolk." (I stored that in my mind, placing it neatly right beside Beppo's somewhat contradictory insistence that the Gluck men didn't know how to take care of women.) "She told me no, Arlo wouldn't ever know it was me. Said she wanted me 'cause I had good genes. I asked her how she knew I had good genes and she said, 'You used to fly, didn't you?' Like there wasn't anything else on earth that mattered. And then she told me I wouldn't have to worry about the baby, she wouldn't ask me for anything for it. Said Arlo would think it was his."

. . . . .

And that was the only lie she told, I thought. The two stories, Jan's and Arlo's, jibed. So nobody had killed Julia because she was married to one man and carrying another man's baby—not unless Arlo had done a real good job of flipping out, and I didn't think he had.

"And you used to be a flyer?" I stumbled a little over the word, because to me a flyer is somebody like Harry, who pilots aircraft. By now I knew the circus meaning of the word, but it still didn't feel right to me.

"Yeah," he said. "But it was a long time ago, damn, it was close to forty years ago, and it didn't last long. I don't want to talk about it, okay?"

I did want to talk about it. But legally I couldn't force him to, and the misery on his face made it plain he wouldn't willingly discuss this topic he'd put off limits.

"Thanks," I said.

"Does that say anything to you?" He was watching me keenly. "I mean, her wanting a baby from me? Because I'm telling you, it makes no sense to me."

I could have told him how it made sense. But I didn't feel I had the right to; it was Arlo's business, not mine. So I went back to his earlier sentence—"Does that say anything to you?"—and answered it. "I think it says neither you nor Arlo killed her."

"Hell, lady, I could have told you that from the start," he said. "And I think I did. I know I was pretty drunk, but I think I told you that."

When I went back through the kitchen Mark was still under the stove, and I still didn't know what he was looking for. Nor did I particularly want to know.

It took me a little while longer to gather Arlo, Beppo, and Luisa all together, around a table in the dining room because the dressing room would be claustrophobic with four people in it. "Look," I said when I finally did, "the three of you probably knew Julia better than anybody else did. At the moment we're not even sure the crime was aimed specifically at Julia—there are other things that could have been meant, which would have caught Julia almost incidentally, just like those two men were caught—but if it was aimed at Julia, why? Each of you individually has told me there was no reason, but can the three of you together think of anything at all, no matter how far-fetched it might sound, that might make somebody want to kill Julia?"

The silence stretched on, as all three looked at one another and back at me. Finally, very timidly, Luisa asked, "Is it okay if it's *really* far-fetched?"

"Right now I'll listen to anything," I assured her.

"Well, it's our grandmother."

Six
. . .

I CANNOT, IN all honesty, say that I have never heard of a grandmother killing her granddaughter. I have. And the truth is that people are more likely to murder their relatives than they are to murder strangers.

But it was difficult for me to visualize a grandmother—anybody's grandmother—climbing up that swaying rope ladder to cut ten strands of rope with a sharp knife. Though come to think of it I'm a grandmother and I climbed that ladder (unhappily, to be sure) and helped Irene slash the rope totally in two, to collect for the lab the cut-and-frayed end that had remained up there to match with the cut-and-frayed end on the floor, and of course Luisa and Julia's grandmother would have been climbing ropes like that all her life—maybe I could picture it after all.

What I couldn't picture was any conceivable reason. "Why," I asked, finally finding my voice again, "do you think your grandmother would have wanted to kill Julia? And how could she have done it with nobody seeing her?"

"That's not what I meant," Luisa exclaimed, a horrified look on her face. "Of course she wouldn't have—and she's dead anyway, our grandmother I mean."

"Then what did you mean?" I asked.

"It's because of the war."

"What war?" I had noticed, by now, that Arlo and Beppo, who

were sitting on opposite sides of the table as were Luisa and I, appeared just as bewildered as I undoubtedly looked.

Luisa took a deep breath and poured herself a glass of ice water from the pitcher she'd brought from the kitchen. "I guess I better explain," she said.

"That would be a very good idea," Arlo agreed, staring at her rather blankly, "because if I don't know what you're talking about she dang sure doesn't."

"Well," Luisa said, "I hope I can make this make sense. Okay, between World War One and World War Two the Sarana family was attached to a circus that toured all over Eastern Europe. My grandfather, my father's father I mean, married my grandmother in Serbia, not very long after the end of World War One, and I don't know whether or not it was called Serbia then but she's always called it Serbia whether or not it really was, so when I say she was Serbian I mean I grew up constantly hearing about a country that right then didn't exist. Not just like she was from Serbia. She was like super-Serbian, really patriotic even after she became an American citizen. And nobody in her family had ever been any kind of a performer, but she took to it like a fish to water, there are stories in the family, how Grandma and Grandpa were married just three weeks after they met and she was flying six weeks after that—but her family, they just about disowned her—"

"They *did* disown her," Beppo interrupted. "My poor mama, her family thrust her out and she never saw any of them again." His eyes, suddenly glistening with tears, looked even more like anthracite set in his wrinkled bronze face as he wiped his face with a large blue-and-white-checked dish towel he was using for a handkerchief.

"Well," Luisa went on, "I know it's far-fetched. But there is a war going on over there, and it's a bitter one. Terry says they're still fighting World War One—he says people forget, but World War One never actually ended. The Armistice actually just agreed to stop fighting because flu was killing everybody. And as soon as the collapse of the Soviet Union took the lid off, they picked up their guns and resumed shooting like nineteen eighteen never happened. And Grandma—I mean, I don't really think it's likely that anybody would want to kill my sister because Grandma is—was—Serbian, but—but I can't think of anything else. I really can't. Not Julia. Everybody who ever knew Julia loved her—I wish I could make you believe that—" Her voice broke for a moment, then went on determinedly. "And you did say not to worry about how far-fetched the idea sounded. That doesn't sound very likely, though, does it?"

"Not really," I said, "though I guess it's not impossible." I thanked her for the suggestion without making it any clearer to her that that idea was too far-fetched even for me, though I expect she knew without being told. We went on talking for a few minutes, but nobody had anything to add. It all came back to the same thing: Nobody had any reason to dislike Julia, much less hate her enough to kill her. There had to be some other reason for the whole thing.

More and more, I was coming to agree with that assessment—but the facts remained that she was murdered, it looked to me like a personal kill, and I was no closer to finding out who did it or why it was done than I had been the night she died.

I thanked them all for their help, and as I began to gather together my notebook, purse, radio, and so forth, the three of them headed back up into the flies. They were all working hard, trying to make certain that by the time the Bird Cage opened for dinner everything would look as normal as possible. The last few times I'd noticed Luisa this morning, she had been climbing around with a tape measure; while I was still collecting my belongings she finished whatever she was doing with the tape measure, climbed back down, opened the bolt of purple velvet, and began cutting. By the time I went out the door she was leaning over the sewing machine, industriously sewing a wrong-side-out purple velvet tube.

There was nothing else I could think of to do at the scene right

. . . . .

now. Our stakeout people had long since left, after exploring the entire building thoroughly, and I went looking for Mark.

He was still under the gas range, lying on his back, with only about five inches of his brown corduroy trousers and his black socks and brown suede shoes visible.

He was snoring loudly.

Disgusted, I leaned over to wake him, and his hand snaked out to grab my wrist. "Fooled you," he chortled.

I twisted free quite easily, and stood up. *"Bastante, amigo,"* I told him.

"Enough what?" he asked in mock innocence.

"Cool it, Mark, okay? You're embarrassing me. Be as silly as you want to when it's just cops, but civilians don't understand."

"Es la verdad," he said ruefully. "But don't you even want to know what I found?"

"All right, what did you find?"

"Come on under here and I'll show you."

Before today, if Mark Brody had said that, I would have crawled under with him, assuming he really had something to show me. Today I was not about to. "Just tell me," I said. "Did you really find anything?"

"No. I hoped I would," he said, scrambling out from under the stove and dusting himself with both hands. "But it looks like whoever replaced the gas line replaced it all the way from the outlet to the range. It's this twisty metal flex kind of thing, same as the other ranges in here have, so probably it's the same thing this one had to start with. It looks like it would be pretty easy to cut across one of the thinner parts. If it was cut underneath, right on a flex crease, there'd be absolutely no way of seeing it. There'd be just a little bit of gas leakage, because the way the hose curls would partially seal the cut, but it doesn't take much to create a real danger, if it's a little leakage over a long period of time."

Our trip back to the police station was notable only for the fact that

Mark did not sing *"La Cucaracha."* Instead, he sang *"Alla en el Rancho Grande"* and a Spanish-language version of "Jingle Bells"—*"retiñid, retiñid, retiñid all día"*—despite the fact that it was only September. All these, mind you, were songs that can be found in just about any high school Spanish book and certainly had been in mine. He was not expressing his culture; he was amusing himself by working at annoying me, and I hadn't the faintest idea why and wasn't about to ask.

Fortunately, he did settle down when we actually got into the building. He and I together took the letters down to Irene Loukas in Ident to be fingerprinted—Irene said that considering the quality of the paper, which was poor, it was unlikely we'd get very good prints, but she'd try, and it would take her about three days, oh and by the way the rope had been cut with a sharp knife—and then we went up to let Captain Millner know what was going on. He was, as usual, roaming up and down the halls looking in on all the squad rooms, sitting in whoever's chair was vacant long enough to look over reports and keep track of what everybody was doing. When Mark and I stepped off the elevator, Captain Millner preceded us into the Major Case Squad room and sat down on Wayne Carlsen's desk. "What did you get?"

"Nothing," I said flatly, and then went on to make a fairly succinct, for me anyway, oral report.

"What possible suspects do you have, if any?" was Millner's next question.

"None that are more than extremely vaguely possible," I admitted. "Nobody that feels probable to me. But I've given some thought to Jan Pender, because if he was afraid Arlo would find out he was the father of Julia's baby he might have wanted Julia dead in—call it a sort of cockeyed self-defense. He out-and-out told me that if Arlo knew what was going on Arlo would kill him—which, by the way, doesn't jibe very well with Beppo's insistence that the Gluck men don't know how to take care of women."

"But?" Millner said.

. . . . .

I must have looked rather blank, because Millner said impatiently, "He sounds probable to me, all things considered. You said you don't consider him very probable. Why not?"

"Oh," I said, mentally shaking myself. "Well, if he'd done it I figure he'd have done it a long way away from the Bird Cage. From all I can tell, he's not lying when he says everything he owns is tied up with that place, and no insurance covers a restaurant that folds because people are afraid to eat there."

"But insurance would pay off on an accidental gas leak that led to an explosion," Millner said slowly.

"Yeah—if something like that had been repeated, I might be looking at him pretty hard," I said. "But this kind of thing—"

"Did he have any kind of insurance on her?" Millner interrupted.

That was something else I hadn't thought of. Any normal life insurance would be handled by Arlo and Julia themselves, but businessmen who feel their success depends on one or two key individuals have been known to arrange to insure those individuals for very high sums. That was worth looking into, and look into it I would. But how high a priority should I give it? I'd need to think about that some more.

"Who else?" Millner asked.

"Arlo Gluck, because of Julia's pregnancy and his knowledge that he wasn't the father. But again, I don't really believe that. My own feeling is that Arlo was telling the truth, and besides that, it's obvious that Julia's act was Arlo's livelihood as well as Julia's. I mean, sure, he could have done it as well as she could, but how many people would pay to see a floor show of a man dancing in a birdcage?"

"Gay bars," Mark suggested, the corners of his mouth trying to twitch into a burst of laughter he was trying to look as if he were trying to conceal.

Ignoring him, I went on, "But yes, I'll check to see what kind of insurance he carried on her. Third, Luisa, if she was jealous of Julia's act and wanted it for herself. But she's been crying her heart out, and also it's pretty evident that she *doesn't* want this act. She's just staying on now as a favor to Arlo and because she's working her way through college."

"Or so she said," Millner commented.

"She was convincing."

"Anybody else?"

I shook my head. "Sure, we can theorize all we want to that there really was somebody totally unknown to Arlo, Julia, and Pender, somebody just getting into the protection racket and feeling his way, who decided to make Pender his example for his other victims. But in that case, how could such a person gain entry into the Bird Cage when nobody else is there—which would probably be from about three to about five o'clock in the morning—and climb up that rope ladder, cut ten strands of the rope, and resew the velvet around it, without ever being seen and without anybody noticing any sign of forced entry the next morning? Or cut a gas line, or leave letters on Pender's desk, which is inside a locked office inside a locked building? I guess it's not impossible. But it doesn't feel likely."

"And that leaves you nobody."

"And that leaves me nobody," I agreed. "So my own opinion is that the best thing to do at this point is go on trying to create leads, since we don't have any to follow. I guess Mark and I will go on talking to restaurateurs today, just in case there really is a protection racket going on—and so that we can rule that out if there isn't. I'll check on insurance tomorrow. And I'd like to get Jan Pender on a polygraph."

"Get—what's his name?—Arlo, the dead woman's husband?"

"Arlo Gluck," I said.

"Get him, and her sister, this Luisa Sarana, on the polygraph too," Millner said.

"I thought about that, but I don't want to try that until at least after the funeral."

"Which is when?"

"I haven't even asked," I admitted.

. . . . .

"It's Saturday," Mark said softly. "I asked," he added. "That kind of thing, you always want to know."

That is true. Although the theory that the murderer always goes to the victim's funeral is as full of holes as the theory that the burglar always returns to the scene of the crime, still it's true that *sometimes* the murderer goes to the victim's funeral and *sometimes* the burglar returns to the scene of the crime. Which means that in the case of murder it's always advisable to have a police officer on hand at the funeral.

"Well, let them know it's coming, anyway," Millner said.

I knew why he had said that. Guilty people who really believe a polygraph is infallible will often confess before they even get to the place where they're supposed to be tested.

"That other fellow you told me about, Beppo Sarana," Millner said. "Do you think it would do any good to test him?"

"I doubt it. He felt sort of like squirrel bait to me."

"Then forget about him. But the others—has Pender consented to the polygraph?" Millner asked.

"I haven't asked. I wanted to discuss it with you first."

A polygraph—lie detector—test is not admissible in court, and rightly so, because it is somewhat less accurate than many people assume it to be. It can indicate lying in a truthful but very nervous person; a very calm person—or one loaded down with pills as simple and easily accessible as aspirin—might be lying through his teeth and still appear to tell the truth. A person who knows how to do it can make it look like he's lying on even the simplest personal questions, which are used to standardize the machine for this person, so that later, on questions he is lying on, he won't look much different. At best it indicates that a person is telling what he believes to be the truth, or believes to be a lie, no matter what the objective truth is.

Newly employed officers, often too eager to believe polygraphs, and newly graduated defense attorneys ditto and outraged because they can't get the results into court, are told the story of the man who believed he was Napoleon. He was incarcerated in a mental institution from which he very much wished to depart. He assured his psychiatrist he no longer had any kind of delusions. The psychiatrist put him on a polygraph. And when the man insisted he wasn't Napoleon, the machine indicated he was lying.

So at best, a polygraph isn't perfect. But it can be a good investigative tool, and that was what I wanted to use it for today.

With Millner's agreement, and assurance from the polygraph operator that he could be available at any time, I telephoned Pender. He was inclined to yell. I was not surprised. "Are you telling me I've got to do this?" he demanded.

"No, sir, I am not. You are not required to take a polygraph examination. It's entirely voluntary. It would help me rule you out if you would, but you don't have to."

He blustered and fussed some more, and finally he said he'd have his attorney call me.

I waited for ten minutes, exploring the contents of my in-basket to see how much of it I could get out of reading, until the phone rang. I grabbed it. "Major Case Squad, Ralston speaking."

"Detective Ralston?" I recognized Ted Siebenborn's voice before he identified himself. "What's this about you wanting to run Jan on a polygraph? I'm not really a criminal lawyer, but it seems to me—" He paused, apparently waiting for an answer.

"As I told him, he can't be required to take one. I'd just like to do it," I said. "At this point, I honestly don't think there's a chance in the world that he's guilty of anything involved with this case, but a more objective person looking at the situation might see him as a suspect. What I'm trying to do is eliminate him a little more than I can just on my own hunches. My own opinion is that he'll sail through the test."

"Let me talk to him," Siebenborn said, "and I'll call you back."

I waited, continuing to make my way through the in-basket. If the city of Fort Worth really expected me or any other detective to read the entire contents of his or her in-basket every day, they'd have to hire somebody else to do the detecting, because the stack of papers that appears in everybody's basket every morning is about as thick as a Russian novel, except that the paper is 8½ by 11 and usually single-spaced with small margins.

I looked over at Mark, to tell him there was nothing at all in my in-basket about any new, or old for that matter, protection rackets in the Metroplex. But Mark really was asleep this time, leaning back in Dutch Van Flagg's desk chair with his feet on the desk and his mouth open. I wondered again what in the world was the matter with him; I'd known him for years, and he'd never acted this way before. And sure, divorce can be traumatic, but why should it have changed him this much?

My musings were interrupted by another call from Ted Sieben-born. "He wants to know if he can go on and do the polygraph test today."

"I don't think so," I said. "Let me have the polygraph operator call you and make the arrangements."

Having done so, I woke Mark up. He told me, amiably, that since gangsters ignore city limits, he thought he should go back to Arlington and talk to restaurateurs there while I checked Fort Worth. He appreciated my telling him what was in my in-basket but, he pointed out, he was in the Metro Intelligence Unit and that's the organization that would generate anything for the in-basket about adult gangster activity. So he'd just mosey on out.

That was fine with me; I wanted to go get a somewhat belated lunch, and I emphatically did *not* want Mark Brody to go with me.

With a paperback whodunit tucked in my purse—yes, I still carry a purse, although now it's a combined purse and briefcase, and I wear my pistol in a shoulder holster—I decided to go to Red Lobster and lunch on salad, baked potato, and broiled fish in solitary splendor, reading as I did so. I excused my gluttony by going, after I finished lunch and returned the book to my purse (it is hard to look official when reading, even if it is quite an interesting mystery—the two best things about fictional mysteries are [a] they always come out right in the end, and [b] I don't have to do anything about them), to talk with the manager and see whether she had heard anything about a local protection racket.

She had not, and she pointed out to me that most of the time such people leave the large chains alone.

That was true. But I happened to know a restaurateur who had nothing to do with large chains. Leon Aristides was the cooking end—head chef, as well as original senior partner, now sole owner—of Helen's Club, about a thirty-minute drive northwest of where I was at the moment. His junior partner, business-and-glamour-end Helen Thorne, had been messily murdered a while back, but I knew the club was still in business because Harry had taken the whole family there for dinner about a week before Hal left to go on his mission. The whole family included not only those then living at our house—Harry and me, Hal, Lori, and Cameron—but also our two married daughters and their husbands and children, as well as my mother. The meal, I may truthfully say, wound up costing about a week of my less-paltry-than-it-used-to-be salary. Harry considered it worth it. I had offered to make Hal a good-bye dinner at home, but Harry said that wasn't festive enough and anyway it was too much work for me.

Well, that part of it was quite true, especially considering everything else that was going on at the time.

Anyhow I called Helen's Club from the pay phone in front of Red Lobster to see if Leon was there, which he was, and if he had time to talk with me, which he said he'd make. Considering that it was now two o'clock in the afternoon, that serving dinner the way Helen's serves dinner from six to midnight means starting to cook before sunup, that Leon is head chef as well as sole owner, and that Helen's has a full-and-people-waiting dinner crowd every night, that was a more generous concession than it might sound.

I went in the back door, trying unsuccessfully not to remember the first time I entered this door to see Helen Thorne's hacked-up body in fragments on the floor among the fragments of her equally hacked, but far less bloody, computer.

The office was neater than I had ever seen it. There was actually desk surface visible, and there were far fewer printouts than there used to be and those few were stacked neatly. The dozens of binders and catalogs that had hidden the desktop were now shelved in a metal bookcase. A stately blonde was sitting behind the large desk, and Leon Aristides was sprawling on the couch looking all arms, legs, and belly.

Unlike the office, Leon was not neater than I had ever seen him. But then, he never is.

To look at Leon, you'd never think he was capable of turning out anything fancier than French fries and cheeseburgers. A short-order cook in a greasy spoon restaurant, maybe—his apron was always dirty, his chef's hat (when he wears one) is always askew, and his chin always looks as if he shaved sometime last week. You'd expect him to be talking around a cigar, but in fact he doesn't smoke.

I could neither spell nor pronounce most of the dishes he prepared, but the only two things that kept me from eating them all the time were the cost in calories and the cost in money.

"This is Helen Johnson," he told me, gesturing at the stately blonde. "My new business manager. She's real good, Deb, you notice how good she's got this office looking?"

"I certainly did," I assured him.

"And you wouldn't believe how she's taken over and sorted out the tax records and that kind of thing. I could have hired just any business manager," he went on, "and I had a lot of good applicants. But I thought—Helen's Club—we really got to have a Helen. A Helen who looks, you know, like Helens ought to look. Not that it matters to *me* you understand, I got a wife and six kids, but this club, you know, any club, it has to have an image. So I wanted—well, you know. But she had to be a good manager too. And Helen, she's good."

Helen Johnson half smiled at me from behind Leon's back; it was clear that she agreed with me that first name and appearance were an odd basis on which to select a business manager.

"It's nice to meet you, Mrs. Ralston," she said to me. "Leon's told me a lot about you."

"Oh dear," I said faintly, remembering the day I had climbed into, and dug all the way through, the Dumpster behind the building looking for a murder weapon that turned out to be in a paper bag half a block up the alley.

"All good," she added, her eyes twinkling.

"And I thought," Leon went on slightly belligerently, "she might ought to sit in on this discussion. I mean, considering what you said you called about. Gangster activity. I don't know anything about gangster activity, except those filthy kids that write all over the building every night. I mean, we have to be out there with spray paint just about every day of the week covering up the graffiti. Can't you cops do something about those kids?"

"We try," I said, "but the parents need to do more too."

"Well, they ain't going to, and that's that," Leon said. "If one of my kids got mixed up in something like that I'd blister his butt real good. It's tough for me to keep my hands on everything at home, considering I've got to work almost every night, but I've got a good wife. And my kids, they learn to work. They work at home, and they work down here when they're old enough. Cleaning floors, busing tables, peeling potatoes, I don't care so long as they're working. Clarissa, that's my oldest girl, she's turning into a real good pastry chef. Studying French so she can go to Paris to study. Paris, you know, that's where you've got to go if you really want to be a chef and not just a fancy cook. I had to learn French when I got there. Let me tell you, that's the hard way to do it."

"I'm sure it is," I said politely.

"Okay, what did you want to ask about exactly?"

I explained.

Leon swelled up like a pouter pigeon. "If anybody tried something like that with me, I'd—well, I don't know what I'd do. But I'll bet they'd have to call you by the time the dust had cleared."

"Maybe you'd better call me first—"

He grinned. "Maybe so. But no, I haven't heard about any protection racket going on in this part of town. Helen?"

"No," she said instantly. "Deb—I'm sorry, I shouldn't be calling you—"

"Deb's fine," I assured her.

"Well, good, because I try not to call people by their first names until I've been invited to. But that's what Leon always calls you, and so of course I think of you that way. Would it help any if I gave you a printout of good restaurants in Fort Worth, the size that might be the target of that sort of thing?"

"It certainly would," I assured her. "How long would it take you to get it?"

"Is five minutes fast enough? We're in the local restaurateurs' association, so it's all on disk. I'm sorry this printer is so slow, but—"

"Five minutes would be wonderful," I assured her. "We had a printer just like that one, until a couple of years ago when my husband got a Hewlett-Packard."

She looked up from the keyboard. "What kind did you get?"

"A Three-P."

"Because I'm thinking about getting a better printer up here, this one is so noisy sometimes I can't hear myself think. How do you like it?"

"Well, I don't use it much," I said, "but he seems to love it. And it's certainly fast and quiet."

The printer abruptly began chattering. She was right. I could scarcely hear myself think, and certainly conversation was out of the question.

I took the printout back into the office with me and started making telephone calls.

. . . . .

By the time I had talked with about fifteen restaurateurs, none of whom had heard of a protection racket, I was about ready to consider Luisa's suggestion. Maybe somebody *did* murder Julia because her grandmother was a Serbian patriot.

· · · · ·

Seven
. . . . .

USUALLY, WHEN I'M on a complicated case, I halfway dread quitting time because it's so confusing, trying to shift gears and become a normal wife and mother while somebody's murder, and the fear that somebody else might be murdered, hangs over me. But this time I was rather relieved. I had a very strong feeling that whoever it was, whyever it was done, it wasn't going to be repeated very soon if at all. Of course I hoped, as we all hoped, that the culprit, or at least one of the culprits, would be picked up tonight, trying for the money. But I wasn't holding my breath on that one, I thought as I parked my car in the driveway, woke Cameron up and unloaded him from his car seat (he had gone to sleep as soon as I picked him up from day care, probably because he hadn't slept much the night before), and set him on the ground because he's too heavy for me to carry anymore. He was so tired he walked right past Pat, who was trying to kiss him.

I paused long enough to scratch Pat's ears and then went on in the living room. Lori, Hal's girlfriend who now lives with us, was sitting cross-legged on the couch in jeans and a sweatshirt, watching television (a quiz show, not MTV, which she will watch with Hal but doesn't really like) and doing her math.

As recently as a month ago, that would have been unthinkable. Then, she was still running frantically in circles trying to do ten times as much as she should have done, trying to make amends for imagined sins, sins she was accused of by the aunt she had gone to live with after

. . . . .

her mother's suicide. We had liberated her from that aunt about five months earlier and were now her legal guardians until she turned eighteen, which she would do in a few more months. Over and over Harry and I tried to make it clear to her that we didn't expect or want that kind of hysteria; we simply wanted Lori to be the best Lori she could be, and that was something she'd easily achieved as long as we had known her.

She and Hal are not officially engaged. The LDS Church does not forbid young men or young women from becoming engaged before leaving on their missions, though it strongly discourages it. But I was well aware that the gold CTR ring—the initials mean "Choose the Right," from a song that begins "Choose the right, when the choice is placed before you"—on the ring finger of her left hand was matched by one on Hal's left hand, as he trudged about trying to convert the entire state of Nevada. But his weekly letters home (required by all mission presidents of all missionaries, mission presidents being well aware of the propensity of young postadolescents to forget their parents exist) bubbled with optimism.

Lori had finally settled down, to do no more than the normal chores that would be expected of a daughter of the house. Usually she was the first person back home on weekdays; she would bring in the mail from the rural mailbox still required in our neighborhood, open the connecting gates to give Pat access to the entire yard, put the breakfast dishes in the dishwasher if nobody had taken the time to do it in the morning, check the dog's and cats' water, and then settle down to television and/or homework. She does not date; she had made it plain to everyone that she would consider her dating, while Hal was on his mission, to be a form of infidelity; but she does go out with other girls, high school or church friends, now and then, and she takes off in Harry's truck when Harry isn't using it, just as Hal used to do when he was home.

"Are you okay?" Lori asked, and I realized I had been standing stock-still in the middle of the living room for at least two minutes while Cameron dashed back outside, awake enough now to take his belated affection to the dog who adores him.

"Sure, I'm fine," I said, "just thinking." I set my purse down on the coffee table to take out Cameron's penicillin, a bottle of pale pink goop his nursery school teacher had handed me with the explanation that Harry had left it there and the next dose was due at 8 P.M., and go into the kitchen to put it in the refrigerator.

"There wasn't any mail today," Lori called after me, continuing to look at her paper as I returned to the living room. She wrote down a five-digit number and stared at it, then shook her head.

"I knew there wouldn't be," I told her. "I had to leave Pat in the front yard."

"Oh," she said, "yeah. Well, that explains why he was in the front yard when I got home." She wielded her eraser vigorously and frowned at the equation, which in all its permutations took up a fourth of the page. Then she looked at me again. "Joanie's mom gave me a ride home, and she told me the Perrys' house was hit today. And the Davises'."

Joanie, a high school friend whose family had bought Lori's aunt's house when she sold it to move into an apartment, lived about four blocks away. The Perrys lived two blocks down from us, on the same side of the same street. The Davises were back-to-back with us; as this subdivision does not have alleys, that meant that our back fence was also their back fence.

"Any idea what they got?" I asked.

"Mostly guns, at the Davises. Pistols."

"Lovely," I said sarcastically. Reuel Davis's pistol collection was fairly well known in the neighborhood. The pistols were not antiques. They were ultramodern stainless steel, and several were even of a form of high-tech plastic I consider particularly detestable because, unloaded, they will go through a metal detector without triggering anything. Their ammunition was stored with them, and Reuel Davis didn't have the good sense to keep them in a locked gun case no matter how many people told him he should. Even granted that he might feel safer with one gun out where he could get at it in a second—and frankly I feel the same way, the way violence seems to be escalating all over the world—the chances of his needing more than one loaded pistol in any kind of sudden emergency approached infinitesimal, and certainly the others should be locked away. Even Harry, who's been an NRA member since he was fourteen, keeps all but one of his guns locked up (even that one is well hidden from Cameron, on a shelf he is incapable of reaching even if he climbs a ladder), and had tried to talk Reuel into doing the same. Maybe now he'd believe us. But meanwhile all those pistols were now out on the street, and I was not filled with boundless glee.

"That's what I thought too," said Lori, who had been around police—and police thinking—all her life; she was the daughter of two dead police officers, so I didn't have to spell out my train of thought. "A television and VCR, at the Perrys. The Davises have this big TV and VCR combination that I guess the burglars thought was too big to carry off. Oh, and they took all of Mrs. Perry's medicines." She cocked her head slightly and looked at me, the corners of her mouth twitching suspiciously.

"It's going to cost her a lot to replace them," I tried to say gravely, "and she can't wait to do it till it's convenient." But I couldn't help it. I flopped down on the couch beside Lori and howled with laughter, as she joined me.

To know Lucille Perry is to know Lucille Perry's medical history, and it was obvious these burglars had never read a *PDR* and thought all drugs, no matter what their intent, must be usable for recreation. What they had gotten would have been an assortment of vitamins, thyroid tablets, asthma inhalers, high-blood-pressure medicine, diabetes medicine, and heart medicine. Mrs. Perry is not a hypochondriac—she is genuinely that ill—but I could not imagine what use anybody else could conceivably have for her medicine. "Actually it

. . . . .

may not be all that funny," I added, finally sobering, "because if one of the burglars overdoses on Diabinese he'll have a hypoglycemic attack he won't forget in a hurry, and if he overdoses on digitalis he'll be dead even faster. But I sure do hate to hear about more burglaries in the neighborhood."

"So do I," Lori added, "and I guess I'm glad Pat was in the front yard. But I did want to get the mail too."

The regular mail carrier on our route had warned us there would be no mail delivery anytime the dog was running loose, and they consider him to be running loose even if he is inside a fence in the front yard, because he is perfectly capable of standing on his hind legs and biting somebody putting mail in a box on the fence post. My pointing out that he has never actually bitten anyone—all he ever does is stand on his hind legs and bark—made no impression whatever.

So the choices were to leave Pat confined only to the backyard, which would make it easier for the neighborhood burglars to come in the front door with impunity; to leave the connecting gates open, which would keep the house perfectly safe from burglars but would prevent mail delivery; or to put Pat in the house, which would protect the house from burglars but not from Pat, who chews on furniture and poops on the floor. Maybe if I got Harry to put up a new post and mailbox about six feet away from the fence, on the other side of the driveway . . .

But he couldn't do that right now, because I needed him to do other things.

"Deb, you *sure* you're okay?" Lori was looking at me quizzically, the pages of numbers, xs, and ys totally ignored for the moment.

"Really, I'm fine. I'm just thinking—we've got a money drop at the Bird Cage tonight, that extortion thing, and I'm hoping it all goes okay. We think there's a good chance we'll pick up the killer, or at least one of his friends. But you know how I get—wondering if everything will work out." It was safe to tell this to Lori; like most cops'

• • • • •

children, she knows that cops sometimes have to blow off steam at home, and that things of this nature are never to be repeated outside the house.

"You want to go back out there tonight?" Lori asked.

"Well—"

"Because I'd be glad to watch Cameron again, honest. He looks like he's just about over the earache, and I'll bet he'll sleep like a log."

"You sure you don't have anything planned?" I asked cautiously. I do not ever want Lori to think even for a second that we asked her to come and live with us so that we'd have a built-in baby-sitter for Cameron; she's been through far too much already to cope with that sort of suspicion.

"Ward activity night this year is Tuesday," she reminded me, "and there's nothing going on at school. I was just going to stay home and study for a Spanish test after I finish this darn algebra, and I can do that okay with just Cameron and me here."

There was, of course, no idea in either my mind or hers of my going alone; although Harry doesn't accompany me on regular police calls even if they do come at odd hours, he loves to go along when I'm off duty and checking things out on my own time. He likes to play cop.

We could not afford dinner at the Bird Cage two nights in a row; that was out of the question, or at least I considered it out of the question whether we could technically afford it or not. (No, we didn't *have* to pay last night—nobody there when the birdcage fell did—but Harry quixotically insisted on paying anyway.) But maybe a drink for Harry, a club soda with a twist of lemon for me, maybe a salad—we'd get there late, fairly near closing time, because closing time and afterward was when anything that was going to happen would happen. "I'll see how Harry feels about it," I said. "Really I would like to go back out there, but I won't even want to leave until after Cameron's gone to sleep. So it shouldn't interfere with your evening at all."

"Okay," she said placidly, and returned to her math and her televi-

116

sion show as I went to change clothes. It's odd, really: I'd feel naked at work without that shoulder holster I've worn for years, but the moment I walk in the door at home the holster becomes a maddening encumbrance. Why I can search a house or car wearing a shoulder holster, but cannot cook dinner wearing one, is beyond my comprehension. It would probably take a shrink to explain it, and I have other things to discuss with my shrink. I went into the kitchen, started the spaghetti sauce, and when I could leave it to simmer I went back to the living room to read the newspaper.

"That smells good," Lori said twenty minutes later, as I laid the paper down and headed back for the kitchen to put on the water for the pasta. "Is there anything I can do to help?"

"Not really," I said, "and you're busy anyway." Indeed she was; she seemed to be using the eraser more than she was the pencil lead.

"Well, but the math can wait." She looked at the math book, a quizzical expression on her face. "It might as well."

"If you're anything like me," I said, "math can always wait. Well, if you want to do something about the lettuce—"

I whack off a quarter of a head of iceberg lettuce and chop it with a paring knife, no matter what my homemaking teacher told me a hundred years ago when I was in high school. Lori, who is still in high school and still taking homemaking, carefully separates every lettuce leaf from the head and tears every lettuce leaf into two dozen pieces. Neither of us thinks the other's method makes much sense, but we do not quarrel over it.

Supper was ready by the time Harry got home; it was memorable only for the fact that Cameron brought Pat in so Pat could have spaghetti, and I had to go take Pat back out (without spaghetti), pour a sufficient quantity of Purina Dog Chow into his bowl, replenish his water, and wash my hands. And Cameron's hands, of course.

Harry was, to tell the truth, underwhelmed by the idea of my going back to the Bird Cage, probably because as it turned out he couldn't go with me no matter how much he wanted to. This time he'd be tied

. . . . .

up all evening on Elks Lodge activity. But he grudgingly agreed it made sense for me to go. "Would you mind taking the car and letting me take the truck?" I added.

He stared at me for a moment, and then said, "Don't tell me why. I have a hunch I don't want to know." He vanished into the bedroom, coming back moments later with a briefcase full of papers he evidently had to take with him to the lodge.

I stuck the dishes into the dishwasher and straightened the kitchen. Lori was now crying over the algebra, which neither Harry nor I could help her with in the slightest. I offered her a Kleenex and sympathy, got Cameron to bed, and went to take a little bit of a nap before taking off again. About eleven, with Lori already in bed and Harry due home from the lodge momentarily, I got up and dressed decently for the Bird Cage, which involved putting my pistol in my purse instead of my shoulder holster, and took off.

As anybody with any knowledge of human nature could have predicted, I had trouble finding a parking place; in fact, I wound up leaving the truck on the street just outside the parking lot. The restaurant was jammed. I think that was when I began to wonder about the accuracy of a statement I'd made earlier in the day, that Pender, if he was going to commit murder, would do it a long way from the Bird Cage, to protect his investment. Would he? Or would he count on this reaction?

Would anybody kill a beautiful, much-loved young woman—a pregnant one at that—to make his restaurant succeed?

And more to the point, would Jan Pender kill to make his restaurant succeed?

I didn't think so. But I've been known to be wrong.

When I got inside, Pender, who was behind the reception counter looking at reservation lists, pounced on me as if he had been expecting me. "What in the hell is all this about a polygraph?" he demanded.

"I told you over the phone—"

"Tell me again face-to-face."

. . . . .

"Right here in the lobby?" I inquired. There were at least ten people in the lobby, presumably waiting for tables.

He glanced around as if he expected to see a room full of spies rather than customers. Then he said, "My office."

I followed him down the hall, passing the bar on the way, where I glanced inside to see Trish Warner, her hair replaited into a much neater version of the braids and beads she had been wearing earlier in the day, her face carefully made up. She was now clad in a slinkily elegant white cocktail dress with strappy gold sandals, and looked like somebody one might encounter in an elegant bar in Beverly Hills. As she talked she was holding, and gesturing with, a glass containing what looked like and probably was weak iced tea, and the three males sitting at the table with her and drinking what certainly was *not* weak iced tea were gazing at her admiringly.

I did not go out and look in the Dumpster to see whether Dennis Nelson also was on the job. I took it that he was and let it go at that.

Pender's office was no more tidy than it had been earlier in the day, and its crowding had been increased by one small blue suitcase, cosmetic size, lying on its side on the floor; Pender had to walk around it to get to his desk chair. "Is that the money?" I asked.

He glanced at it. "Uhhh—I couldn't get all the money they asked for," he said. "It's ten thousand dollars. You remember, I told you this morning I had it." He put the suitcase up on the desk and opened it.

Ten thousand dollars, in hundred-dollar bills, is one hundred pieces of paper. Neatly banded, it takes up less space than a ream of paper. No wonder the suitcase was small.

"What's that?" I asked, seeing a white envelope loose in the suitcase.

"It's a letter telling them I'll get the rest but they've got to give me time." He was closing the suitcase, returning it to the floor, as he spoke. "Look, I know you think this is stupid, but I don't want anything else to happen, and—" His voice trailed off. He began shaking his head and forgot to stop, until he sat down behind the cluttered

. . . . .

desk and dropped his head into his hands. "Dammit, it's like I've been living in a nightmare." His voice was muffled. "When is it gonna end? I keep thinking—she can't really be *dead,* not Julia, she was about the most alive person I ever knew—but then I know she really is dead. I didn't want Luisa to go up tonight, but she told me she was going to anyway and Arlo and Beppo backed her up on it. I just—sometimes I wonder if it's worth it. Any of it."

He looked back up at me, his eyes wet. "So why do you want me to take a lie detector test? You think I killed Julia? Is that what you think? You told me you didn't—" He was shouting at me now, his voice violent.

Deliberately making my own voice soft in hopes of defusing his rage, I began, "Jan—"

"I know my name. You don't have to remind me of it." His voice was still raised, but he probably wouldn't be audible past the kitchen now. "Why do you think I killed Julia? Julia and the baby? My own baby, even if I never was going to be able to say it was? What kind of person do you think I am? You think I'm a murderer?"

"I don't think you're a murderer," I said.

"Then why—"

"Jan," I began again, and this time he let me finish. "I don't think you're a murderer. I don't think you killed Julia. But I can see why other people, looking at the evidence I've got and not seeing you in person, might think so. That's why I want to be able to tell anybody who asks why I haven't taken a warrant for you that I've ruled you out. A polygraph—with the results I expect to get—will rule you out. And that'll give me more time to investigate and find out who really did it."

He gestured toward the suitcase. "What if you—your stakeout people—what if they get him tonight? Then what?"

"Then I might not need to put you on a polygraph," I said, "but I might still need to, because the person might be very convincing that yes, he was doing the extortion and yes, he was responsible for the fire

. . . . .

in the kitchen, but he didn't kill Julia Gluck. Jan, I can't run on hunches, do you understand that? I have to run on facts. A polygraph isn't conclusive; that's why it can't be presented in court. But the results of polygraph tests are facts."

Pender took a deep breath. "Okay," he said, and tried to grin at me. "What does your husband think it's like, going to bed every night with police protection? You sleep with a pistol? Your husband, does he sleep in a bulletproof vest?"

"No," I said, understanding that he was lashing out at me in hopes of diffusing his own rage. "At home I'm a wife. If you had a wife you'd understand that. Or have you ever been married?"

That was the wrong question to ask, and I didn't know why. Obviously I had said something, in those few words, to trigger something in Pender's mind, because he dropped his head in his hands again and wept for fully five minutes.

I watched him uncomfortably. If this weren't a police investigation, I could leave. If I knew why Pender was crying, I could say something that might be at least a little bit consoling. But this was a police investigation and I didn't know why he was crying this time—though I had a hunch I was going to have to find out—and so I waited, uneasily. I finally sat down.

Pender quit crying, finally. "Stay here," he said thickly. He stood up, pushed his coatrack aside, opened a door behind his desk that I hadn't really noticed before, and went inside. Before the door slammed shut, I caught a glimpse of sanitary facilities, not very clean.

The executive washroom? I wondered.

I sat. I waited. After a while, Pender came back out. He had washed his face, removing most but not all of the evidence that he'd been crying. "You here for dinner?" he asked.

"Just something to drink will do," I said. "Club soda with a twist of lemon, maybe." The fact was I didn't even want that, but I did want to be out in the dining area, and to be there without anything at all would make me very conspicuous.

. . . . .

"It'll be on the house. You didn't have a very good experience last night. I don't know why your husband insisted on paying."

"I already ate," I said, as politely as I could. "I just wanted—I wanted to be here, Jan, in case the person is caught tonight. And I wanted to see Luisa's act. Remember, I never did see how Julia's was supposed to conclude. Does Luisa do all the same things Julia did?"

"Every one," Jan said. "And that's right, you didn't see it, did you? Well, come on, the show's starting in ten minutes."

He paused in the hall to lock the door to his office, and then I followed him back out to the dining room. After a whispered consultation with a waiter, he said, "No tables available, which I expected. We've got a long waiting line. I told them to quit taking reservations at eleven, unless they're for tomorrow night. If we lock the doors at twelve we'll still have people here till one. But they always keep my table open. So join me there. What can I offer you? You don't really want club soda, now do you? Wine, cocktails, beer? We got it all. I'm paying." He was trying to sound jovial. He was not succeeding. But if I refused to sit at Jan's table, if I refused his offer of something to drink, I'd create more awkwardness instead of less.

"Just some kind of sparkling water with a twist of lemon or lime," I said. "And thank you."

"That's all? I've got good *vino,* none of this supermarket stuff."

"Just water," I repeated. "Really. I can't drink anymore."

"Monkey on your back?" he asked sympathetically. "Well, I can understand that." I blushed as he called a waiter over to get my sparkling water. But if he wanted to assume I couldn't drink because I was a recovering alcoholic that was fine with me. I didn't want to try to explain my religion at this time.

Last night I had been paying more attention to my food than to the preparations for the show. This time, I drank the sparkling water almost absently, watching the ceiling carefully. When I had entered the dining room, Beppo, in white leotard and tights—and despite the fact that he had to be in his seventies he looked good in them—was stand-

* * * * *

ing on the platform, and Arlo, also in white leotard and tights, had climbed a rope to get to the top of the room where all the cables were attached. I watched him as he finished checking them and then slid back down a rope to leap six feet and land, as lightly as a squirrel, on the platform. Then Arlo and Beppo pulled lines that drew the gilded cage with its trapeze bar toward them. The two of them held it, as Luisa, decked out in a yellow bird costume (and where had she gotten it? She couldn't possibly be wearing Julia's) carefully climbed in and arranged herself. They pulled more cords, and the entire swing assembly moved back out to the center of the huge dining room before Luisa began to swing.

Attempts were made at this point to distract the attention of the audience from the necessary business that preceded the show; the singer, dressed in clothing that would befit the 1890s more than the 1990s and talking through his megaphone, was imitating old vaudeville routines, making lame jokes that were so unfunny that, paradoxically, they were funny, while the band tuned up in a rather loud and seemingly uncoordinated way that accented the worst of the jokes and added to the hilarity.

It was camp, of course, and maybe a person has to be just the right age to appreciate camp, but I must be that age.

I noticed tonight, as I hadn't last night, that Arlo and Beppo (and where was Beppo last night? He wasn't in the dining room when Julia fell; I didn't see him afterward; and of course there was no reason for me to notice beforehand) pulled more ropes toward them, so that the swing's cables and the swing and cage themselves assumed a position that was almost horizontal to the floor. At this point Luisa was leaning backward for balance, sitting on the trapeze and clinging hard to both sides.

When they released the ropes, the trapeze assembly swung forward well past its point of suspension. By the time it moved back toward that point again, Luisa was standing. She pumped rhythmically as a child pumps a playground swing, sometimes standing, leaning her body backward and forward, sometimes sitting, leaning her body in one direction and her legs in the other direction.

Another thing I hadn't noticed last night was that as she began to swing there was no more cable from the suspension point to the trapeze bar than a child would have on that playground swing. As her swinging continued to strengthen, Arlo and Beppo let out more and more line until, like her sister last night, she was swinging in twenty-foot arcs out over the diners.

By now—and I hadn't even noticed when he'd made the transition—the singer had abandoned the attempts at humor and was singing. As last night, he began with "I'm Only a Bird in a Gilded Cage." Other singers joined him, from where I couldn't tell, until an entire barbershop quartet complete with straw hats and waxed handlebar mustaches was singing and gesturing, as overhead Luisa danced on the trapeze with a brilliant smile that told no one it was her sister who had fallen to her death from that same spot twenty-four hours earlier.

I watched Arlo and Beppo maneuver the ropes; she was still at least partially under their control. Gesturing toward them, I asked, "Jan, is that how they always do it?"

He answered me absentmindedly, his eyes on Luisa. "Oh, yeah, that's the way it's done."

That was when I remembered the rest of what I wanted to ask him. "I'd really appreciate it if you would tell me a little about your circus background."

This jerked his attention back to me. He wasn't watching Luisa at all as he answered, "Do you really need to know?"

"I'm not sure," I told him. "But the problem is that I won't know whether I need to know until I *do* know."

"Well—" Once again, he wasn't looking at me; his eyes were fixed on Luisa. "When I was a kid, you know, I wanted to be a gymnast. My parents, they came here from Hungary in nineteen fifty-seven, changed their names and Anglicized them, and I was old enough then I knew that the whole USSR had a good gymnastic reputation. In fact

· · · · ·

I'd gotten started in Hungary, before the rebellion."

"I remember the rebellion," I said.

"I thought you might. We came here after the rebellion—managed to get out before the Russkies closed the border, spent about six months in West Germany before getting to the United States. And—I still wanted to be a gymnast. You know, Olympic gold and all that? I got pretty good at it, but to win the prizes you've got to be small and lithe. Small-boned especially; it's okay to be fairly tall if you're small-boned. If you're too big, tall or heavy-boned either one, it doesn't matter how good you are; it just doesn't look right. And by the time I was sixteen it was pretty evident I was going to be too big, too tall and too heavy-boned both." (That rather surprised me; he looked short and slim enough to me.) "And besides that, by then I had figured out you've got to have a good coach, an expensive coach, and in the free world you've got to pay for it yourself. And except for a little stuff at the Y, I was pretty well self-taught after I was eleven. But I kept working out, trying to think of a way I could use the abilities I'd learned. I thought about going to Hollywood and being a stunt man, you know, but then when I was sixteen the circus came to town and I went to it—never had before, not since we left Hungary, because my folks never had the money to take me, but they knew I was feeling blue 'cause the gymnastics dream was over. Well, I saw the flyers, and *man!* So I rigged up a trapeze in the backyard, my folks were always as sympathetic to what I wanted as they could afford to be, and when I graduated from high school I went down to Florida, you know, Sarasota, where the circuses live when they're not at work, and I got into flying. You know, aerial acts. I was good. I was damn good. But you know, these circuses, the flyers and so forth, they tend to be families. And they'd rehearse with me, I learned to fly and to catch, but when it came to traveling with the show, well, that was mostly family and nobody would admit to having a place for me. And flying, it's not like lion training, you can't do it alone and look good, except for something like that." He gestured at Luisa. "And that's not really

. . . . .

flying. So I performed at Circus Circus for a while, you know, in Las Vegas, they don't insist on families, they'll let individuals come in and learn to work together, and then I got accepted at the Moscow Circus for a while despite being Hungarian-American and that was great, Russia had some really good circuses, except I don't speak Russian very well." He grinned. "I didn't speak Russian at all, until I got there. But I learned, real quick; I was there about three years. But they were having budget cuts, and let me go. I came back home and I couldn't find any kind of work for a while. I mean I was working in a restaurant, busboy, waiter, that kind of thing. And you know, I like restaurants, I really do, but the kind I like you have to be a real chef to cook for them, and I never had the time or money to go to chef school. But then—then I got one of the troupes in the United States to accept me."

"How'd you do that?" I asked.

He shrugged. "I just did. I told you I was good. So I traveled with the circus about four years, United States and Europe, but then I had a real bad fall. Arm and shoulder injuries, and they just didn't heal right. Sure, I could do the kind of thing Luisa is doing now, not that anybody would want to see me do it, but real flying, catching, no, I just couldn't do it anymore. But I had my insurance, you know, through Lloyd's of London."

There was considerable pride in his voice when he said that, and he glanced at me, looking to see if I was adequately impressed. I had recently watched a television news story about Lloyd's of London, and I knew quite well that the various insurers who work under that blanket will insure a trained flea if they're paid well enough. It is meant to sound like a prestige factor, and even now some movies that are supposed to be extremely scary will advertise that they are insured by Lloyd's of London against somebody dropping dead of fright while watching the show. You'd think that kind of thing alone would convince people that there's no glory at all to being insured by Lloyd's, but apparently it doesn't.

. . . . .

"So," he went on, "the other thing I was always interested in, like I told you, was restaurants. I mean, I can't cook, not like that, but I damn sure appreciate good food. So I thought I could sort of combine the two, like I did here. I took the money from my insurance and I hired a good chef and some performers, and I opened up my first restaurant, in Las Vegas."

"Nevada?" I asked.

He stared at me. "What other Las Vegas is there?"

"Probably several others," I said, not saying that the one I knew best was in New Mexico and had nothing whatever to do with gambling.

"Yeah, it was in Nevada. But there were too many other good restaurants in Las Vegas, and people don't go there for food and circus acts, and even if they did I couldn't compete with Circus Circus. But they don't, they go there to play blackjack and feed the slots. So finally I sold that one, and I sank everything into the Bird Cage."

"Why Fort Worth?" I asked.

He shrugged. "Damned if I know. I just like the idea of Fort Worth."

"You mentioned insurance," I said. "Did you have any kind of insurance on Julia? I mean special insurance, not just your normal business liability insurance. Like you had on yourself, through Lloyd's?"

"No," he said. "I guess I should've. But what she was doing—that was so easy. I guess I never thought of anything happening to her."

"And why did you pick Saranas and Glucks to go to work for you?" I asked.

He stared at me, a sort of don't-you-know-anything stare, and said, "Who wouldn't, if they could get 'em?"

The restaurant locked its front doors to the outside, not to the inside, at midnight. As Pender had told us, it took until past one for the building to be empty except for cleaning crew; I remained there, but

. . . . .

I had arrived in Harry's pickup truck in hopes of misleading anybody who might be watching for my car. Trish, no longer acting her call-girl role, joined me in Pender's office, where I had a radio. "I never found anybody who looked or sounded suspicious," she told me. "Not that I expected to. But it was a place to look."

"Pender's leaving now," Dennis Nelson's tinny voice said quietly. "He left the suitcase on the left side of the back door. He's driving away. . . ."

I finally decided to leave at 3 A.M., when the last of the cleaning crew departed, leaving Trish in the office and Dennis in the Dumpster. Both of them would stay until the first pastry cooks arrived in the morning. Their car was parked three blocks away, so from all anybody could tell the restaurant was totally deserted.

Before closing the back door, I armed the intrusion alarm with the number sequence Pender had given me. Then, in the forty-five seconds the system allowed before breaking into whoops, I dashed on out the door, closed and locked it, and headed toward Harry's truck.

From the Dumpster, Dennis said, "Deb, how long do you want me to stay here?"

I stopped, turned. "I thought we discussed that."

"We did. But I didn't think it was going to be this cold tonight. Dang, it's not but September and feels like January."

I looked at my watch. "I'll see if I can get somebody to come out and relieve you in about an hour."

"Good."

I went on toward the truck. I was no more than ten feet away when the truck exploded, and I dropped flat on the pavement just in time for the entire hood, and one of the doors, to sail over my head.

Eight

. . . . .

I HIT THE ground flat on my face, arms over my head (as if that would do any good), and lay there for a second (which felt much longer) listening to the sputter of additional small explosions. How many boxes of ammo did Harry have stored in the camper? What caliber was it? And was it all pointing straight up? Because if it wasn't, anybody within a mile or so of that truck was in danger right now.

So far it seemed to be. But I could still feel the heat moving toward me—until I noticed that it wasn't the truck at all. My skirt was on fire! As I rolled over, I saw that red-yellow-blue flames from something under the truck were leaping thirty or forty feet into the air. I sprang to my feet, prepared to run hell-for-leather back toward the restaurant. Except that if I did that I'd be creating the perfect environment for the fire on my skirt to flame on up. I slapped it out, or approximately out, because I was pretty sure it was still smoldering, with the sleeve of my jacket, yanked off the jacket, which now was also beginning to flame, and then ran as a stream of sparks blew toward me.

There is a fire extinguisher in every police car. There *was* a fire extinguisher in Harry's truck. But Harry's truck no longer existed, and the car Dennis and Trish arrived in was three blocks away.

All restaurants have fire extinguishers.

By now Trish and Dennis were visible; Dennis was out of the Dumpster and yelling into his radio, and Trish had opened the back door without knowing the alarm code, so the alarm was blaring into the night. Seeing my plight, she let it close behind her as she ran toward me, using her hands to slap out the small fires on my hair that I hadn't even noticed yet.

Great. She didn't have a fire extinguisher. She didn't have the keys to the door. I did—except they were in my purse, which I had dropped when I hit the deck, which meant we weren't going to be able to get back into the restaurant to get a fire extinguisher, not that a fire extinguisher could do anything about that incredibly huge blaze, but it might have helped my skirt, and besides that there was cold water inside the restaurant.

The hell with it. I stepped out of my skirt just in time, because seconds after I dropped it, it blazed up again. I sat down and then hastily got back up. It was, I guessed, going to be a while before I could sit comfortably again.

Dennis stopped yelling into his radio, to turn on an outdoor water faucet he'd spotted near the Dumpster and then back away, as Trish and I both tried to get as much of our anatomy as possible into the water. Well, mainly her hands, but I seemed to be hurting in more places than I had noticed to start with, and right now I wasn't up to distinguishing between burns from a fire and asphalt burns from where I hit the ground.

And Dennis was right; it was cold. The air was cold and the water was cold—though that helped, as it took some of the fire out of the burns—and I was cold, cold clear into my bones, and I sat again and then unsat again, deciding to try lying on my stomach across the cold cement back loading dock, if I could do it without knocking over the small blue suitcase containing ten thousand dollars—What small blue suitcase?

Maybe it had already been knocked off the dock—

At my insistence, Dennis began looking for it, while I crawled back under the water faucet—given the choice between fire and ice, I didn't like either one, but I disliked the fire more. I emerged from the water again, shivering violently, just as another dull *whoomph!* of ex-

. . . . .

plosion took out a large section of the street, and more flames shot up so that the block began to look like San Francisco after the World Series earthquake. For the first time I realized, in one part of my increasingly shocky mind, that it hadn't been a car bomb. Nobody had put a bomb in Harry's pickup truck. It was the gas main under the truck that had exploded.

By now I could hear a lot of sirens—police cars, fire trucks, ambulances, I supposed.

I couldn't possibly have gone to sleep. There was no break at all in my consciousness, but EMTs were there and they had wrapped me in ice packs and were loading me onto a stretcher—"I don't need to go to the hospital," I protested hazily, shoving one of the ice packs away.

"Sorry, ma'am, you do," an EMT who looked about the same age as my nineteen-year-old son told me, neatly replacing the ice pack.

"Wait a minute—Dennis, did you find—"

"No, I didn't, it's gone."

I couldn't believe this. A suitcase full of money had vanished in seconds right in front of three police officers.

The flames were falling—somebody up the line must have turned off the gas feed to the main—

"I don't know how you do it, Ralston," Captain Millner said. *"Other* detectives go home and have a cold beer, but *you* go home and the next thing I know I'm getting a call from the hospital at three-thirty in the morning—"

"I never did it before," I pointed out, rather drowsy from the 800 milligrams of ibuprofen I'd swallowed on arrival.

"Not at three o'clock you didn't," he readily agreed. "You want a list of the other times?"

"No, really I don't," I told him. "I just want to go home and go to bed."

To my astonishment, I was going to be able to. The burns, though painful, were superficial, all first-degree except for two small spots of second-degree that were no worse than some sunburns I have had. Outside of singed hair I looked perfectly normal. Harry, somewhat more upset over the injury to me than over the destruction of his beloved truck as well as the camping gear and the four boxes of rifle bullets he'd promised never to store in a vehicle again, had gone to get me something to wear, as I declined to go home either in a hospital gown or in a blouse and panties, even though Millner *had* managed to retrieve from near the fire my purse, which, amazingly, considering it contained a loaded gun, hadn't exploded also.

"Well, it looks like Pender after all," Millner rumbled, almost as if he were talking more to himself than to me.

"What makes you say that?"

He glanced at me. "You said it. You mentioned that if there had been another fire you would have suspected Pender—"

"I would have, if the fire had been inside the restaurant," I said. "But it wasn't. It was designed to put the restaurant out of business for as long as possible, without doing any physical damage to the restaurant itself that might be covered by insurance."

"Hmmmm," Millner said. "Let me think about that. Ralston, don't come in tomorrow unless you really feel like it, okay?"

"Okay," I agreed. "You always say that."

"I know I always say that. And you never pay any attention."

"I must like my job," I said.

"You must. Or else you're a glutton for punishment."

By the time I reluctantly crawled out of bed Friday morning two hours later than usual, my subconscious had been on the job all night. Despite what could be considered as evidence for the extortion theory, I was increasingly certain that this was *not* an extortion attempt gone wrong but rather the deliberate murder of an innocent young woman caught up in something she couldn't have known about. And if I was right, if I wanted to clear this case, I was going to have to learn something fast about circuses, circus performers, and particularly aerialists, of whom I had never before even heard of any but the Flying Wallendas. In terms of the new vocabulary I had been learning, it rather confused me that I had heard of the Flying Wallendas only in terms of tightrope walking. Flying, I now knew, involved trapeze acts, though not all trapeze performers are flyers. Some are catchers.

I had permission to stay home. Obviously I was not going to do it. Despite Captain Millner's insistence, I don't think I am a glutton for punishment. I'm not even sure that I'm a particularly dedicated cop. It's just that I have this driving need to *know*. I have a love-hate relationship with mysteries; I'd go nuts if I didn't have something to worry at mentally, the way a dog worries at a bone, but once I have a mystery I have to do my best to clear it up at once. If I'd been Alexander I wouldn't have cut the Gordian Knot, and I wouldn't have done one other thing until I had sat down with that knot and worried at it and worried at it until I had it completely untied.

In fact, I remembered my brother Jim and me having contests with each other, each of us trying to invent or create a knot the other couldn't untie. Come to think of it, maybe we were still doing that, in view of the fact that I'm a cop and he's a defense attorney (though fortunately in Houston, which is several hundred miles outside of my jurisdiction).

While I was thinking through these things, I was dressing, in the softest cotton panties I owned and the softest, most often washed slacks in my closet. My upper story was fine, except for the singed hair, which I trimmed off with nail scissors until I could get to Peggy's to have it cut right—and it might be very interesting to see what Peggy was going to say about my hair this time, considering some of it seemed to have melted and stuck together as it cooled.

Cheerios and skim milk and a banana—there, I ate breakfast so I could take another 800 milligrams of ibuprofen—now can I go to work?

My conscience was apparently satisfied. It said nothing as I got my car keys—Harry was using a rented car until he could replace the truck—and headed for the door. Then I hesitated. There was one more thing I had to do, though I wasn't especially delighted with the idea.

I reluctantly decided I'd better call Mark Brody. I have a metro line, so the call to Arlington wouldn't be long distance, but I did not have any great desire to talk with him.

He was in his office at the Arlington Police Department, and he was on good behavior—what I would, in the past, have assumed to be his normal conduct. "Did you come up with anything?" I asked.

I half expected him to act confused by the question. Fortunately he did not. He just answered, "No, every restaurateur I've talked with knows nothing about a new protection racket. There are a few more places I want to check, but I'd say it's going to be a water haul. Speaking of water hauls, what's this about your car being bombed last night?"

"My car didn't get bombed. It was Harry's truck, and it was sitting on top of a gas main that blew up."

"So why'd the gas main blow up?"

"My guess is somebody rigged it. Mark, this is going to be personal, there's no use you going on working with it. I talked with about fifteen restaurateurs yesterday after we split up, and I didn't get anything either. If there were anything to get surely one of us would have gotten something."

I hoped we were both right, for several reasons: first, if it was a personal kill rather than an extortion attempt gone bad, I was looking in the right places at the right people—a personal kill is always easier to clear than an impersonal one—and second, if there was no protection racket then I didn't have to cope with Mark Brody anymore, and the way he'd been acting lately, that would suit me just fine.

"Are you okay?" he asked, sounding genuinely anxious. "I mean, were you in the car I mean truck when it—"

"Obviously not," I said more sharply than I meant to. "I'm still walking around. Mark, I'm sorry, I didn't mean to snap at you.

. . . . .

134

But—"and it just occurred to me right then—"if I hadn't stopped to talk with Dennis I *would* have been in it when it went."

"You suppose somebody meant you to be?"

I excused myself politely, went to the bathroom and threw up, rinsed my mouth, and then returned to the telephone. "I hope not," I said. "But I think you're right. I think maybe somebody *did* mean me to be in the truck when it blew. And I have no idea who it could have been or how they knew where I was. Mark, I—until I know more about it, I'd rather not talk about it much, okay?"

"Okay," he said, sympathy oozing through the phone. Then he changed the subject as obviously as possible. "You heard anything about the money drop last night? Was it picked up?"

"Oh, it was picked up," I told him. "It was picked up sometime between the time I saw it on the loading dock as I left and the time I got back to the loading dock without my skirt and half my hair. And there was *nobody* there but Dennis and Trish and me, and I know what all three of us were doing."

"Shit, Deb, maybe it's poltergeists," Mark said earnestly. "Look, kid, take care of yourself, okay? And let me know if there's anything else I can do."

I thanked him and then went out to check on the dog and found that Harry, in addition to voluntarily taking Cameron to the day-care center (and even remembering to take along his penicillin), had shut Pat properly in the backyard. I left him there. Burglars in the neighborhood or no, I do like to get my mail occasionally. Unless there is a major emergency, missionaries are allowed one telephone call home a year, at Christmas, so mail was the only way I was going to hear from Hal. And maybe I'd be lucky. Maybe the burglars had taken the day off.

Then I headed for the office, intending to glance through my in-basket, pick up a radio, and dash out to the library.

That was when I encountered the next delay, my late arising having been the first and the telephone call to Mark, the second. Detective

. . . . .

Marty Cubbins, the polygraph examiner, cornered me. "Where in the hell have you been?" he demanded crossly. "I've got those three people from your case coming in today and I've got to know what to ask them. I've read the case reports, but that doesn't tell me enough."

Those who have never had or seen a polygraph examination frequently assume it works on the basis of surprise: the person is asked an unexpected question and responds strongly. But that's not right. In a polygraph test, there are no surprises. The polygraph examiner discusses the situation extensively with the person doing the investigating, writes down the questions to be asked, and then discusses the gist of the questions—though not always the questions themselves—thoroughly with the examinee before hooking up the polygraph, which measures minute changes in blood pressure, respiration, and pulse rate. Presumably the examinee, knowing the significant questions are coming, has time to sweat, worry, and anticipate the question, thus increasing rather than decreasing the intensity of the response.

Usually this works. Often it does not, either because the person is a nonreactor (either naturally or as a result of overdose of something as mild as aspirin) who shows no response whether or not he's lying, or because the person is a hyperreactor (again, either naturally or as a result of overdose of something as mild as caffeine) who responds to every question. Fortunately neither aspirin nor caffeine work for everybody, so most people, no matter how much they try to bluff the polygraph, don't succeed.

But it sometimes happens that a person who is not guilty responds as if he were lying because the question is very emotionally loaded for him. This is another reason why a good examiner will discuss the questions, and often the expected or actual responses to them, with the examinee as well as with the investigator, both before and after testing. The machine itself does not tell whether somebody is lying or telling the truth. The machine merely makes note of physiological responses, and as the paper spews out of the machine the operator notes the number of the question being responded to. Then it is up to the operator to decide whether or not lies are present or whether the results are inconclusive—which happens more frequently than most people realize. Like so many other things, proper readings of polygraph results come about through expert interpretation. The machine doesn't do it all.

"It's just as well you haven't drawn up your list of questions," I told Cubbins, "because there's a lot more we need to talk about. But are you sure they're still coming in? I mean, there was a big fire last night—"

"They're coming in," Cubbins said. "I talked with that lawyer on the phone ten minutes ago. Come on up here and let's get these questions settled."

Cubbins and I talked for nearly an hour before we both felt comfortable with the list of questions drawn up for Jan Pender, Arlo Gluck, and Luisa Sarana. *"Now* I'm going to the library," I told Cubbins.

"Oh, no you're not," he retorted. "This is your case. Pender will be here in ten minutes. You stick around till I'm through. I might need to talk with you between tests."

Pender was not there in ten minutes. We waited, and waited, and finally I called Pender's house and got no answer. Then I called the restaurant, where one of the pastry cooks told me the gas was back on (which surprised me) and Pender had been there but had left again. Presumably he was on his way here. He could have got caught in a traffic jam; he could have had a fender bender; he could have got cold feet and be out somewhere trying to decide what to do.

Or trying to decide what to say, if in fact he was guilty. Because a good many guilty people first agree to take a lie detector test, and then become increasingly worried and frightened, finally deciding to confess rather than be faced with a piece of machinery that seemingly can read their thoughts.

. . . . .

At eleven-fifteen, Cubbins shrugged. "He's not coming," he said. "I have Sarana scheduled at eleven-thirty and Gluck at twelve-thirty, but they told me they'd get here together."

They did, at eleven-twenty. The desk guard called Cubbins to let him know they were in the lobby, and I went down and got them.

I sat in on Cubbins's discussion with Luisa, as he explained to her what he was going to ask and—again standard procedure—modified some of the questions in the light of things she told him. "Do you have any questions?" he asked finally.

She shook her head.

"You remember that you answer everything yes or no, you don't try to explain anything?"

"I remember."

"And you remember you're supposed to lie on several inconsequential questions at the beginning."

"Yes," she said. "Do you want me to tell you which ones?"

"Definitely not," he said. "I can probably tell just from the answers, but if I can't tell from that *or* from the machine then this isn't going to work anyway. But I think you'll be a good reactor."

The polygraph is in one of those rooms, ubiquitous in police departments, that have what appears from the inside with the lights on to be a mirror but, from an adjacent room (in this case Cubbins's office) with the lights off, to be clear glass. I watched through the mirror as Cubbins carefully arranged Luisa's arms on the arms of the chair, put a blood-pressure cuff on her, and attached several leads (they always look to me like octopus tentacles) to her. "This looks like an electric chair," she joked nervously.

"Oh, it is, it is," he said. "But it's a different kind, and you're perfectly safe. Now, are you comfortable?"

"Yes," she said, and tried to smile at him. The smile was a dismal failure, and once more I had to remember that her sister was to be buried Saturday. We had originally planned to wait until after the funeral for this, until Pender (who hadn't showed up) insisted it be done immediately, but actually it was better to do it now. With every passing hour on any killing the trail gets colder.

"Now, just sit there and relax," Cubbins told her.

He walked over behind the equipment and began turning switches. I happened to know that he could turn the whole thing on and have it up and running in about twenty seconds, but as always, he deliberately took about three minutes, long enough for Luisa to relax fully but not long enough for her to get bored and start fidgeting. Then he asked, "Is your name Luisa Sarana?"

"Yes."

He numbered the printout with a red marker. "Do you live in France?"

"Yes."

Another red mark.

I couldn't, of course, see the dials of the machine or the paper printouts, but I could see Cubbins's back, and there was an almost imperceptible relaxation in it. Evidently her reactions were going to be strong enough for him to read.

"Do you live in Fort Worth?"

"No."

"Have you ever been to Fort Worth?"

"No."

"Are you in France now?"

"Yes."

"Are you in Forth Worth now?"

"No." I could see her smiling, very slightly.

"Do you like circuses?"

"Yes." Clearly, she wouldn't lie on that one even to calibrate his machine.

That must have been the end of the control questions, because the next thing he asked was, "Was Julia Gluck your sister?"

"Yes."

"Is Julia Gluck alive?"

· · · · ·

"No."

That would be a very emotionally loaded question for her; he was now getting a look at the difference in her chart between emotional response and lying.

"Is Julia Gluck dead?"

"Yes."

"Do you think she was murdered?"

"Yes."

All these questions had been emotionally loaded; it was time now for some innocuous questions to calm her before he went on to the next loaded question. "Are you engaged?"

"Yes."

"Do you like eggs?"

"Not really—ooops! No."

"That's okay, that happens to everybody at least once. Just try to remember to answer yes or no. Do you know Arlo Gluck?"

"Yes."

"Is Arlo Gluck your brother-in-law?"

"Yes."

"Have you known him all your life?"

"Yes."

"Is Arlo Gluck your lover?"

"No!" Visible anger at that question; my guess was the emotional response was so strong Cubbins wouldn't be able to tell whether or not she was lying.

And so it went, a delicate interspersing of emotionally loaded questions, neutral questions, and questions directly related to the crime. I left the mirror after the first five minutes and went out in the hall to sit with Arlo and try to keep him from getting too wound up for the polygraph to work. The examination took fifteen minutes; to Luisa, it probably felt like two hours. She came out, finally, damp with sweat, and Arlo went in.

The whole thing was finished by one-fifteen, and Luisa Sarana and

Arlo Gluck departed together. "What have you got?" I asked Cubbins, after going into the office where he was looking at the charts the machine had printed out.

"Well," he said, "both of them are concealing things. But that's nothing odd; people are always concealing things and thinking they're not, and these all seem to be on personal matters. I got inconclusive answers on several questions, but not on any related to the crime. I don't see any evidence at all that either of them knows anything about Julia's murder or that either one of them knows what happened to the gas line. I don't think they're sexually involved with each other."

"Really? It looked to me like she nearly blew up at that question."

"Oh, she did, the first time. Stronger response than I got on any of the questions she was lying on. But I went back to it about six more times, and—well, see for yourself." He pointed to squiggles on the page, with question numbers written and circled in red marker at fairly regular intervals. They meant nothing to me, and I said so.

"Then you'll just have to trust me on it," he said with finality. "Neither of them knows any more about the extortion demands than they learned listening to you guys talk about it yesterday. I did ask about Julia's pregnancy, as you suggested. They both know Julia was pregnant. Luisa thinks Arlo was the father. Arlo doesn't know who the father is but thinks he was probably a gymnast at one of the colleges in the area—that's one of the areas that was a little inconclusive, on the polygraph. He was emotional about it. But what man wouldn't have an emotional response if he knew his wife was pregnant by another man? My own feeling is, it was an emotional response, but it didn't mean lying, when you put it together with everything else. And neither of them thinks the pregnancy had anything to do with Julia's death. That one *wasn't* iffy. And that's it," he said, looking up at me. "That's all I can give you, unless you can get that Pender fellow in here for me. I wish I could do more."

"Thanks for what you've got, anyway," I said. "Let me try again to call Pender."

I still didn't find him, and Cubbins said, "You might as well go get lunch."

"What about you?" I asked.

"I brought mine." He pulled a brown paper bag out of his desk drawer and sat down under a poster of Dr. Seuss's Bartholomew Cubbins and his five hundred hats to begin unwrapping sandwiches.

As late as I had eaten breakfast, I hadn't the slightest desire for lunch. But the library was about two blocks away, and I definitely needed to go there. After picking up a hand radio and putting it in my purse, I called Dispatch to tell them where I'd be, signed out on the whiteboard in the office, and took off on foot.

I didn't want just any librarian to help me; I wanted to work with Maria Amado, widow of my friend Carlos Amado who was killed on duty several years ago. When I was looking for something work related it was always easier to work with Maria, because I'd found that, possibly because she'd been a cop's wife, she could understand what I needed better than other people could. I had telephoned over there earlier, and Maria had told me she'd be back from lunch by one and she'd be available at least for the next two hours after that.

When I reached the library, an impressive gray stone-and-glass building across the street from the Tandy Center, to which it is connected by an under-the-street tunnel, Maria was standing at the desk talking with a woman who looked to be my mother's age. I couldn't tell how long the conversation had been going on, but it must not have been for long, because Maria was offering to help the woman learn to use the catalog computer.

"Oh, I couldn't learn that," the woman said rather proudly, as if not learning to use the computer were a mark of genius. "That" came out as two syllables, the first ending in a level tone and the second in a falling tone. "You'll have to help me."

Not visibly gritting her teeth, Maria said, "Well, let's go on over to the computer. Now, you wanted—"

Never mind the next five minutes; I waited as Maria fielded in-

. . . . .

creasingly unreasonable demands, until the woman finally snapped, "What do *you* read? Comic books? Or can you even read at all?"

Maria still managed to keep her temper under control. "I read archaeology books, and a lot of Anne Perry—"

"Then what's *her* newest book?"

Maria had her mouth open to answer, but the woman forestalled her. "You just don't know anything, do you?" she said. "I should have known better than to ask a *Mesican* to find anything. I'll find a White person to help me."

"You do that," Maria said sweetly, and looked over at the checkout counter, where one librarian (White) was checking out forty-odd books for an ambitious reader or, more likely, someone doing research. The other librarian, who clearly had heard the discussion, instantly became very busy checking books in and refusing to allow Maria to catch her eye. I didn't blame her. She was Black.

"They all seem to be busy," Maria said. "If you'd like to wait—or maybe somebody downstairs will be free—"

"Never mind, I'll go look on the shelf." The woman stalked off toward the elevator leading downstairs to Fiction.

"Which she should have done to start with," Maria said under her breath, to me.

"Do you get much of that?"

"Not very many people are that obnoxious. But you'd be surprised how many people are afraid to learn to use the computer. And it's nearly always older people; kids come right in and read the instructions and don't even ask for help. I suppose it's because they have computers in school. And some older people have learned it, of course. But the ones who won't—I don't know, Deb, most of them aren't like her—my guess is she's just bone lazy besides being hateful. Oh well—people are people. So—what can I help you with?"

I explained, and she started hitting keys. "I can do that," I offered, feeling highly self-conscious because I had been so sorry for myself over Captain Millner's orders to me to learn to use a computer.

. . . . .

143

"I know," Maria said, grinning briefly at me before returning to the keyboard, "but you might not think of all the subtopics I can think of. It's probably faster this way."

Wishing like mad I'd driven to the library instead of walked, I left a few minutes later with a double armload of books about circus customs, circus acrobats, circus aerialist acts, and related material.

I certainly wasn't going to haul all that up to the detective bureau and then back down again. I went in the front door of the police station and out the back door, to stash all but one of the books in my car. Then, with that last book in my purse (now you know why I carry a big purse, besides the fact that I have to carry my pistol there when I'm off duty), I went on up, to find Captain Millner and tell him I intended to go home and read the rest of the afternoon but I was still on duty.

"Read what?" he asked. "I think you should just rest. Trying to come to work when you were just about blown up last night—and I already said you need to wait to restart that computer thing when it's quieter around here."

"Which will be the day after a heavy snowfall in hell. I'm reading circus books."

He stared at me for a moment, and then asked, "How relevant do you think that will turn out to be?"

"I don't know," I said. "And I won't know till I've read them. What did they find out about the explosion?"

"The federal bomb squad was out on it, as well as ours and the state," he answered. "Traces of plastique. Fragments of a detonator. But it doesn't look like it was on a timer. It was detonated with some sort of radio control device."

"Ducky," I said heavily. "That means somebody was trying to kill me."

"Yeah," he said. "I'm afraid that's what it means. You might also be interested to know they had the gas main temporarily repaired and operational again by nine A.M. Did you and Brody find out anything on that extortion series? Because the money's gone, you know."

"Obviously I know; I was there when it went missing, and dammit, I don't see how it could have. As far as any extortion series is concerned, if you mean other than at the Bird Cage, we found out there wasn't one, or at least we haven't found one so far. Brody talked to a lot of restaurateurs in Arlington and I talked with a lot here, and neither of us found anything at all. I sat out there for hours last night and nothing happened until I looked the other way."

"Yeah, I was going to talk to you about that," Millner said. "Being out there yourself, I mean. You're hiring a dog and trying to bark yourself again. That was Trish and Dennis's job, not yours."

"They were there too," I said.

"I know. I talked with them. What happened on the polygraph exams? And what's the case number?"

I told him about the polygraph and gave him the case number, and he turned around and started hitting keys on the monitor. Meanwhile, standing rather than sitting at my desk, I picked up the telephone to try once more to call Jan Pender.

This time I got him. About thirty seconds later, I wished I hadn't. He was yelling. He did not intend to stop yelling. The gist of the yelling seemed to be that he thought the suitcase was under observation all night.

"It was, until it was picked up," I said.

"The hell it was picked up, when I got in this morning it was sitting right here in my office. And if it was under observation all night, would you be good enough to tell me how in the hell it happened that I opened it this morning and there was nothing in it but a newspaper?"

I sat down, hard, and immediately wished I hadn't. "Run that by me again."

"Ten thousand dollars. You saw it, yesterday. Gone. Nothing in the suitcase but a Fort Worth *Star-Telegram*."

"Jan," I said, "that suitcase was under direct observation from the

. . . . .

145

time you put it out there until the time it was taken."

"Then, lady, one of your cops must have helped himself."

"Jan," I said, "I almost got killed last night when your gas main blew up. One of the stakeout officers was helping me put out the fire on my skirt and in my hair, and she burned her hands pretty badly doing it. The other one of the stakeout officers was talking over his radio to the dispatcher, trying to get somebody out there to put the fire out before it spread on into your restaurant. And that's when the suitcase vanished. In view of the fact that these demands for money, and these assaults on your business, have been going on for months, isn't it more likely that somebody who works in your restaurant helped himself while we were all busy? Like maybe the same somebody who gets into your office in the middle of the night when it's locked to leave notes on your desk? The same somebody who manages to cut gas hoses in the kitchen and cables in the dining room without being seen by anybody? The same somebody who puts plastic explosives and radio detonation devices in the parking lot under my husband's pickup truck that I was driving?"

I could hear him sputtering. When I finally let him talk, he said, "Nobody told me anybody got hurt last night."

"Then maybe you should ask a few more questions. And answer a few. Starting with, Who in your organization knows anything about explosives?"

"Nobody," he answered promptly. "And I still say it was one of the cops last night, because if it was somebody who works for me who took the money, why did they put the suitcase back in my office and why did they put the newspaper in it?"

I absolutely couldn't think of any answer at all. Finally, not expecting any useful results, I asked, "What date is the newspaper?"

Not unexpectedly, he snorted. "I'll check," he said then, and laid down the phone. But in the background I could hear a suitcase opening, paper rustling. Then he said, "Huh?"

I wanted to ask him what the "huh" was about, but he wasn't

holding the phone. Finally he came back to it. "I correct myself," he said stiffly. "There was a newspaper and a note. The newspaper is yesterday's. You want to know what the note says?"

"Yes, if you don't mind."

"Oh, I don't mind, I don't mind at all. It says, 'You called in the cops. Now your insurance premium'—he spelled it *p-r-e-i-m-u-m* but I guess he meant 'premium'—'has gone up again. Your coverage for the month is thirty thousand dollars.' That's the part of it that's typed, that it looks like he wrote in advance. Underneath it he's added, in pen, 'Your partial payment has been accepted. But there are late charges. Leave another twenty-five thousand by the end of next week. And tonight is a little reminder of what happens when you call in the cops.' No cop left that note," he admitted, "but you were going to catch him—"

I started to say something. He resumed yelling. "And dammit, don't tell me you and Ted both told me that would happen. I know you did, and I don't like 'I told you so' any better than anybody else does. But why didn't you catch him? I mean, I'm sorry you got hurt and all that, but why didn't you catch him?"

"You know what, Mr. Pender? The answer is I don't know."

"My office was locked, dammit!"

"Wasn't your office locked the times those notes turned up on your desk?"

Long silence. "Yeah," he finally said.

"Can you make me any kind of list of who would have access to your restaurant, or to your office, even if you weren't there?"

"Half of Fort Worth, it looks like from my receipts from last night."

"Never mind customers," I said. "Your employees. Your suppliers."

"Well, yeah, but I'm the manager. I don't have an assistant manager, just a floor manager and a drop safe for receipts. Nobody but me is supposed to have an office key. I mean I don't even let the cleaning people in unless I'm here."

. . . . .

"Keys are pretty easily come by. Just make me the list, if you'd be so good. And I think I'd better go on out there and get the note and the newspaper—"

He interrupted me in a hurry. "The hell you say! Lady, you're not coming near me! What do you want, the demand to go up to forty thousand dollars? The restaurant itself to get bombed?"

"I believe the demand will go up whether or not I go out there," I said. "And whatever will happen to the restaurant will happen whether I go out there or not. And I believe you know that."

There was a long silence at the other end of the line. Then he sighed. "All right, yes, I know that. But right now—he's given me a little bit of time. And whoever he is, he knows you. That's pretty obvious. And I'm afraid he'll do something else if he sees you. To me *or* to you. I know I can't stop you coming out here as a customer; I would if I could. But other than that—keep away until—unless—I say you can come back."

I couldn't force him to turn the evidence over to me. Even if I didn't agree to stay away, Ted Siebenborn would tell him that in a hurry. I could probably get a court order, but it wasn't worth causing enmity, when my guess was that if I didn't push him he'd change his mind in hours anyway. "All right," I said finally, reluctantly. "In case you change your mind, here's my home phone number." I gave it to him and hung up.

"Report," Captain Millner said.

I reported.

"Go home and read your books," Captain Millner said. "And for cryin' out loud, get some rest. Unless it's something else happening at the Bird Cage, or something happening to somebody involved with that case, I'll see to it you're not called out. But take a radio with you just in case. And look, take a city car. I don't know what's going on with the Bird Cage, and I want you to be able to go straight to the scene if something else pops."

Great. That meant I had to go back and get the unmarked car I had turned in, drive it into the police employees' parking lot, transfer the library books into it, and then go home.

But on the good side, it also meant that if I got a call-out in the middle of the night, and like Millner I wouldn't be at all surprised if that happened, I wouldn't be burning my own gasoline. Harry would yell, of course. He always does when he sees that I went home in a police car, because it means even more inroads into our family life, which is already fragmented enough. But I couldn't do anything about that. Despite the enormous raise Harry got when he moved into management, he still felt very strongly that I had to have a job too. I didn't feel that strongly about the financial end of it, but I did feel that if I had to have a job it was reasonable for me to have one I liked and was good at.

It was two-thirty when I turned onto my own street. But I couldn't park in my driveway. A very rusty panel truck, which appeared to have been brush-painted green with house paint, was already there, and what looked like Harry's computer was sitting on the tailgate. The front door was standing wide open. Pat, in the backyard, was about as close to hysterical as a pit bull could get. And the sweet strains of Hal's worst acid-rock tapes were wafting out on the breeze.

I had no questions as to what was going on. Parking my car across the end of the driveway so that anybody trying to leave would have to go through the car—I wouldn't have done that with my personal car, not only because my insurance wouldn't cover it but also because my car, being a Ford Escort, was so light it wouldn't stop the truck for more than a few seconds—I radioed in my location. "Wait for back-ups," the dispatcher instructed me.

"I've got a backup," I said. "Namely my pit bull. He's in the fence in the backyard. Get me a uniform car en route fast, but don't let any uniform officer go back there. He hates uniforms."

. . . . .

"Ten-four on that."

Then I took my pistol out of my holster, left the car door open so nobody could hear it slam (as if they could, over that obnoxious noise), and headed for the front door.

Nine
· · · · ·

PROFESSIONAL BURGLARS ARE as silent as possible, so that they can hear the approach of any possible counterintruder.

Professional burglars open every possible exit as soon as they get inside, so they can flee quickly no matter which door the counterintruder is entering through.

In this case, there were only three possible exists, unless they—from certain things I had heard from neighbors, I assumed there were more than one—wanted to resort to going out a window: the now-splintered front door, which I was standing directly in front of; the door into the garage, but the garage had been turned into such a maze of small interconnecting rooms that anybody would practically need a map to reach the outside; and the door into the backyard, which would take them directly into the jaws of a very angry pit bull.

And these were not professional criminals. The music told me that.

Pistol drawn—*and where in the heck were those backups?*—I slipped as soundlessly as possible, though I doubted they could hear an elephant over that cacophony, into the front hall and then sort of slithered on into the living room.

Harry's ham radio and CB radio, Hal's boom box (plugged in and turned on), Lori's small portable television, our VCR, every AM and FM radio in the house, and several other small appliances were all piled in the middle of the living room floor. I was particularly annoyed to see, in the pile of items to be stolen, a UPS delivery box that must

· · · · ·

have just arrived, which from its return label I judged undoubtedly contained two new—and very expensive—purses I had recently ordered.

But I'd worry about that later, particularly since the burglars were not going anywhere with our possessions.

I could hear, under the racket, somebody moving around in Harry's and my bedroom. *Good,* I thought in satisfaction, *neither the bathroom nor bedroom window is large enough for anybody over the age of six to get out, and Harry's guns are now all locked up in his computer room.* Though come to think of it they had obviously gotten the computer room open, unless that was somebody else's computer on the tailgate of the truck, and I didn't think it was. But getting the computer room open and getting the gun locker open are two different things. Harry and the builder he'd hired to work with him on that project meant it to stay closed.

I waited until they came out the bedroom door, the girl with the strap of her purse draped over her right shoulder, my jewelry box in her right hand (with the left, she was holding the shirttail of a scruffy sleeveless T-shirt that was being worn by an equally scruffy dog; apparently the shirt served the dual purpose of collar and leash) and the boy with the CPU of my computer in his right hand (which made me nervous, as I always carry it with both hands on the very rare occasions when I move it at all) and six library CDs in his left. Pistol in my right hand, properly braced by my left hand, I yelled, "Police! Freeze!"

The effect, I suppose, was somewhat diminished by the fact that I am five feet two inches tall, weigh about a hundred and fifteen pounds, and have very short graying hair. One criminal I was trying to arrest told me I looked like somebody's sweet little auntie, but to my own mind I probably look (though I hope like mad I don't act) like the mother in that Sylvester Stallone movie *Stop! Or My Mom Will Shoot.* Both of the burglars were somewhat taller than I—the male was over six feet, and the female was at least five feet seven—and both of them had wiry builds.

But, as has been said repeatedly ever since guns were invented, guns are pretty good equalizers.

The girl—scrawny, with uncombed, very thin white-blond hair, probably not over sixteen years old, with dozens of bruised needle tracks up and down her arms—dropped the jewelry box, and my jewelry, most of which is cheap costume stuff anyway, scattered all over the living room floor. At the same time she turned loose of the T-shirt, and the dog, who seemed the most intelligent of the three, didn't bother to look back at Pat, who was trying to claw his way through a glass door, before bolting. Even if he didn't know what a pit bull was, he knew better than to mess with a larger-than-him dog making that sort of noise.

Their dog seemed to be a slightly overgrown cocker spaniel. The only dogs that like cocker spaniels less than pit bulls do are Rottweilers. (One day in the vet's waiting room I heard a teenage girl, who was holding a cocker spaniel in her arms, complain to her mother that Rottweilers don't like cocker spaniels. "Nonsense, my dear," the mother replied. "Rottweilers *love* cocker spaniels." As the teenager started to protest, her mother added, blandly, "To eat." I couldn't have said it better myself.) But unfortunately for this cocker spaniel, he wasn't going to get very far. I had closed the front gate. On the other hand, as long as the gates between the front and back yards were closed Pat wasn't going to reach him unless he learned to climb over the fence, and so far he hadn't managed that.

The girl turned as if she were intending to chase the dog, again caught sight of my pistol, and froze again.

By then the boy—equally scrawny, equally blond, equally needle-tracked, probably about twenty—had dropped the CPU. I didn't *hear* anything break, but I was definitely going to have to ask Harry to look it over carefully before I plugged it in again. I started reciting a Miranda warning. They both stared at me; then the boy interrupted, "You got this all wrong, lady. The—uh—the people who live here, they asked us to move some stuff for them."

· · · · ·

"That's funny," I said, "I never saw you before, and I'm sure my husband would have told me if he wanted all our electronic stuff removed."

"Oh, shit," the boy said, sounding more dispirited than angry. "I thought you said you was a cop."

"I am a cop. And this is my house."

"Yeah, but lady, you don't really want to use that gun, now do you?" He began edging toward me, hand thrust out in front of him toward my pistol. He was almost close enough to grab the barrel. Legally I could fire now. But he was right: I didn't really want to use that gun. I had killed one person because I had no other choice, either for myself or for the other people he would have killed if he hadn't been stopped, including a woman who was at that moment giving birth. I never wanted to have to kill again if I could possibly keep from doing it.

But I certainly wasn't up to a wrestling match, given both the size disparity and my recent burns, and if I didn't stop him fast, he might make me have to use the gun. I took two steps to my right and opened the patio door. Pat surged in, snarling, barking, and howling, and the boy and girl both cowered back against my bedroom door, the girl with her hands over her face. I knew Pat wouldn't hurt them. But they didn't. And now the boy, whoever he was, wouldn't make another try for my gun.

But I had forgotten about the cocker spaniel. Pat couldn't spare a glance for the people in the house. He tore in through the patio door and right back out the front door, after that other dog who had dared to enter his universe.

The girl screamed something incoherent and went after the dogs.

The boy tried to go after her.

I stuck out one foot and tripped him.

Not exactly Marquis of Queensberry rules, but it worked. I planted my left knee in the middle of his back—not gently—and had him handcuffed before he'd gotten back the breath the fall had knocked out of him. About that time the cocker spaniel rushed back into the living room, yelping, with Pat right behind him and the girl right behind Pat and screaming at him. I dropped the pistol safely out of the girl's reach, stomped my right foot on it to be sure, and grabbed Pat's collar. The girl grabbed the tail of the cocker spaniel's T-shirt. She looked once more at me—I still had one knee in her partner's back, one foot on the pistol, one hand on the handcuffs, and the other caught in Pat's collar, rather like a game that used to be advertised several years ago—and then she picked up the cocker spaniel and bolted out the door. Pat wished to follow. Pat struggled wildly. But fortunately he thinks I can restrain him, so I can.

I could not chase the girl without removing my foot from my pistol and my knee from her partner's back, and although it is difficult for a person whose hands are manacled behind his back to stand up from a facedown position, it is far from impossible. I didn't want him to move. So I was still half on the floor with my knee in his back when I heard the truck start up. Over the frustrated yelling of the boy, of which *bitch* was the most intelligible word but I couldn't tell whether he meant his partner, me, or both, I heard the crash as the back end of the truck hit the passenger's side of the detective car I had driven home. The truck's engine ground and whined, but it wasn't strong enough for the truck to push the car away and keep going. Frontward it might have been, but not backward.

I very much hoped that Harry had everything on his hard drive backed up. I hadn't backed up anything on mine, and we might at this point have two computers at least temporarily out of service with hard-drive crashes as well as mechanical damage. I hoped Harry wouldn't take that as a mandate to go out and buy a third to use while the first two were, if necessary, being repaired. I feared that he would.

Subliminally, I had been hearing sirens for a while, I didn't know how long, but they'd been getting nearer and nearer. Then I heard one cut off.

Danny Shea, whose police ability had improved considerably since

. . . . .

my first encounter with him, came in, holding the neck of the T-shirt of the now-handcuffed girl about the same way she had earlier held the tail of the T-shirt of the cocker spaniel, who now ran in beside her dragging his shirttail on the floor and occasionally tripping over it. He—Shea, not the dog—kicked the door shut, or at least as shut as this door was ever again going to get, behind him. "Does this belong to you?" he inquired pleasantly.

I tightened my grip on Pat even more securely. "You made the collar, you keep her," I replied, rather out of breath more from excitement than exertion.

"Cricket, you stupid bitch!" the boy yelled from the floor. "Tryin' to take off and leave me here—we could have taken her, if you'd stayed here and helped me—and if you hadn't had to turn on that damn radio we'd have heard them coming—but no"—he made that three syllables, rising, falling, rising—"you had to have music. Couldn't wait till you got home—"

"Shut up, they're listening to all this!" the girl yelled.

"Like it's gonna do any good now," he snarled, and shut up.

That gave Shea an opening to speak. He addressed me, not either of the prisoners. "Residential burglary, resisting arrest, unlawful flight to avoid prosecution, reckless driving. Strong-arm robbery?"

"Naah," I said. "That ought to do it. Unless we find out about something else. There'll eventually be multiple counts of burglary anyway. Watch this one." Removing my knee from the male's back and my foot from the pistol, still holding Pat's collar, I dog-marched Pat to the open patio door and pushed him out, kept him from returning by planting my knee firmly in front of his chest, and closed the door, removing my knee from the doorway at the last possible moment.

He has a certificate, issued when he finished obedience school, that says he is an obedient dog. The certificate lies. Anyway, Pat cannot read.

After scooping up my pistol and returning it to my holster, I returned to my prisoner, who was still lying facedown. I reached in his pocket to find his billfold. His driver's license—at least one of his driver's licenses, but this one looked the most authentic—told me he was Duane Porter and he was twenty-two years old. His credit cards had numerous names on them, some of which I recognized as belonging to my neighbors. Keeping out the driver's license and most of the credit cards, I tossed the billfold on top of the coffee table, or rather, on top of everything that was on top of the coffee table, including the latest copy of my *Women & Guns* magazine, the latest copy of Harry's *Soldier of Fortune,* and Lori's math assignment, which presumably she had given up on anyway.

By now Shea had the girl handcuffed. He handed her purse over to me. "Hey, that's mine," the girl objected loudly.

"And all this stuff is mine," I retorted, gesturing at my scattered possessions.

"Yeah, but don't you need a search warrant to look in my purse?" she demanded.

"Your purse is very portable," I told her, without adding that I would certainly have to get a warrant before searching the truck unless I could talk one of them into giving me a consent to search. "And before you ask, I also don't need an arrest warrant, not after seeing you in the act of committing a felony. Shea, Mirandize them while I look at this. I started to but got sidetracked."

He started reciting the Miranda warning as I opened her purse. Her driver's license—one of several, actually, but the one that looked most likely to be really hers—told me she was Cricket Porter.

Shea finished the "Do you wish to give up these rights?" and stared at her, waiting for an answer.

"I don't know what Duane wants me to do," the girl said wretchedly. The boy just nodded, awkwardly.

"You have to say it out loud," I told him. "And Officer Shea was telling the truth. You really don't have to. If you don't want us to question you then we won't."

· · · · ·

"You might as well," the boy—Duane—said. "You've got us cold. Yeah. Yeah, lady cop, I wish to give up those rights."

"Are you Cricket Porter?" I asked the girl then.

"Uh-huh," she said wretchedly. "And if Duane says he gives up those rights I guess I do too." She looked apprehensively at Duane.

"Is he your boyfriend, brother, husband, what?"

"Husband," she said. "We hadda get married, well, I guess we didn't really have to but my dad, you know, he was awful mad at Duane and me both and we figured we better not make him madder. Anyway that was when I was fifteen, but then I lost the baby and we—we just, you know, sort of drifted. My folks wouldn't take me back, and his didn't want him neither. I don't guess you want to know all this."

"Tell me anything you want to," I said.

"I guess that's all right now."

I returned my attention to the driver's license. She was twenty, which was rather a surprise; I would have to start considering her a woman rather than a girl. Her credit cards, like his, told me she was several people, some of whom I knew—well enough to know she was not any of them. She also had a couple of checkbooks; the name was not Cricket Porter on any of them. One of them was the kind with no-carbon-required second copies. I glanced through it; the last three checks were written in a distinctively different hand than the others. I never can figure out how forgers manage to get away with their forgery, when respectable people like me have to produce at least two pieces of identification proving who they are before they can cash a check. I've been told that they manage to seem very respectable and very convincing, but how respectable and convincing can a person seem with needle tracks all over her arms?

Laying the checkbook on top of Lori's math book, I went on searching. There were a couple of credit-card receipts in the bottom of the bag. "Credit-card fraud, forgery," I added to Shea. "Go find out who the truck belongs to. Porter, you can get up and sit on the couch now."

"With my hands behind me?" he snarled.

"You're not going to do it any other way," I answered.

With some help from Officer Groves, who had come in as Shea went back out, he managed, though he kicked viciously at the leg of the couch on the way. I didn't care. The leg of the couch had been attacked by cats, a dog, and a toddler. And Porter was wearing sneakers with the toe out. The kick definitely hurt him more than it hurt my couch.

While Shea was standing in the front yard checking automobile registrations, Lori arrived home from school and dashed into the living room, looking somewhat pale and stopping abruptly when she saw the two people in handcuffs now sitting on the edge of the couch. "Deb," she demanded, "are you okay?" Assured of that, she went on. "What's going on? Are these the burglars? Did they break the door in? Were you in the car when they hit it?"

"Got it in one, except I wasn't in the car," I said more cheerfully than I felt. "I was already inside." Because regardless of how pleased I was to have stopped the burglary wave in our neighborhood, the fact remained I was getting no farther on the murder I was supposed to be working or on a matter of even more interest to me, namely the question of who had tried to kill me last night.

Which reminded me. "Go get my radio out of the car, please, Lori," I said.

"Uh—the car is kind of bent," Lori said. "I don't know if I can get it open."

"See if you can. If not, see if you can get it just reaching inside. It's on the seat. Or at least, it *was* on the seat."

She came back with the radio and a report that the driver's door would open. "The other one won't," she added. "And the radio was under the seat. Deb, I kind of think the car is totaled." I kind of

· · · · ·

159

thought so too, from the sound of the crash, but I hadn't had a chance to look at it yet. "You want me to call Harry and ask him to come home?" she added.

"I wish you would," I said. "Thanks for thinking of that."

I figured the truck belonged to one or both of the Porters. It didn't. Shea returned, seconds after Lori left the room, with the information that it belonged to one Charles Gardner, who lived eight blocks from me though I had never met him, and it had been listed as stolen three weeks earlier. *Hallelujah,* I thought tiredly, *we don't have to get a search warrant after all. Now if I can just convince the Burglary Squad to let me bring those of my possessions that are outside back inside, and put the others away properly, after they're photographed, instead of leaving them in the evidence room until the case is disposed of, I'll be very happy.*

Then, using the radio Lori had brought me instead of my own telephone—I will freely admit that I was a little rattled—I gave the names and birthdates from the driver's licenses (the ones, that is, that looked most likely to be authentic) to Dispatch to run on NCIC, the big national crime-information computer system. The answer came back fast. As young as they were, both of the Porters had been in prison twice. In Texas, as in many other states, three strikes and you're out. Theoretically they would both be in prison for the rest of their lives; actually they probably wouldn't be there much over seven years, but that would be plenty to put an end to whatever amount of their youth heroin had left them. I could see from the looks on their faces that they'd figured that out too.

"You don't have to answer this," I said, "but knowing about the three felony convictions law, why on earth did you pull this?"

They both went on looking at me. Finally the girl—Cricket—shrugged awkwardly and said, "What else was there to do? Everything always goes wrong for us anyway. At least when we're on the shit we don't have to think about it."

That left me totally speechless. I can think of absolutely no situation in which there is nothing to do but burglarize houses in order to get money to buy drugs to anesthetize oneself from reality.

I could have talked to her about decisions. I could have pointed out how many of the things that go wrong in the world are caused, totally or partially, by the decisions human beings make. But I didn't have any legal right to do so now, when I was acting in my official capacity despite the fact that it was my house that had been burglarized, so I kept my mouth shut.

"What's going to happen to my dog?" She eyed the cocker spaniel, who was trying to climb into her lap.

"I guess he'll go to the pound."

"They'll kill him," she said, and burst into tears. "I know they will. We got him from the pound. They had *five* cocker spaniels that day, and about fifty other dogs, and they said they would have to kill the other cocker spaniels and most of the other dogs, because nobody wanted them—just because they weren't show quality—and I don't care if he's show quality! None of this is his fault! Him's a sweet-ums—" She nuzzled the dog's head with her forehead, and the dog licked her face. "I won't be able to get him back; they sure won't keep him seven years and even if they would there's no reason *he* ought to be in jail and he wouldn't know me seven years later anyway."

Then she looked at me. "I know I don't have any right to ask—but it's for Ivy, not for me—and you look like a nice lady, would you keep him?" -

Comments have been made before, from friends and family, about my propensity for taking in strays. We have a dog and two cats. Although city zoning laws would allow us one more dog, where would we *put* another dog? But I was aghast to hear myself saying, "I guess I can keep him, at least long enough to find him another home."

"Would you? Oh, would you?" Just for a moment I could see in her briefly dazzling smile a little of the girl she must have once been. "He's a nice dog. His name is Ivory because when I first got him that's what he looked like, but I usually call him Ivy. He's, you know, fixed, and he's had all his shots and everything. And it's not his fault he's dirty right now. I just didn't wash him. I should have—"

"I'll go wash him right now," Lori said, clearly glad of something to do. Since calling Harry she had been wandering uneasily around the house, trying not to get in the way but too wound up to sit down. She picked up the cocker spaniel and headed purposefully for the bathroom she and Cameron shared.

Meanwhile I was asking myself what in the world I had gotten myself into. How was I going to persuade a pit bull and a cocker spaniel to share one yard, even temporarily? And how was I going to explain to Harry what I had let myself—and the rest of the family—in for?

In the midst of all this the telephone rang. I turned around mechanically to answer it. "Jan Pender," said the voice at the other end. "Look—I—uh—I wasn't thinking straight a while ago."

Restraining the urge to tell him he certainly wasn't, I just said, cautiously, "Okay."

"And I've been thinking—I don't want you at the restaurant, not tonight, but, uh—do you know where Cattleman's is?"

"Yes."

"Can you meet me in the parking lot there in, say, half an hour?"

I looked around the living room. "Jan, I really can't," I said.

"Well, I can understand—" His voice sounded stiffly formal now.

"No, I don't think you do," I said. "I got home from work to find two burglars in my house. They're still here" (I ignored the squawking noises now coming from the telephone), "and so are a couple of uniform officers, and the Burglary Squad is on its way, and you wouldn't believe the state of my house. Could we make it, uh"—I looked at the clock—"five-thirty?"

We agreed on five-thirty, and I hung up with Jan's good wishes ringing in my ears.

Harry and the Crime Scene Unit, in the person of Irene Loukas, arrived almost simultaneously, just past four o'clock, with Captain Millner and Detective June Winters from the Burglary Squad right behind them. Millner and June came into the house without knocking, and Millner, who does not under normal circumstances go to the scene of a burglary, drawled, "Two vehicles totaled in two days. That's some going even for you, Deb."

"I wasn't driving either one of them," I pointed out.

"That's true," he admitted. "But I thought you were working on that mess at the Bird Cage. When did you transfer to Burglary?"

"About the time I got burglarized," I retorted. "June, after Ident gets through with everything, can we have it back? That's Harry's computer in the back of the pickup. I don't know what else of ours is in the truck—I'll have to look to be sure—but all of this is ours."

She looked at "all of this." She leaned over thoughtfully, picked up an Avon ring that appeared to have been stepped on, and handed it to me. I glanced at it. The bezel was now bent over on its side. In view of that, together with the fact that I hadn't worn it in eight years, I tossed it into the trash can.

"I haven't photographed that," Irene yelled. "You ought to know better than—"

I bent over the trash can, removed the ring, stood up, and handed it to June. June carefully restored it to where she had found it. "Is that better?" she asked, a little sarcastically.

"I guess," Irene said. "Deb, what in the world did you have in your head, to put a good dead bolt on a hollow door?"

"I had my financial situation in mind," I answered carefully, "or at least I would have if I had been the one to do it. In fact Harry did it. But you know as well as I do that even a solid steel door isn't going to stop somebody who's determined."

She did know it, and she knew I knew she knew it. She and I together had looked, several years ago, at a solid steel door with a dead bolt that went through the door frame and two inches into a solid wood wall, and burglars still managed to get in. Admittedly those burglars had been professionals, in search of the drugs and drug money presumably inside that particular house, but still it proved that no lock is totally secure. Irene did not, however, desire to admit to that knowledge. "I guess," she said grudgingly, "but it would still make more sense to have a decent door. I mean, really, a hollow wood door—"

"Will you quit criticizing my doors and take your pictures?" I inquired, trying not to look at Harry, who was swelling up like a pouter pigeon with the desire to defend himself, though in fact he'd only added a good lock to the door that had been on the house when we bought it.

"I'm trying to. Now if everybody would get out of my way—"

We wound up sending Shea to transport the two prisoners and keeping Groves to make sure the pickup truck was left absolutely alone until the accident people arrived. As the burglars left, the girl was crying quietly about having to leave Ivy, but the splashing noises in the bathtub and the occasional yips, followed each time by Lori's most soothing tones, reassured her he'd be cared for.

Then we all stood out in the front yard fidgeting, with Harry having a fit to get at the computers, until Irene had taken all her pictures and otherwise examined all the evidence.

I couldn't see any need for fingerprints, since we had found the burglars in the house and almost every surface they had touched was too grainy to hold prints anyway. But Irene insisted on fingerprinting the door glass, despite the fact that I literally could not remember the last time I'd washed it. Even she couldn't find anywhere else to fingerprint.

Then we were able to get Harry's computer, which turned out to be the only thing of ours actually in the truck (although there were a good many other things, some of which I recognized as belonging to May Rector, so I told Groves to go on over there, and some of which I did not recognize at all), and Harry took it tenderly back into the house to examine it.

By the time everybody else had left except the accident people, who were still waiting for a tow truck to come get the stolen truck and the police car it had run into, Lori had finished washing the cocker spaniel. She brought him out into the living room, nicely brushed and blow-dried and wearing one of Hal's T-shirts, which was a good bit too large for it. "What is that?" Harry demanded.

"He's a cocker spaniel," I said.

"What is it doing here? Never mind, don't tell me, I don't think I want to know. Deb, you distinctly promised me *no more livestock!* And anyway why is it wearing a shirt?"

"But we couldn't let him go to the pound; they would kill him there!" Lori protested, hugging the dog. "And he won't wear the shirt all the time, just until we get him a collar!"

Never mind the rest of that conversation. By the time we got through, Lori and I had picked up most of the mess in the living room, the stolen truck and the police car I drove home had been towed away, Harry had pronounced both computers well ("Lucky neither one was turned on," he remarked. "They're a lot tougher when the heads are locked.") and was busily hooking them back up where they belonged, and Harry and I had agreed we would keep Ivory only if Lori and I could convince Pat to accept him, and only temporarily. "Now feed him something," he added grumpily.

Now that Harry had gone from calling him it to calling him him, I suspected we would get little more argument about keeping him. In the meantime, we would put Pat in the front yard, to defend the unlockable front door from further invasion, and leave Ivory in the backyard because we didn't dare leave him inside a house he didn't know while Harry, Lori, Cameron, and I went to Cattleman's, to meet Jan Pender, take custody of his papers, and—incidentally—have a meal ourselves. After that, Harry would drop me by the police station, where I would use my own judgment on whether to get another police car to drive home or whether to drive home in my own car, while Harry went on to the hardware store to buy a new door and hope he could get it hung before he went to bed. Without Hal's help, it would certainly take longer than it would have taken when Hal was at home, unless Harry decided to ask friends to help him, and it was pretty short notice for that.

Finally having the time to think about personal things, I sat down with the UPS box and happily opened it, with Lori (and Ivy) looking over my shoulder. "Wow, those are pretty," Lori said.

Harry abandoned the computer he'd been testing in the living room (regardless of the fact that his new computer room is part of what was once the garage) long enough to ask, "Are they satisfactory?"

By now I had the first purse out and was examining it. "I think," I said, "that they will be highly satisfactory." So was his comment. I assumed, and hoped, it meant he had forgiven me for the dog.

Having finished with his own computer, Harry headed into the bedroom to get mine up and running, which, to my astonishment despite Harry's assurances, proved possible to do. I followed him in there. "Harry," I asked, "do you know anything about the Internet?"

He looked at me, clearly surprised. "Sure," he said, "I use it all the time."

"Why didn't you ever tell me that?"

"You never asked." He sounded quite bewildered by the entire discussion. I decided not to explain that I had gone today to set up my own Internet account. "Well, look," I said, "if I wanted to know more about circus aerialists, is there anybody on Internet who could tell me?"

"Babe, there are people on Internet who can tell you *anything*." He sounded distinctly more cheerful. Maybe he would finish forgiving me for another dog, especially one here only temporarily, if I asked him enough questions about computers. "Look, I'll tell you what—I'll just put a question on right now, and then we can check the answers when I get home tomorrow, okay?"

I guessed that was okay. At least it had better be. I had no idea how much use it would or would not be, and still less how much time it would take and how many answers I might get, but it had to be better than nothing.

After fiddling with the computer (his, still in the living room, not mine, which he gladly abandoned) for about five minutes, he asked, "What sort of information do you want? If I send in a question this broad I'll get enough to fill ten books."

"Anything you can find out about the Saranas and the Glucks. And about whether Jan Pender was an aerialist, and what anybody can tell me about him. About anybody mixed up with any of them who might know how to do explosives. Did you get onto Internet through work?"

"Uh-uh," he said, "I go in through Delphi." I must have looked uncomprehending, because he added, "One of those on-line services I pay for. You know, like Prodigy?"

"Okay," I said.

"Why, do you want to use it?"

"The city just created an Internet account for me," I said, "but I don't know what to do with it."

"I'll teach you," he said, extremely happily.

I had no doubt that he would.

It was just after five-thirty when we pulled into the parking lot at Cattleman's, and Pender was waiting for me in a deep maroon, almost black, Chrysler. He handed over a manila envelope. "I tried to handle them the same way you did," he told me. "So maybe the fingerprints on them will be better. Look, I'm sorry I was so hysterical this afternoon, but I hope you can see how scared I am about somebody else getting hurt. I wouldn't mind having stakeouts again tonight, but they would have to be different ones, because I think you're right, I think whoever it is probably works for me and somehow knew about the first two that came out. Somebody new, somebody he didn't recognize, well, that might work."

"I'll have to call and see what I can work out," I said.

"You can order dinner first," Harry pointed out after Pender had left and we were going into the restaurant. "Then you can telephone while we're waiting."

Usually while we were waiting for the main meal I ate salad, but salad doesn't take a hundred years to eat and I ought to have time. I told Harry what I wanted for dinner, and then I went not to the pay phone inside Cattleman's, lest by some remote chance it really was a protection racket and they had somebody inside Cattleman's too, but to the closest pay phone I could find outside.

By the time I came back in, two new stakeout people, neither of them people who had been to the Bird Cage before, were en route, and Ident had been alerted that I'd be coming in later with paper to be fingerprinted in connection with the case. I will admit now that none of that accomplished anything at all.

Considering everything that had gone on, it was still surprisingly early by the time we finished dinner. Harry dropped me by the police station and then headed for home. Driving another unmarked police car home, noticing the circus posters all over town, I got this bright idea.

$\mathcal{T}\varepsilon n$
. . . .

"THE CIRCUS?" HARRY snarled. "Are you out of your mind? You can't even sit still long enough to finish a meal, and you want to go to the circus? *Tonight?* You're supposed to be resting, and I've got to get this door put on." He didn't mention that he also had to remove what was left of the previous door, which would close adequately for very early fall weather but definitely would never lock again, and after doing that, before he could replace the door he had to replace about half the door frame. He also didn't mention that it was past sunset and he was working by dim yellow porch light, under the very interested stare of the new (to us) cocker spaniel, whom he had let inside again.

"I took some ibuprofen when I got home. And tonight is when the circus is here," I pointed out. "And anyhow I don't see how you can put the door on before the varnish dries." I thought the matter over and added, "If we leave Pat in the front yard—"

"If we leave Pat in the front yard we don't get any mail," Harry said morosely, standing back and looking at the door. "Can you keep the cats in the house till this dries?" He continued to look at the door. "You're right, it's got to dry." As he had chosen clear polyurethane spar varnish and the door was oak, it was actually going to be quite handsome as well as low-maintenance once it was finished. I very carefully had not asked its price. I was quite certain that I did not want to know.

"Sure, if you want to get their cat boxes back out," I answered.

Normally the cats use their boxes only in winter; in the summer they prefer to go outdoors, and the boxes were stored away. "And I mean to leave Pat in the yard just for tonight," I added, returning to the earlier discussion. "I mean, tomorrow is Saturday and it's probably going to take all night for the varnish to dry anyway, you can finish then—"

"How do you know there are even any seats left?"

"I called and asked. And then I reserved them, with the Master-Card. I can cancel them if you would prefer." I was tempted *not* to tell him they were premium seats, but since I wanted to be truthful, and also I didn't want to get into a quarrel at the box office, where he would notice the price even if they were going on the MasterCard, I added slightly guiltily, "They are kind of expensive. But Harry, I really do need to do this."

Never mind the rest of the discussion. Harry got out and refilled the cats' boxes, and Lori corralled both cats in her bedroom and locked the cat door while Harry shut the damaged front door adequately to restrain and confine the cats so that the new door would not carry, in perpetuity, feline footprints. Lori then opened her bedroom door and the cats stalked out, looking very peeved. After banging her head on the cat door four or five times, each cat then stalked across the room to sit down on the raised hearth (they wound up on opposite ends like firedogs), to lick her paws, wash her ears, and pretend for the sake of her feline dignity that she didn't really want to go out anyway.

Ultimately we departed for the circus in two vehicles, the kids and me in the second police car I'd taken home and Harry in the rented pickup truck he'd exchanged an hour earlier for the rented car when it dawned on him that he couldn't possibly bring a new door home from the lumber store in a sedan. The idea was that he could get the kids and himself home, safely though not comfortably, if I happened to get a call-out while we were there. He stayed right behind me the whole way, so that if I got a call I could pull over to the side of the road and we could transfer Lori and Cameron into the truck. I had my pager clipped to the waistband of my slacks and my radio, along with my pistol, in my new purse, the first one I'd ever owned except for a uniform bag that was designed to carry a pistol.

We parked side-by-side some eight blocks from the circus, which was being held in the Cow Palace vicinity. Despite the crowds on the street, I didn't mind having a pistol with me, as well as an ex-Marine (limping as a result of a helicopter crash several years ago, when he was test-piloting a new prototype that set itself down, hard, on its side, in the middle of a field, but still far tougher than he might look to a street punk) beside me. And Lori and I had our pepper spray in our pockets as we walked that eight blocks at night. The streets of Fort Worth are probably safer than most large city streets, but crowds have their own dangers, which I am probably more aware of than most women, and if something happened I wanted to be ready to react fast.

When we arrived at the ticket booth, while Harry was picking up our tickets I splurged ten dollars for a lavishly illustrated souvenir program that purported to tell the entire history of the circus as well as complete biographies of all the performers in this unit. Harry positively oozed disapproval, but he said nothing at all. In this, I have been authoritatively assured, he differs greatly from most men who overspend and prefer that their wives not do likewise.

I doubted very much that a hundred heavily coated glossy pages, at least half pictures, were going to provide me a complete history of this or any other circus, to say nothing of a complete history of circuses in general. But there was an outside chance that the booklet might say something I'd find useful.

Neither Harry nor I had been to a circus since we were ten years old. Lori and Cameron had never been to a circus, and no matter what my purposes were, they were both totally enthralled.

As Arlo had gloomily pointed out, there's no big top—the huge circus tent, with its acres of canvas—anymore. But I found that Luisa also was right: circuses still smell like circuses. Still look like circuses. Still feel like circuses. I had forgotten how much fun they were.

· · · · ·

But I did not allow myself to forget the real reason I had come to this circus on this night. I watched with considerable, though not total, interest as the grand promenade opened the show, after which the clowns rushed into the ring while equestrians stood erect, arms folded, on the backs of prancing white horses, ending their performance with a wild interwoven gallop partly to distract everyone's attention as the cage of lions and tigers was brought in. I watched lions and tigers and bears, and elephants and horses. I laughed and marveled as fourteen clowns climbed out of one small play-sized car, reflecting that if I'd seen this on television I'd just have assumed it was trick photography—which is one, but by no means the only, reason why the circus doesn't translate well to television.

I sat even straighter, with much more concentrated interest, as the ringmaster screamed, "And now, ladies and gentlemen, the Marvelous Montañez Family! Let's welcome Mario, Maria, and Marty Montañez back from a three-month engagement in Las Vegas! The Marvelous Montañez Family!" He fairly shrieked out the last four words, and the applause he had so eagerly invited rang out loudly.

I had not had a chance to see Julia's act all the way through. Although I had been at the Bird Cage last night throughout the last nightly performance of Luisa's act, which was presumably the same as Julia's, I had not seen all of it either, because people kept distracting my attention by talking with me and showing me things. This time, I was going to watch all the aerialists through their entire acts—provided I was allowed to, I thought, feeling like swearing at a woman who was threading her way through the seats and pausing directly in front of me while juggling six boxes of popcorn and six paper cups of Coke. Slender though she was, her behind blocked my entire view.

But as she moved on to block Harry's view, turning the other way now so that Harry very unwillingly had his head at approximately her crotch level, I could see the three young people, all clad in sequined leotards covered with glittering capes, with nylon tights and practical-looking tough, gaudy, but totally flexible boots, trotting around the ring and repeatedly, as they reached each section of seating, bowing together while spreading their capes with outstretched arms. Not one of them looked to be over thirty years old.

After completely circling the ring, the three flung off their glittering capes without watching where they would land, which was in the arms of an older man wearing more sober colors but no fewer sequins. As the three stretched their arms out triumphantly above them, smiling brightly on the audience before scattering in different directions in what seemed almost an excess of enthusiasm, the older man hung the capes over wooden pegs stuck at eye level in the side of a standing pole and then turned to pull on a rope, holding it tightly while someone else, similarly dressed, did something else I couldn't quite make out.

Obviously I would see far more, tonight, than I would have if I had sat through ten, twenty, even a hundred of both Julia's and Luisa's acts. Everybody who seemed to know had assured me that what I was seeing at the Bird Cage wasn't real flying at all, was something a child could do once the child got past being afraid of the heights.

Maybe so . . . but are all children afraid of heights? I remember when I wasn't; I would climb every tree I could find, no matter how tall it was. I would swing the playground swings so far up they were nearly parallel to the ground, desisting only when a teacher, alerted by children frightened about what I was doing, came and told me to stop at once, and then swinging lower, more slowly, until the teacher and the tattletale were out of sight. The weightless moment when the swing stops at the top of its path before reversing directions delighted me. I played on the monkey bars more than any other kid in the entire school, swimming through the air so fast that no one could catch me, and I could climb the metal climbing pole on the playground faster than anybody else I knew.

That is, until the day when I was about eleven that I, with about ten other kids, perched in the top of a large sweet gum tree that grew right beside the front porch of my aunt's house in Marshall, Texas; I don't think I've ever seen a sweet gum in the Fort Worth area. Somehow I got knocked out of the tree. Even then I kept my head, while my mother and my aunt screamed in terror, sure my head would hit the corner of the concrete porch and crack open like a coconut. I knew there was a short branch, part of its shoots broken off, about six feet above the porch, and I managed to twist myself around so that I caught it by my knees, dangling head-downward on the branch until I could get my hands up onto it, reverse my position, and clamber on top of the branch to scramble shakily to the ground. I think, now, I'd have been all right, emotionally as well as physically, if they'd sent me right back to climbing.

But they didn't; they made me go in the house and lie down, where I had nothing at all to do but relive, over and over, that moment of stark terror when I first felt myself falling and heard my mother and aunt screaming, terrifying myself more with each repetition. I have had to climb since then, sometimes, at work. But I've never done it without feeling a giddy dread and horror of falling again, this time without a branch to catch me, without a way to stop the fall.

Would I do now what Julia and Luisa did?

No way.

Would I have done it when I was eleven, before I fell out of the tree?

Almost certainly.

Would I do what I expected to be seeing shortly at this circus?

Never. Not in a hundred thousand million billion years. No way.

Would I have done it when I was eleven, before I fell out of the tree?

Probably, but why worry now about what might have been? I needed to stop thinking about that, and go on and watch the show.

People—including several of the clowns—ran to ropes, to pull on them and rearrange things, as the three athletes—the woman in glittering red, the men in different shades of glittering blue—swarmed up rope ladders and leaped out onto trapezes, which, using ropes from the ground, were gradually moved to different areas. They used a net, I noticed, but it was so low to the floor that if anybody actually hit it the net would probably give so much the person might as well hit the floor to start with. I assumed it was more a sop to insurance requirements than anything anyone seriously regarded as a safety precaution.

I studied the way ropes were snubbed around supports and other ropes; I paid attention to the various arrangements of rings and pulleys, and to the way people on the ground unobtrusively helped to secure ropes people were using up above. I watched, and went on watching.

People at the Bird Cage had explained to me the difference between a flyer and a catcher, and I was interested to notice that there was some difference between the body builds of Maria and whichever man was the other flyer and secondary catcher, and the body build of the man who was the main catcher. All three were quite muscular despite being lean and rangy, but the catcher's muscular development, particularly in his thighs, chest, and upper arms, seemed much heavier.

Here there was none of the strutting and dancing that I had seen at the Bird Cage. This was pure action, as dramatic and seemingly (and probably really) dangerous as it could get. Toward the end of their performance I watched Maria swing higher and higher, hanging by her knees with her long hair trailing beneath her, until she suddenly flung herself into the air and flew like a flying fish across the empty space between the two trapezes, her arms flung out to be caught by a strong man's hands. Held only by her hands around his wrists and his hands around her wrists as the trapeze kept on swinging, she agilely turned her entire body so that her knees caught the bars beside his. Then their hands released each other, and she twisted her body again, so that finally she stood on one foot only, leaning off the left-hand side of the trapeze, which now swung at an awkward slant with its heavier edge leading.

The other man launched himself into the air then, to be caught and to rearrange himself until all three were on the same trapeze, the woman and the lighter man leaning to either side and the heavier man in the center. Swaying their bodies then, they increased the speed of the swing, which had let up slightly.

Then the heavier man, the catcher, launched himself into the air from a standing position, flying like an arrow to land with his waist across the trapeze the woman had left only moments earlier.

The lighter man and the woman went on swinging, went on swinging, and the heavier man watched them, his swings mirroring theirs now instead of matching them. Then the lighter man rearranged himself so that he was hanging by his knees with the side ropes of the trapeze wrapped around both ankles, obviously for further stability. Maria, standing, somersaulted off the trapeze, to be caught by her wrists as she grasped his wrists. But this time, instead of facing forward, she was facing backward. The two went on swinging.

The music of the circus band, which had been a scarcely noticed background to their act, faded out. Drums, their snares silenced, beat out a quickly ominous tattoo, and then they too went silent.

"Ladies and gentlemen!" the ringmaster shouted. "Maria Montañez will now attempt a quadruple backward somersault in the air, an incredibly difficult accomplishment never seen in the ring since nineteen fifty-seven, when a German trapeze artist fell to her death in her thirteenth performance! Hold your silence, ladies and gentlemen!"

I took this announcement with the grain of salt it deserved. It was undoubtedly true that Maria Montañez would attempt a quadruple backward somersault in the air. It was undoubtedly true that it was extremely difficult and dangerous, and it might well be the first time it had been seen in the ring since 1957. It probably had indeed led to the death of a German trapeze artist, though I had no particular reason to assume she had died on her thirteenth attempt. But it certainly was not the first time Maria Montañez had attempted it.

Even without what I had been told by Arlo and Luisa and Jan, I would have been able to guess from what I was seeing this evening, even if I couldn't from what I remembered from childhood trips to

. . . . .

the circus, that everything circus aerialists did called for split-second timing. That sort of timing doesn't happen by accident; it occurs only when people rehearse the same thing over and over and over, not until it becomes routine—I could not believe that this sort of thing ever could become routine—but until it becomes nearly a conditioned reflex, until a glance can tell the acrobat whether or not everything and everyone is in the right position and it is the right time to let go and fly.

To a steady roll of the Scotch drums, Maria and the lighter man swung back and forth, with her body increasing the length of the pendulum; the heavier man swung back and forth, watching the woman intently and adjusting his timing to hers. Then, after a nod from the heavier man so nearly imperceptible I wouldn't have recognized it if I hadn't been watching for it, the lighter man spoke briefly to the woman. He swung backward one more time, almost up to the rafters. Then, as the trapeze reached almost the top of its forward swing with her feet literally brushing the rafters, she leaped away from the lighter man's hands, drawing her knees up to her chest and putting her arms around her knees, turning over—and over, and over, and over—stretching her arms and hands blindly above her the fourth time, to be caught by the outstretched hands, to catch the outstretched wrists, of the heavier man.

I don't know many people were even breathing, during those interminable moments she was in free fall. I don't think I was; only after she was standing beside the man, throwing kisses at the crowd with both hands, did I become aware that Harry and I were holding hands so tightly my fingers felt crushed. "Wow," I heard Lori say beside me. "I don't see how anybody could ever do that."

Neither did I.

But no matter how much I marveled, I watched carefully to see how each trapeze artist got back down from the trapeze. That was one of the things I hadn't seen; Julia of course had fallen, and when Luisa was getting down, somebody—I think it was a waiter—was standing in front of me talking. Did someone pull their trapezes back to the platform where they had climbed on? Did they scramble through the web of ropes to retreat to the platform? Jan had said something about a rope—

I should have known better. Neither of those exits would be glamorous enough.

The heavier man, arm outstretched to the right, slid to the floor with his left hand on the rope and the rope wrapped around his left ankle. (I assumed, but could not see, that there was something—some covering, some tool—on the rope he used to protect himself from rope burns.) The slimmer man, arm outstretched to the left, slid to the floor with his right hand on the rope and the rope wrapped around his right ankle. And finally Maria, her arm outstretched to the left, her right hand on the rope, her left knee raised with toes pointing down and the rope wrapped around her right ankle, slid to the ground, to pose dramatically between the two men with both her arms flung up in a silent victory yell while she smiled dazzlingly at the crowd.

With repeated bows, throwing kisses from both hands to the audience, all three fled out a door.

Screaming, cheering, clapping, stamping continued until all three ran in again, circling the ring, smiling and throwing more kisses. This time, when they exited, they didn't return.

There wasn't much more show after that. It was just as well, because anything else would have been an anticlimax.

We walked away from the Cow Palace in the darkness, Harry carrying Cameron, who, although he insisted volubly that he was not tired, was asleep in Harry's arms before we got back to the car. Cameron was quite offended, after we got home, when I insisted on bathing him and getting him into clean pajamas before putting him to bed.

I returned to the living room after that to find Lori sitting with the back door open and the patio light on. Judging from the scratching I could hear, both cats were once again locked in her room. She was holding Pat and talking to both him and Ivy, who was sitting on his haunches in front of her. Harry, in the recliner chair he insisted on getting but very rarely actually uses, was watching open-mouthed. As I paused beside him, he glanced around at me and put his finger to his lips before returning his attention to the scene at the back door.

Lori was addressing both dogs, explaining to Pat that Ivy had come to live with us because his other people couldn't take care of him anymore, explaining to Ivy that Pat was the top dog here and he had to understand that. She was talking to them as if both dogs understood English and knew exactly what she meant. Both dogs seemed to be listening to her attentively.

When she let go of Pat, he stood up and wagged what was left of his whacked-off tail. Ivy rolled over on his back, in what even I could recognize as a posture of abject surrender. Pat nosed at him, and Ivy stood up again. He and Pat sniffed amiably at each other's hindquarters, and then both trotted off toward the water dish. Apparently Pat was demonstrating to Ivy where it was, just in case Ivy hadn't learned yet.

"I'll be darned," Harry said, as Lori closed the door. "I'd never have believed you could get those two to get along for a second, let alone this fast."

"Dogs are pack animals," Lori said, rather more smugly than was completely seemly. "You just have to let them know who is and isn't part of the pack." With that, she also headed off to bed, letting both cats back out when she opened the door. I suggested that Harry and I do likewise: go to bed, not let the cats out.

"I think I'll just have a look at Internet," he said, "to see if we've got anything back on your query."

"It can wait till morning."

"I just want to see what there is now."

I shrugged and, for the first time that night, went on into the bedroom. The little orange light on the answering machine was flickering. After picking up a pen and a memo pad, I pushed the button.

"Deb, this is Luisa, please call me whatever time you get home. It's 555-6893. It doesn't matter how late it is."

She sounded virtually hysterical.

I didn't look at the clock; I just picked up the phone and started dialing, and she answered on the first ring.

"This is Deb Ralston," I said.

"Thank you so much," she said, half sobbing. "Deb, I don't know what to do, Arlo's missing."

She had my full attention. I asked for details.

"I don't know," she said, "he's just *missing*. He left right after the last show tonight, and he was going to come back and get me and take me home only he didn't come back, and he wasn't at the Cage, and I waited and waited, and finally one of the janitors took me home, and I thought maybe he'd forgotten me, he's been so upset, so I looked where he parks, and his car wasn't there, and he hasn't been home, and he hasn't called—" She caught her breath in a sob. "I don't know what to *do!* Deb, I *know* he didn't kill my sister, so why—?"

"I don't know," I said. I didn't like any of the things I was thinking. Despite all our assumptions to the contrary, could he be the killer?

Or could the killer have gotten him?

I got a description of Arlo's car, the license number, a description of the clothes Arlo had been wearing when he left. "I'll take it from here," I said. "And I'll call you when I know something. I'll call you in the morning whether I hear or not."

"Thank you," she said.

"And you try to get some sleep," I added, knowing when I said it how idiotic an idea that was.

"Oh, sure," she said, and hung up.

I called the station and put a lookout on Arlo's car and Arlo. There ought to be a lot of other things I could do. But for the life of me I couldn't think of one right now.

Lost in thought, I wandered back into the living room, where

. . . . .

Harry, staring intently at the computer screen (and I wondered how long his computer would stay in the living room this time before he returned it to its designated location in what used to be the garage), asked, "How much of this do you want me to print out?"

"How much is there?" I asked, my mind back on the task at hand.

He studied it. "Oh, it'll come to about five hundred pages."

"Are you kidding me?" I demanded, getting up from the couch to look over his shoulders. "Five hundred pages? In this short a time? How many people answered, for crying out loud?"

"Not many. Probably three or four hundred," he said casually. "There'll probably be a lot more in the morning, and we'll go on getting answers for a couple of weeks."

"I'll read it on-line," I said weakly, not even wanting to think about the volume of paper all that would take to print. "I hope you don't want the computer again tonight—"

"It's not on-line now," he said, in a rather aggrieved tone of voice. "I got it off. I've downloaded it to my disk. Why don't I go put it on your computer?"

"Because that would involve transferring it from your hard disk to a floppy to my hard disk—"

"That would only take about five more minutes," Harry interposed.

"—and I might be reading late tonight, and I don't want to keep you awake when you've got that door to work on tomorrow."

"Oh," Harry said, "yeah. Well, give me five minutes."

The five minutes, as I had fully anticipated, turned into an hour as he checked various on-line services—Prodigy, Delphi, AOL, and I didn't know what-all else—for his E-mail and his favorite bulletin boards, occasionally laughing, reading a note out loud to me, or replying to somebody, during which time I called the police station again to be sure the dispatcher had sent the lookout to all neighboring police departments and put it on NCIC. But eventually Harry yawned several times, retrieved the file he'd downloaded from Internet, showed

. . . . .

me how to print out anything I wanted hard copies of, and wandered off to bed.

I had spent most of the hour, what time I wasn't on the phone, leafing through the souvenir program and reading what looked most interesting. As I had feared, there was really nothing on it that was of any use to my investigation, though the pictures were excellent. After that, I had turned to my library books, first doing what I should have done before even taking the books out of the library, namely checking the index of each one for references to anybody named Gluck, Sarana, or Pender. The references were few, and each one, when I turned to it, was laudatory or historical but told me nothing that could have related to the Bird Cage except that the Sarana family and the Gluck family had repeatedly intermarried, which I could have guessed without the books.

I started through the E-mail file expecting to find just about the same thing, and to start with that was what I got. I don't know how many screens I browsed through until I came to exactly what I wanted.

I didn't even know how to tell who it was from. I'd have to ask Harry, tomorrow, to show me that, because my informant—if he or she was speaking from personal knowledge—might need to be subpoenaed as a witness.

"Connections between Saranas and Glucks go back several hundred years," my unknown informant began:

> Most recent I know of is marriage of Arlo Gluck and Julia Sarana about seven years ago in Sarasota, Florida. Most recent prior to that began in 1947, when the Saranas and Glucks joined forces for what turned out to be about ten years, working with several different circuses that toured Europe, going from free areas to Communist areas without much hassle from either side even when the Berlin Blockade was going

on. That coalition came to an end in 1957 in West Berlin, when sixteen-year-old Pamela Sarana fell to her death attempting, without a net, to leap from the hands of Barthold Gluck of the Gliding Glucks to those of novice aerialist Jan Pender, making a quadruple somersault on the way. The autopsy demonstrated that Pamela was six weeks pregnant, but the question of who the father was remains open; her fiancé Barthold Gluck insisted he was not, but there seemed to be no other likely suspect. The Sarana-Gluck coalition, which had lasted only ten years, broke up at that time, although Pender remained with the Glucks until his own serious injury a year later.

Barthold Gluck continued to perform. He later married one of his cousins, with whom he performed for the next thirteen years, until he retired from active performance at the age of forty-three to work as a trainer.

Aerialists Eugene Sarana (who now performs under the name of Marty Montañcz), his wife, Maria, and her twin brother, Mario Montañez, were trained by Pamela's father, famed aerialist and trainer Beppo Sarana, who taught Pamela the secret of the quadruple somersault first performed by his wife, the former Margaret Harrison, who, like Pamela, died doing the act. Beppo has since left the circus to work with his niece Julia Sarana and her husband Arlo Gluck, who have taken up nightclub performing.

The signature was a series of letters, numbers, and punctuation marks incomprehensible to me.

I highlighted the information and told the computer to print. Here was a definite link to what had happened at the Bird Cage.

The ringmaster also must be wrong, I thought; it wasn't a German aerialist who fell, but the accident occurred in Germany.

Here, too, was ample reason for Beppo Sarana to dislike the Glucks, to dislike Jan Pender. So why was he working for Jan Pender, why was he working with Arlo Gluck? Had he been able to forgive all involved to that extent? And how, I wondered, could the death of his own niece fit into the picture? If it were Jan or Arlo dead (and maybe Arlo *was*) then Beppo would be the obvious suspect—but Julia? I just couldn't see it.

Suppose it were Beppo—then why would he kill Julia? That was the stumbling block I couldn't get past. I could see a picture evolving, but I didn't like it and I didn't really believe it . . . besides, if it were true, where would the explosives come from? Because by now I'd made that quick telephone call that had let me know the federal bomb people were now saying that the radio detonation device was pretty sophisticated, and the bomber definitely knew what he was doing. And even my wild imagination couldn't believe that trapeze artists normally are skilled in the use of high explosives.

But all the same, when morning came I'd start checking out all the ideas that had come to me as I read this message, just in case one of them turned out to be connected.

I grabbed the sheet off the printer, automatically closed the printer tray at once lest a cat jump on it and break it off, and lay down on the couch to think about it. A while later Harry came in and informed me it was 2 A.M., and I promised him I'd come to bed in a minute.

I woke, on the back on my couch with the sheet of paper lying on my chest, when Harry's rented pickup truck roared out of the driveway driven by Lori on her way to early morning seminary.

Eleven

· · · · · ·

OF COURSE IT couldn't possibly be Lori going to seminary, I realized as I went to wash my face and so forth, because this was Saturday, and seminary is Monday through Friday. I felt much better; the burns seemed to be healing adequately. And the time—I looked at the clock and was aghast to see that it was almost eleven. I couldn't even remember last time I'd slept this late. And I had promised to call Luisa in the morning.

The poor girl must have been sitting right beside the telephone all morning, if not all night. She answered instantly. But she could tell me no more than she could the night before, except to add that she'd kind of found out Arlo had his knife with him. Which knife? Oh, that special knife he and all the males in his family were given when they turned sixteen. A big one. Very sharp. Yes, she guessed you could call it a hunting knife, but she thought it was more of a commando knife. No, she hadn't ever seen him use it, what would he use it for? It was really more of a ceremonial knife, not one to use.

Her sister's funeral was in half an hour; she was grateful I had called so she could leave. If Arlo wasn't at the funeral—

If Arlo wasn't at the funeral I'd have to pick up a photograph of him afterward. And I'd have to add a little to the lookout: a little like *may be armed, may be dangerous.*

May be suicidal.

May have killed his wife.

· · · · · ·

But why, dammit, why, why, *why?* And if he had, he was one of the best actors I'd ever seen in my life.

I couldn't get out of my mind, now, that inconclusive result Cubby got on the polygraph, about Arlo maybe not telling the truth about not knowing who his wife was pregnant by. But what difference did that make? He did know she wasn't pregnant by him. So why would who she *was* pregnant by make any difference in whether he would kill her?

I had a headache. Clearly I needed some medicinal chocolate. Then I needed to get back to work.

I wasn't *officially* working today, but the last circus performance was tonight, and by midnight the circus train would be loading back up to move on to the next booking. That meant that if I wanted to talk with the Montañezes—and I did; that was the obvious next step—I would have to catch them during the day today.

But normal household duties don't stop just because somebody wants to talk to somebody. I went into Cameron's room; he was not in his bed, which meant either he was outside playing with one or both dogs, or he had gone with Harry. I pushed open the door of Lori's room very slightly; she was sound asleep. Last year I read some-where that for some reason teenagers, no matter what their body schedules were before they hit their teens or will be in adulthood, tend to be night owls who sleep very hard and very late in the morning whenever they have a chance. I was now on my fourth teenager, with presumably only one more to go, and I could well believe that state-ment.

I checked the whiteboard on the inside of the door that led from the kitchen to the ex-garage. Harry had installed that for me several months earlier, and now all grocery items and toiletries somebody wanted to have restocked, all telephone messages for somebody to call somebody back, all requests for somebody to do something, all ap-pointments anybody had coming up, and all destinations and expected times of return were supposed to be written there. We'd found it worked very well, and my only regret about it was that neither Harry nor I had thought of it earlier, when we had more children at home and one of them was Hal.

As I had hoped, Harry had written a note in blue marker: *Gone to hardware store. Cameron is with me. Be back whenever.*

I checked the dogs, who were both in the backyard and getting along quite amiably. No need to check the cats—Harry had left the front door open, which presumably meant the cats had been released from durance vile and were now headed for a vacant field to catch mice to bring in the house, this being their usual custom after they had been locked up for a while. Anyway, it was September, and they like to stock their winter hunting grounds. I made a note on the whiteboard to buy mousetraps and d-Con.

After eating a bowl of Cheerios and drinking a mug of hot chocolate, I headed for the telephone book. Locating the Montañezes and getting them to talk to me might be easy or it might not. I didn't want to guess at which.

There is a saying that after you've done your homework—that is, checked all reasonable reference sources—you can lay your hands on any fact you need, provided it is neither a government secret, evidence of criminal activity, nor a proprietary trade secret, with a maximum of five telephone calls. When I heard that I absolutely did not believe it. It sounded too unlikely for words. But I went and tested it, and I've been using it ever since. So far the highest number of phone calls I've needed has been four, and that was only once. I never needed more than three at any other time.

So who were the right people to start with this time?

I made a telephone call. That person didn't know, so I asked, "Who do you think might be likely to know?" Armed with that name, I made another telephone call, and got another name, and made another phone call, and got the name of a motel. I called its switchboard, asked for Maria Montañez, and waited briefly until the phone at the other end of the line began to ring.

. . . . .

"Hello?" said a rather sleepy voice.

"Miss Montañez?"

"I'm not doing any more interviews. I'm sorry, but that's in my contract, and—"

"I'm not asking for an interview," I interrupted. "I'm a police officer."

Dead silence for a moment. Then she asked, warily, "Have I done something?"

"Good heavens, no!" I said, trying to sound jovial, which is rather difficult as I am not a jovial person by nature. Friendly, yes, I hope, but not jovial. "No, but I'm working on a very complicated problem and I think you and your husband and brother might be able to help me with it."

"What kind of problem is that?"

"I'm trying to find out who murdered Julia Sarana Gluck—"

Maria Montañez screamed and dropped the telephone, and I could faintly hear the commotion in her room as she yelled, "Gene! Gene! There's a cop on the phone, and she says Julia's dead! Somebody killed Julia! Gene—"

The phone was moved around several times, and then a male voice said, "I'm Eugene Sarana. What's this about my sister?"

"Your sister?" I repeated, utterly appalled. "Julia Gluck was your sister?" Of course I should have guessed, given what I knew. I guess I had assumed they were cousins. I guess I had assumed if he'd been anyone close to her he'd have called me. Mainly I guess I didn't think.

"What's this *was?* What are you talking about?"

"I'm so sorry, I wouldn't have notified you this way if I'd known. But I would have expected Arlo or Luisa to get in touch with the family—"

"They probably did." His voice was rough with grief. "But nobody told us. It's sort of a rule in the family, you don't give people bad news when they're performing if there's any way you can keep them from finding out. We've got a four-day break starting tonight, they'd probably have told us tonight after the last show. So what—"

I told him. After a long pause, he said, "I could understand a fall. Especially with that idiot Arlo convincing her the circus is dead— that's enough to depress anybody. But something like this—what did you say your name is?"

"Deb Ralston."

"And you're some sort of private eye?"

"No, I'm a detective with the Fort Worth Police Department."

"Detective Ralston," he said, "I am telling you, and I suppose you probably won't believe me but it's the truth, that there was not one human being in the entire world who had any reason at all to dislike Julia."

"I've been hearing that from everybody," I said, "and I do believe it. But I'm sorry to say the fact remains that somebody murdered her, and I don't know why, and it looks like on this one I'm going to have to find out why before I can find out who. So if I could meet with the three of you—"

"It's eleven-fifteen now," he interrupted. "Can you be here by noon? We'll be having breakfast then—I'll have it sent up, Maria's sure not up to going out—and you can join us. Mario will be here too."

"You're not going to the funeral?" I blurted out.

There was a brief silence. Then he said, "I don't think that would be a good idea. So be here at noon if you can."

I had to say one more thing, even before I agreed to meet them at noon. "Mr. Sarana—I know this is none of my business—but I wish your wife wouldn't try that quadruple somersault tonight, as upset as I figure she'll be. I mean, I know all about the show must go on, but—"

After a short bark of hard laughter, he said, "Don't worry about that. She won't. The show doesn't have to go on to that extent."

"And . . . I guess Luisa's your sister too. . . ."

"That's right."

. . . . .

"She's doing Julia's act now."

"So?"

"That's how Julia was murdered," I said, and began to explain, not telling him for now that Arlo was missing.

"I'll talk some sense into her head, too," he told me roughly. "As soon as I get through meeting with you. You'll be here at twelve, then?"

I rushed to shower and don slacks, a shirt, socks, and sneakers; since I was off duty and wanted to enjoy my new purse anyway, I used it instead of my shoulder holster. Then I added my note to the whiteboard below Harry's: *Gone to talk to the Montañezes, back whenever. Sorry!* That last was necessary: although I have done detecting when I was technically off duty as long as I have been a detective, Harry still tends to resent the practice, as he considers that my free time belongs to the family, not to the police department. (Oddly enough, nobody seems to believe that my free time belongs to me. But I believe that is a universal problem among women.) Surely even Harry would understand this time, though. I certainly couldn't wait and talk to the Montañezes Monday if they were leaving town Saturday night.

Harry was driving up as I backed out of the driveway. I rolled down my window and pulled my car up beside the rented truck, the two of us pointing in opposite directions so that the driver's windows were side by side. I told him what I was doing, and he said, "Okay, I'll be finishing up this door, because it looks like rain. And you've got about another seven hundred pages of replies on Internet; I checked this morning."

"Are there that many people in the *world* who keep track of what's happening in circuses?" I asked. "Harry, I only got about a third of the way through what you had last night, and that was just skimming."

"You want me to go look and see if any of it seems relevant?"

I hesitated. Theoretically I wasn't supposed to involve my husband in police work, but I did it all the time anyway, and I'd kept him pretty well posted on this. "I wish you would," I said finally.

. . . . .

"I'll get hold of you if I need to. Good luck. And Deb—stay out of trouble."

As I headed down the street wondering how much trouble I could get into just visiting the Saranas, Harry turned into the driveway.

I called Eugene Sarana again from the motel lobby, and he gave me the room number and told me to come on up.

Seen up close, Maria Montañez belied my memory of the ballerina who came to our high school. She looked even better face to face, without makeup, than she did from a distance in heavy stage makeup: small, trim, totally in proportion, with long wavy black hair, dark brown eyes, and long eyelashes. She had been crying, though, and was still crying off and on.

Eugene Sarana, the slightly heavier man, the main catcher, turned out to be her husband, and the lighter man was her twin brother Mario. Seen up close, Maria and Mario looked to me as if they were probably in their midtwenties, and Eugene seemed slightly older, maybe thirty. The Saranas—it turned out Maria used her married name when she wasn't performing—had two children with them: four-year-old Will and two-year-old Diana.

Like Maria, Eugene had been crying, although he managed not to while I was there.

As introductions progressed we went through the usual call-me-Deb-call-me-Maria business. Gene had ordered breakfast for me as well as for his wife and brother-in-law, and although I had already eaten I felt it would be churlish for me to refuse—besides, I like bacon, and out of respect for everybody's cholesterol count I never buy it anymore.

I didn't know what I hoped to get from them. As I had expected, all three of them knew Beppo Sarana and Jan Pender as well as Arlo and Julia Gluck. As I had further expected, not a one of them was old enough to remember Pamela Sarana, though they all knew Barthold Gluck.

"I'm sorry to sound like I'm digging up old scandals," I said, "but as

. . . . .

hard as I've tried, I have been totally unable to come up with any conceivable reason for anybody to want to harm Julia as Julia. So all I can figure out is she must have represented something or someone else to her killer. I've looked at the possibility that Julia's murder was an extortion attempt gone wrong, but that doesn't fit either. At this point absolutely all I can think of is that either Julia was killed in revenge for something she had nothing to do with, or she was killed . . ." I hesitated. This was Arlo's and Julia's personal business. But by vanishing, he'd made it much more police business than it ever was before. "Or she was killed because she was pregnant, not by her husband," I said firmly.

Gene nodded. "You're not telling tales out of school. I knew about that. But she told me Arlo knew what she was doing."

"But Arlo's missing," I said.

"There are times I think Arlo's got the brain of a chipmunk," Gene replied. "But I've known him all my life. I think he'd panic, in a situation he didn't know anything about—not in flying, of course. He'd panic, but he wouldn't kill."

"Maybe," I said, "but if so, then this thing in nineteen fifty-seven is the only thing I have been able to come up with. And even knowing about it, I don't see why Beppo, or anybody else for that matter, would have harmed her as revenge for it. So anything you can tell me, anything at all—even if it's just old rumors, because sometimes people believe rumors and act on them."

Gene and Maria were looking at each other. Then Gene said, "I guess I'm the appropriate person to talk. Okay—first, I think you can rule out Beppo. He's a religious nut, always has been, and I can't see him killing anybody under any circumstances, especially not Julia. I'm not even sure he'd kill for self-defense, except in wartime. Beyond that—I can't think of anything."

"If you rule out Arlo and Beppo there's nobody left," I pointed out. "But *somebody* did it. It didn't just happen."

"I can't make any suggestions at all," Gene said.

. . . . .

"Then just give me background," I suggested, feeling rather hopeless at seeing both of my possible leads evaporating before my face.

Eugene drained his coffee cup, set it down hard, and said, "I don't know what you know about old-time circus families. I gather you've been finding out as much as possible, but there's so much nobody is likely to think to tell you because it's so far in the background nobody really thinks about it. The first thing that's important, I guess, is that there's so much inbreeding that the family trees tend to look more like braided rope. And that's inevitable, for several reasons. First, most people wind up marrying people they know—"

Maria giggled through her tears at that. "Really, Gene."

"All right, but you know what I mean. It's a little different now, because the children go to public school in Sarasota part of the year, but up until the last, say, fifty years, a circus person had almost no chance to meet anybody in any other occupation. A second reason is that of what you're used to and what you accept as normal. Suppose, say, that I had married somebody other than Maria, somebody from outside. How's she going to take to my performances, after she gets past the glitter and glamour and starts to realize that's her husband up there risking his neck just about every night for six or so months out of the year? Or suppose Maria had married somebody from outside. The same feeling and probably worse, because she's a woman, and what call do women have to risk their necks?"

I nodded. This was an attitude I was quite familiar with, though I'll admit I don't get it from Harry very often. But I remembered when I first went to work for the police department. Clint Barrington—he was my first partner, that was before he went over to the sheriff's office—and I were waiting to testify on a burglary when three prisoners got hold of a bailiff's gun and ran. We knew they hadn't got out of the courthouse. So the courthouse was evacuated of all civilian personnel, and all the police fanned out to search.

This was immediately after I had gone onto the department, before I had even gone to recruit school. I was in plainclothes at this time because I was so short they were having to have uniforms specially made for me, and I didn't even have a uniform purse then. So I had a Colt revolver with a five-inch barrel because that was the only conceivably acceptable service revolver Harry had in his arsenal and we couldn't afford quite yet to buy me a new pistol (having fairly recently purchased Harry an airplane, a matter we still can't discuss without me yelling), and I was carrying around a purse the size of a doghouse so that I could conceal the Colt in it—and I don't even like Colts; that darn two-stage trigger drives me nuts.

Even then, with no training at all, I had better sense than to hunt three armed escapees with my pistol in my purse. So, having no other choice, I had left my purse in the judge's chambers and was carrying the pistol in my hands.

Clint and I had been good friends before I entered police work. I had worked in a doughnut shop for a while, after Harry left the Marines but before he went to work for Bell Helicopter, when we needed money badly, and Clint had talked me into trying out police work because it paid a lot better than a doughnut shop and the shifts couldn't possibly be worse. He hadn't bothered to tell me it was interesting work because by then he knew me well enough to know I'd figure that out quickly on my own.

But I think that until that day, when he saw me—and in those days, in my midtwenties, I was pretty if I do say so myself, as short and slender as Maria Montañez and looking about as harmless—pushing open a door with my foot, with that five-inch Colt held in both hands, Clint hadn't fully let himself realize that by talking me into trying police work he was taking me from the comparative safety of the doughnut shop—only comparative, because any woman working alone at night in a convenience store or anything like that is subject to robbery, kidnap, rape, even murder—and putting me on the front lines. When he saw the gun in my hand, that realization hit him hard, full in the face.

He said absolutely nothing to me, that afternoon in the hall of the

. . . . .

194

courthouse. He simply looked at me, and his face blanched, and he went his way and I went mine, and eventually two deputy sheriffs caught the escapees in the attic ready to surrender. Neither Clint nor I ever mentioned that day to each other, and it was a long time before I ever told Harry about it.

Most men dislike seeing women risking their lives a lot more than they dislike seeing themselves, or other men, do it, unless it's something quite unavoidable, like childbirth, and even then some of them seem to really prefer not to be around. (Harry would have been there if he could have been; it wasn't his fault I gave birth to Cameron in a hospital in New Mexico while Harry was in a hospital in Texas.)

Gene Sarana was right in what he was saying. If Maria had married outside the circus, it would have been extremely difficult for her to continue following the profession she knew and loved.

Gene had broken off his monologue long enough to grab Diana and suggest, rather firmly, that she quit chasing Will in circles with a water gun and sit down and eat her breakfast. Now he returned to what he was saying.

"I don't want you to think that we're the Jukeses and Kallikaks. We don't marry our brothers and sisters and usually we don't marry our first cousins, and just about every generation two or three people will bring outside mates into the family, or leave the family to go with outside mates, so the size of the performing family stays fairly stable, growing when it needs to and shrinking when it needs to. All this has several results, and the one that's probably most important to you, to what you're doing, is that which families are most prominent is constantly changing according to who has the most children, who brings the most new people into the family, who has the most children that leave the family. Sometimes one family name will be the most important for a generation, then for the next generation it might be a different name. Right now I'm performing as a Montañez even though I'm a Sarana. Next generation who knows? Maria and I have already produced two Saranas who might decide to perform as Montañezes or might decide to perform as Saranas. But just about all of us are related in some way—more or less distant cousins, or at the very least more or less distant cousins-in-law. So—yes, I know what happened in nineteen fifty-seven. Unless you've done a lot of digging, I know a lot more about it than you do."

"Are you willing to tell me?"

Unaccountably, his face reddened briefly. "It's no secret. Uncle Beppo married an Englishwoman, Margaret Harrison, in the thirties sometime, and Aunt Margaret took to flying as if she'd been born to it."

"So that's how their daughter got the name of Pamela," I said. "I'd wondered about that. It sounds so very English."

He grinned, briefly. "A lot of the family—all the families—didn't much care for Margaret, I'm told, because her English habits seemed prissy to them. That's why I think Pamela was pressured into agreeing to marry Barthold Gluck—sort of, say, to redeem Beppo's crime not just of marrying outside the family but of marrying an Englishwoman. I don't think either one of them, Pamela or Barthold, I mean, was in a big hurry for the marriage, which is part of why it never happened, besides her age of course. Dad told me he had the feeling Pamela especially wasn't interested in Barthold after she met Jan Pender. Jan—well, let me back up. Through the first half or maybe two-thirds of this century—We all have passports, of course, you've got to have passports to travel, especially in Europe, or at least you did then, but— it was like we were international. Like the circus was above politics. And the Saranas and the Glucks were traveling together right then, and they'd come to the United States, been here for a while, and then some people wanted to go back to Europe and some didn't and there was a big row about it. A few other people were traveling with them, and Jan Pender was one. He was an outsider trying to turn into an insider, and from all I've heard he was good, he was damn good. So the decision was made, go back and try a few more years in Europe, see how it felt, and if it didn't feel right then we'd—they would, I mean, of course I wasn't born then—all ask for permanent residence status in the United States, which is the first step toward citizenship."

"Would they have gotten it?"

"I guess so, because they *did* get it, a little later. Anyhow—Beppo was a flyer for a while, and then as he got older he started thickening, like I'm doing"—Gene gestured deprecatingly at his chest—"and then he decided it would be best for him to let up some on the flying and become a catcher most of the time. And Margaret—I've seen home movies of her. She was damn good. The official line is that it was Beppo who thought up the quadruple somersault thing and taught it to Margaret. The reason it's so dangerous, by the way, isn't that it's difficult. Just about anybody can turn four somersaults in a row. It's just that it's got to go so *fast,* because gravity doesn't change its rules for somebody who wants to turn four somersaults in the air and then be caught by somebody else in the air. So, as you saw last night, you've got to be at the top of the swing, just about as high as you can possibly go, before you start the somersaults, and your catcher has to be at just the right place when you're through, and that takes just an incredible amount of coordination. But—though he claimed it later, it wasn't Beppo that thought the thing up, the way I heard it; it was Margaret. Not that it matters who thought it up, I guess, but Margaret . . . She died in nineteen forty-two, back in England because of the war—the whole troop was there, you don't go doing circuses in a war zone and most of the men were gone to the war anyhow and not many women are able to catch very well. It's not lack of strength or ability, it's just the fact that some of a woman's muscles are attached slightly differently from a man's muscles. But Margaret tried to do the quadruple somersault anyway, performing somewhere—actually I think it was in Scotland—with a young Gluck boy, about sixteen, swinging her, and one of her sisters-in-law was supposed to be catching her and they missed. I don't know really what happened and neither does anybody else; nobody was filming it; all I know is Margaret fell a long way and she was so far off balance she landed on the side of her head and broke her neck. She died instantly. Beppo—was in Eastern Europe at the time, I don't know exactly where. He couldn't even get home for the funeral. He said the quadruple should never be tried again; a triple should be enough for anybody.

"But there were a lot of home movies of Margaret's quadruple, and when Pamela was fifteen she wanted to do it. Started working on it, with Barthold Gluck swinging her and Jan Pender catching. Beppo was fit to be tied, but he let it go on—from what I've heard he couldn't do much about it anyway. Pamela was hardheaded.

"A movie camera was running when Pamela fell, so it's pretty clear what happened. Barthold did everything he was supposed to and Jan did everything he was supposed to, but Pamela was a long way off her intended position and nobody knew why until the autopsy. She hadn't told anybody she was pregnant. And—sure, you can fly when you're pregnant, for a while—Maria, how far were you when you quit? Four months? Five months?"

"Four months the first time. Five the second, because I was a little more used to it. But," she went on, having been handed the floor for a moment, "the thing is, you do have to be aware, both consciously and subconsciously, of what is happening to your center of balance, and you don't attempt the really hard things. I wouldn't try a quadruple—probably not even a triple—if my period was three days late. The baby then is so small it's invisible, but you've already started holding water and your ligaments have begun to change just a little bit, and so your center of balance might be off. Just a little—not much—but it doesn't have to be much. See what I mean?"

"Yes," I said. "So Pamela was pregnant and nobody knew whose the baby was—"

"Then," Gene said.

"I don't understand?"

"Nobody knew then whose the baby was," Gene said. "Beppo went a little crazy. He accused Barthold of, uh, sexual misconduct—remember Barthold and Pamela were engaged but not married—and

· · · · ·

said he swung Pamela wrong on purpose so nobody would know of the fornication—that was his word, fornication, and he didn't pay any attention when Barthold kept denying the whole thing. But he also accused Jan of fornication with her and insisted Jan deliberately didn't catch her because he was jealous and wanted Pamela for himself—which of course makes no sense at all. And there was a big row because everybody in the family went ballistic, Beppo accusing his own daughter of promiscuity and alternately accusing Barthold of deliberately killing her about it and then turning right around accusing Jan of the same thing. Now, mind you, all this was nonsense anyway, because the movie made it quite clear that it was Pamela, not anyone else, who was off position—and then later Jan admitted he might be the father, he and Pamela had had a little fling, but by then Barthold also had admitted they had, uh, anticipated the wedding. But—what's odd—when the Saranas and Glucks split up over it, Jan went with the Saranas, and even after Beppo knew what Jan said, Jan and Beppo went on working together for another year, until Jan had his accident. So it's pretty clear that after the initial commotion Beppo pretty well got over it, or at least he quit blaming Jan for the accident."

"What exactly happened on Jan's accident?" I asked. "I've never heard a full story."

"I wasn't there. I wasn't born yet, and because Jan wasn't a family member it's not talked about much," Gene said. "All I know is, he fell."

Maria opened her mouth, but Mario beat her to the punch. "My mother was there," he said, and that was the first time I had heard his voice since the introduction. "She was a Sarana before she married Dad. She told me about it. She said Jan was catching for her cousin Maureen Sarana—"

"Excuse me," I interrupted, "but I'm totally lost. I don't remember how anybody is related to anybody. And what's with all the names starting with *M?*"

"To make them easy for audiences to remember," Eugene said.

· · · · ·

"Like me performing as Marty Montañez when I'm really Eugene Sarana. As to how we're related—hell, I don't know if *I* can sort it out. But—Beppo is a Sarana. Margaret was his wife and Pamela was his daughter. I'm his nephew, because my mother was his sister."

"And Maria and I are his second cousins, even though we're not Saranas," Mario put in.

"I am," Maria said.

"But you weren't born one," Eugene pointed out. "Anyway, Arlo is a Gluck, he's Barthold's son, but he's related to both the Saranas and the Montañezes."

"What about Maureen?" I asked.

"Forget about Maureen," Eugene said. "I'm sorry I mentioned her. She's Beppo's cousin, I forget exactly how she ties in, but she's left the circus anyway and lives in Yorkshire now. I just mentioned her because she was rehearsing with Jan when he fell. Okay?"

"Okay," I said humbly, and waited for the lecture to continue.

"So Jan really couldn't fly much, you know, he was always too heavy-boned," Mario went on, "but he had the coordination and he was a darn good catcher. Anyway, Maureen was a little out of position and he tried to stretch farther to catch her, and fell. Well, it was in a rehearsal, not in a performance, and they had all kinds of safety devices up, nets and mechanicals and everything, and Maureen was okay, but whoever was operating Jan's mechanical—do you know what that is?" Mario interrupted himself.

"Arlo told me something about it. Isn't it some sort of rope where somebody on the ground is keeping somebody else from falling?"

"That's good enough," Mario said. "And what Mom told me was, whoever was operating Jan's mechanical got rattled and let it slip, and Jan had a bad fall—messed up his right shoulder real bad, and you can't catch *or* fly with a bad shoulder."

"Do you know who was operating the mechanical?" I asked.

The three looked at each other, and Mario said, "No. I don't think I ever heard."

· · · · ·

Nobody could think of anything else to tell me, and when I asked, without much hope, whether any of them knew of anybody in the Sarana, Gluck, or Montañez families who knew anything about explosives, all three of them stared at me as if I had lost my mind. "You've got to be kidding," Mario said, finally, and it was pretty clear he spoke for the rest of them as he added, "What would we need to know that for?"

Without much hope, I asked about Arlo's knife. "I've seen it," Gene said.

"And?"

He shrugged. "Luisa's right, it's a commando knife. And a damn good one. Blue high-carbon steel, not any of this stainless or chrome that won't keep an edge. If he took it with him he's scared."

"Or suicidal?" I asked softly, thinking, *A knife like that could cut rope very easily, as far through as anybody wanted to cut it.*

"Not Arlo," Gene said. Then he was silent for a moment. "Well, I don't think so," he said finally.

I stopped in the motel lobby to call home and see how Harry was getting along with the door. He had already hung it and was midway of varnishing the inside, with the door now in a vertical position so the cats couldn't walk on it. Then he told me, in tones of annoyed amusement, "Your boyfriend got here a while ago."

"My what?" I repeated, totally baffled.

"One Mark Hanna Brody the third, blue-eyed blond with a good tan and a Hispanic accent, whom I last saw a few years ago at Forth-Con wearing Spock ears. Drunker than a pissant. He seems to think you've agreed to elope with him to Mexico."

"Harry—"

"I took his car keys and pistol away from him and told him to wait for you in bed."

"*You told him what?*" I screamed. "Harry, are you out of your mind?"

"Quit yelling. He told me the story of his life and wound up crying

· · · · ·

201

about Marguerite's defection—sounds to me like she really did shaft him pretty good—and then barfed up half a bottle of Jack Daniel's on the living room floor and—yes, I've cleaned it up—and staggered to our bed. He's snoring his head off there now."

"Can you get rid of him before I get home?"

"That depends on when you plan to get home. I stole his car keys and I'm not sending him anywhere till he's sobered up."

"That really ticks me off," I said. "He was acting thoroughly squirrelly last time I saw him, but then he sounded okay the last couple of times I talked to him on the phone. I had no idea he'd pull a stunt like this. And on top of that I was just getting ready to call him."

"What for?" Harry asked.

"I'm going to the Bird Cage again," I said. "I—Harry, every idea I have seems to evaporate, and I just want to go look at the scene again while everybody's at the funeral, to see if I can come up with any other ideas, and then if Arlo doesn't show up at the funeral I've got to get with Luisa and get pictures and stuff. Mark was supposed to be working with me on this case, so I thought—well, I don't really need him anyway, because he was just assigned to it when it looked like extortion, and it's not going to be."

"Want me to call your office and get you a backup?"

"I don't guess so. Really, Harry, none of the involved people are even going to be there, with the funeral going on. And anyway it's broad daylight and we know this joker plays a concealed hand. I ought to be okay. There's no reason anything should go wrong."

"Except that when you take off like this all too often it does," Harry said morosely and, unfortunately, truthfully.

"I ought to be okay," I said again.

"Are you trying to convince yourself, or me?" Harry demanded. "Never mind, never mind. I'll go look through the rest of the stuff on Internet, and call you if I find anything you ought to know. Just take care of yourself, Deb, okay?"

"I will."

. . . . .

And was I trying to convince myself or him? I wondered as I hung up and walked slowly back to the police car I had been issued Friday night after the burglary suspect wrecked the other one. But really, there wasn't any reason for me to be worried. I was just going to the Bird Cage to check on a couple more things. Everybody there was provisionally cleared. Weren't they? And anyway, as I'd told Harry, they weren't even going to be there.

The Bird Cage does not open for lunch, but based on my experience of restaurants, I felt quite safe in assuming somebody would be in the kitchen.

The street was still blocked off, and there were six trucks from the gas company there. They might have the gas back on, as I had been told, but clearly they weren't through working yet. And when the gas company got through Public Works had to rebuild the street, before it could be reopened.

I detoured, drove into the parking lot, parked at the back door, and rang the delivery bell. A couple of chefs I hadn't previously met came to the door together, and one of them checked my identification and said, "Jan told us all to cooperate with the police. What is it you want to know?"

"Nothing, actually," I said. "I just want to have another look at the trapeze. Is that okay?"

I was glad he didn't ask me why I wanted to look at the trapeze, because I don't think I could have thought of an answer. I was having a gut feeling that hadn't yet made its way into my brain, and perhaps I hoped climbing around on a trapeze myself would help me think.

He hesitated and then said, "I don't see why not. Luisa isn't there, though. We wanted to go to the funeral too, but Jan said somebody had to be here. So there's nobody here that can tell you anything."

"That's okay. I just wanted to look at the trapeze."

"You won't be in our way. Go right ahead."

Alone in the vast, darkened, echoing dining room, I felt like an intruder in a city of the dead. I looked around the room carefully, seeing no one and yet uncomfortably aware that there were a thousand places for someone to hide—and someone who had murdered Julia Sarana Gluck wouldn't be any too happy if I seemed to be closing in on the secret.

But surely Luisa, Jan, and Beppo were all at the funeral. Arlo was who knows where. And now, looking again at all the ropes, seeing how they were like those I'd studied as I watched the performance last night, and thinking in the light of what the Montañezes had told me, I felt sure one of them—Arlo, Luisa, Beppo, Jan—had to be the killer unless—and this wasn't impossible—somebody else from the circus had come here while the circus was in town. But *why*? None of it made sense. Nobody else, nobody without a trapeze background, would have known how to do it—what cable to cut, how high to cut it—or had the nerve to climb that high up to cut the cable even if they did know what to do. But nothing I had gotten so far had given me any reason why *anybody* would do it.

I put my purse down on the table nearest the ladder leading up to the platform and set one tentative foot on the first rung. The ladder swayed, and I was still moving a little stiffly from the burns. *I could have done this when I was eleven, and I can do it now,* I told myself. *It's just because I fell that time that I'm afraid. But this isn't a tree; there aren't ten children on the platform; there's no one to push me. I could have done it then and I can do it now.*

I started up the ladder, feeling it sway with every step until I reached the platform so high above the floor. I climbed a little farther and stepped onto the platform.

Luisa had been rehearsing, or Arlo and Beppo had been checking the cables, or both. The trapeze enclosed inside the birdcage, which usually rested ten feet away from the platform, now hung right beside the platform.

I could have done this when I was eleven.

I took one tentative step onto the trapeze, holding tightly to the ropes on both sides. I took a second tentative step. Now my entire weight was on the trapeze, was held—as Julia's had been held that night—by the two ropes that suspended the trapeze.

Trying not to feel sickened by the height and the ceaseless slight motion, I carefully clung with both hands on to the side ropes as I eased my feet off the trapeze and sat down on it.

Does anybody ever forget how to swing?

I leaned my body forward, my legs backward, but what was under me was a bar less than an inch in diameter rather than a comfortable swing seat. I quit pumping. I didn't want this swing to move.

Clearly I wasn't going to learn anything this way.

Increasingly giddy from the height, I began to reach behind me, to catch hold of the platform preparatory to crawling—and I was afraid I would really be crawling—back off the trapeze, back onto the platform to return to the ground.

And I heard a rope creak, and I was moving, and I couldn't reach the platform with my outstretched hand and I didn't dare try to reach farther because I would overstretch myself and lose my balance and fall.

But what choice did I have?

None at all.

Somebody hadn't gone to the funeral. Somebody who knew which ropes to pull to make the trapeze do things hadn't gone to the funeral. He, or she, was on the platform, and the trapeze was moving out, away from the platform, out over the middle of the floor where I had first seen Julia Sarana's body.

I wasn't in the chefs' way, but I was darn sure in somebody's way.

I looked back, over my shoulder, to see a rabid grin on the face of Beppo Sarana.

I was far out over the tables, and I didn't have a safety net, and I heard and felt the faint jolt as an imperfectly cut strand of cable gave with a final pop.

Beppo had already prepared for Luisa's death.

But now I was going to die in her place.

. . . . .

Twelve
· · · · · ·

I COULD HAVE tried to appeal to him, but what good would it have done? I already knew he was capable of murdering his own nieces, even knowing that one of them was pregnant: What interest could he possibly have in keeping alive a woman he didn't even know—one who, moreover, was interfering with his plans?

But after that first instant of panic, I was in no way willing to die in Luisa's place, especially since Luisa would not be helped in the slightest by my doing so. Undoubtedly if he missed her this way he would—if he lived to do it—go after her another way.

The problem was that I hadn't the faintest idea what I was going to do. I did not even have my pistol; it was down on a table far below me, stuck in my purse. But even if I did have it, what good would it have done? Yes, I could shoot Beppo Sarana. But I would still be thirty-odd feet away from the platform, on a trapeze with one of its support ropes cut almost through. Even if I could get hold of the uncut support rope and climb it high enough to reach the line or lines—this I hadn't studied closely—from which the support ropes were suspended, which I almost certainly could not, the chances of my being able to go hand-over-hand back along the line to the platform were exactly zero. Anyway if I could achieve all those impossibilities Beppo Sarana would be there waiting for me. And on top of that, I didn't even know for sure which support rope was cut. I was assuming it was the one on my left because that was the one cut when

Julia fell, but that was at best no more than a supposition.

I was remaining as still as possible while I was doing this cogitating; surely the swinging that Julia had done, in her act, had hastened the breakage of the last two strands of her rope. But no matter how long I remained motionless, I still wasn't safe. Having cut the vertical line, Beppo was perfectly capable of climbing a little higher and cutting the horizontal line that the vertical line was suspended from. Of course there would be no chance at all of passing that off as an accident, but he knew well enough nobody was going to consider anything he did as accidental by now anyway.

I don't want to get into the question of whether or not our entire life flashes before our eyes when we think we're about to die. From all I've heard about near death experiences, that isn't often true, and personally I can't think how anybody could have enough time for his whole life to flash before his eyes. Mine certainly didn't, although it could be said that I wasn't that close to death. I will say, however, that certain *relevant* parts of my life flashed before my eyes:

I have been in the police department three years. I'm still in uniform division. I have two children at home. I'm in a standoff situation. The armed robbery suspect has a gun pointed at me and I have a gun pointed at him. I don't really want to pull the trigger; I'm gambling that he doesn't want to either. I talk. He talks. We talk, and after a while he gives me his gun and starts crying.

What do we talk about? His wife, his children, my husband, my children. Not about the crime, not about the fact that he's just shot an unarmed convenience-store clerk in the course of a twenty-dollar robbery, except that I manage to convince him the clerk didn't die—it's true, by the way—so it isn't murder, and even if he does twenty years for the robbery, which is vanishingly unlikely for a first offender, it's better than never living to see his children grow up.

I hit his hot button. I talk about what he cares about, not about what I care about.

What is Beppo Sarana's hot button? I asked myself.

Can I turn around on this trapeze that's not much thicker than my thumb, turn around so I can look at Beppo and he has to look at me? Will he find it any harder to kill me, while he's looking at me, than he did to kill Julia without watching her die, because I know he wasn't here when Julia died. Had he planned to be here tonight to see Luisa die?

If I try to turn around, will that be sufficient movement to break the last one or two strands of nylon that are holding me up? Because I don't know how many strands he cut this time. The fact that he cut ten strands the first time says nothing. He might want this rope to fail sooner. He might want this rope to take longer to fail.

But if I want to see his face I have to turn around, whether I can or not. I keep telling myself that if I could do it when I was eleven I can do it now, but my self knows that's nonsense.

Never mind how I did it. I don't know how I did it, and I don't think I ever will know. But I managed, and finally, after what felt like about half an hour but probably was no more than two or three minutes, I was sitting the other way on the trapeze, facing away from the main part of the dining room, looking at Beppo Sarana, who, just as I had feared, had started climbing up a rope. Looking at him was no treat. His glare was, quite literally, diabolical, and I knew that if I got out of this alive it would haunt my dreams for a long time to come.

"Beppo," I said, "why do you want to kill me?"

He looked at me. He didn't answer.

Obviously he didn't answer. He held a knife in his mouth, the blade crosswise in his teeth, and if I didn't miss my guess that was Arlo's ceremonial knife. Had he stolen it earlier, had he used it to cut Julia's ropes? Or had he killed Arlo and taken it from him then?

If Beppo had tried to talk he would have dropped the knife. He kept on climbing.

"I met Gene today," I said.

He went on looking at me, and he went on climbing.

"You know, your nephew, Eugene Sarana?"

Beppo stopped climbing.

"He married Maria Montañez, but you probably know that. He's performing under the name of Marty Montañez right now. He told me about how different names come to the forefront in different generations. They have two children now; they're Saranas, of course, so probably in the next generation the Sarana name will be the most important again." He was actually listening to me now. I must have been doing something right. "Gene told me about Margaret and Pamela. Margaret must have been a wonderful wife to you."

That was reaching him; amazingly, one tear stood out on his face, rolling down from his right eye. "She must have worked hard to do what she thought would please you."

He was still crying, at least enough that a tear now rolled down from his left eye.

"Women ought to do what their husbands say, shouldn't they?"

He continued to look at me. I couldn't tell whether he was still crying now or not.

"You know what? My husband told me this morning to stay out of trouble today."

That was clearly the wrong thing to say. The expression that spread across his face wasn't one I'd like to look at for long. Hastily, I moved the conversation back to Margaret. "That must have been so terrible for you, Margaret dying when you were so far away, and then Pamela dying right in front of you. Gene said it really tore you up, but that you went on working as a trainer."

An incredibly grotesque expression spread across his face, and he resumed climbing. Clearly that, too, was the wrong thing for me to say.

I tried again. "Gene said you were a supergood aerialist. He said you could do things nobody else could." In fact he hadn't said anything of the sort, but maybe flattery would work.

Flattery did not work. Apparently there was no longer anything I could say that would matter. Beppo stopped climbing, now, not because he was listening but because he had reached a sort of nest where several ropes came together from different directions, and he was rest-

. . . . .

ing against one of the ropes so that he could use his hands again.

"What did Pamela look like? Did she look much like Margaret, or more like you? Gene didn't tell me that; I guess he didn't know. Did you and Margaret have any other children? He didn't tell me that, either."

It was no use. He wasn't hearing me; he had chosen not to hear me. I was no longer a person. I was a thing, and I was a thing that had gotten in his way.

Draping himself over a couple more ropes so that he was effectively suspended with no further effort on his part, he moved the knife from his mouth to his hand and started cutting. For a moment I thought he intended to go down with me, which at least would save Luisa's life, but then I realized he had a thick leather belt around his waist and a rope attached to it. Clearly it was some sort of safety device. If I couldn't think of a way out of this, I was going down within the next two or three minutes. Then he would climb down and maybe pretend to discover the accident, or maybe hit the road, to go back after Luisa later.

Quite suddenly, I dropped into that mode we go into in emergencies, that mode in which time seems to stand still, so that no matter how fast the emergency is happening there's all the time in the world for thought. I have been in this mode before. . . .

I am in the top of a sweet gum tree with my brothers and cousins. We are all laughing; we are all playing. Nobody intends to harm anybody, but somehow I am knocked out of the tree, and as I fall time crawls, so that I have all the time I need to think, to react. I fall head-downward; I use my hands to ward off limbs that might otherwise break my arms; I twist around toward that broken-off stubby branch and I move just right as I reach it, so that my knees are over it and I am hanging by my knees just as I have done hundreds of times on the monkey bars at school, except that my bare knees are bent not over cool metal but over scratchy bark.

Laboriously, I curl up, bending at the waist until I am almost bent double, so that I can reach the branch with one hand. Then, with one hand on the branch, I pull myself farther up, so that both hands are on the branch, and I keep curling upward, upward, until I am sitting on the branch, and then I cautiously get to my feet, maintaining my balance by holding to other, smaller and larger, branches. When I am so close to the tree trunk I can hug it, I reach one cautious foot down to a lower branch, and then another, and then another, and then there's that three-foot jump to the ground.

Only when I reach the ground do I feel my legs shaking, so that I have to sit abruptly on the red clay and white sand ground. Only when I reach the ground do I hear my mother screaming.

What is she screaming about? I'm okay. I caught myself, didn't I?

I start to go back up the tree, but my mother yells at me. "Go in and take a bath and go to bed!"

What for? I'm not dirty, and I'm not through playing. It's not even four o'clock and supper isn't till six.

"Go in and take a bath now!"

Thoroughly disgusted by her silliness, I go and take a bath. She won't let me go out and play again. She and my aunt make the other children get out of the tree too. No more tree climbing for any of us, especially not me. My mother says climbing trees might be all right for boys, but I'm a girl, and I'm not to go up that tree or any other tree again.

And only later, in bed that afternoon and in countless dreams since, does time move in real time, so that I don't have time to think, to save myself, as I hurtle toward the corner of the cement porch. But my mother and aunt are convinced they've done the right thing.

I hadn't remembered. . . . It's not just men that won't let women run risks; it's women too, maybe it's more women than men.

My cousins and brothers weren't in this tree with me, and there was no convenient broken branch for me to catch myself on, and the floor beneath was cement. But there must be a way I could escape—

I am at the circus with Harry, my husband, and Cameron, my son, and Lori, who will almost certainly be my daughter-in-law. Cameron is too excited to stay still; he jumps up and down throughout almost all of the show, and Lori keeps wishing audibly that Hal could see all this. I wish the same; I wonder why I never took the children to the circus when they were younger.

I watch Maria Montañez as she begins the quadruple somersault that killed Margaret Sarana and her daughter Pamela; Harry holds my hand too tightly, and there is virtually no sound from all that huge audience gathered in the Cow Palace. As she comes out of the fourth somersault Maria holds her body the way a diver does, her head up, her hands forward, her back arched forward, her knees together, her ankles extended, and her feet together with her toes pointing to what would be the ground if she were standing upright.

She doesn't have to reach far; her husband catches her wrists and she catches his, and then her husband seems to toss her twice and on the second toss she springs upward, to stand beside him.

Mario slides down a rope; Gene slides down a rope; last, Maria slides down a rope. They stand together triumphantly.

If she hadn't died, would Julia have slid down a rope? Yes, she would have. Arlo told me that.

If I had been watching instead of looking at somebody who was standing in front of me, would I have seen Luisa slide down a rope? Surely I would have.

Then where is the rope?

Is it somewhere I can't reach, does the cage have to be in exactly the right spot for a person to reach the descent rope?

But I didn't believe that. No matter how careful a person is in his or her performance, no matter how careful the ground-crew members are, no matter how well everything is planned, something is bound to go wrong sometimes. I knew the Saranas and the Glucks didn't use safety nets, and I was even reasonably sure I could understand the reason. But if they didn't use a safety net, then they had to have some way to get down if things went wrong, no matter where they were.

It had to be inconspicuous. . . . It probably wouldn't reach all the way to the floor, but it would reach far enough for her to dismount safely. . . .

I wasn't just thinking. I was looking and feeling, all the time I was thinking, and as I looked I felt a slight jolt. I looked up quickly. Beppo

. . . . .

was cutting the support rope; the jolt I had felt was the first strand going.

How long had it taken Irene and me to cut off the section of rope we had sent to the lab? We couldn't cut through the entire rope at once, I remembered that for sure; we had cut it strand by strand, and that was what Beppo was doing now. But still—twelve strands. How long did it take to cut twelve strands?

And then I had my hand on the escape rope . . . slightly behind me, so that I had to turn to see it, and inconspicuous, as I had guessed, dropping down from the "door" of the birdcage.

Too bad I didn't know how Maria, Julia, Luisa, Gene, and Mario had managed to go down the rope without acquiring hellacious rope burns. But one thing was sure: I would rather collect rope burns, no matter how bad they were, than leave my four-year-old motherless, than take away from Lori the peace of mind she was laboriously rebuilding after her mother's suicide, than leave behind my husband and sons and daughters and sons-in-law and grandchildren by dying in such a horrible way. I doubt I'm any more afraid of dying than most people are; probably I'm less so than a lot of people, because I don't believe death is final. But nobody with good sense wants to leave this life when there's still work left for him or her to do.

No, I didn't take the time to try to figure out how Julia or Luisa would have made it appear that the gilded bird had flown from the gilded cage. I just turned sideways, slithered through the flexible fabric bars, twisted the rope once around my left ankle (grateful I had worn sneakers and thick socks this morning, instead of the sandals I started to put on), caught the rope in my left hand because if I had to have one hand out of commission for a while I'd rather it not be my writing/cooking/gun hand, and started sliding.

The next thing I found out was that you don't slide very fast if you're wound up with a rope this way and you don't know what you're doing. I had to figure out a way to propel myself down the

. . . . .

rope, because the friction that wanted to keep me where I was was about as strong a force as gravity. Turning my body so that my left hand was working with my right, I started trying to walk my hands down the rope, figuring if my hands went down my torso would go down, and my legs surely would do the same. But it didn't happen. In a crouching position on the rope, I realized that its strands were entangling with my sock. I was going to have to move the rope up above my ankle, above my sock.

That was when I started sliding. That was when the rope began to burn, to cut, the palms of my hands, my left leg above the sock.

Beppo was watching me, his face alive with rage and panic. He hacked furiously, twice more, at the rope and then realized he could not possibly finish cutting through the rope before I got to the floor. He dropped from his perch down onto the platform and then started down the rope ladder, taking three rungs at a time. I could scarcely believe what I was seeing. He couldn't have been younger than seventy, and he climbed faster than I could.

But all the same he was climbing and I was sliding. I hit the floor before he did.

But I had wound up using both hands on the rope, and when I dropped off the rope both my palms were bleeding, both my hands were cut, in places to the bone, and already too stiff to use, and about half my left leg starting about four inches above the ankle and going almost to the knee seemed to have lost its skin and more than I liked of its flesh.

I could not draw my gun. If I had been able to draw it I couldn't have held it long enough to fire. And he still had the knife.

Still had the knife, and was coming at me with it, and I began to wonder just what language the name Sarana was. Obviously the Saranas and the Glucks had been all over Europe for generations, but were they Sicilians?

The Sicilian skill in knife fighting is legendary, and from the pose Beppo had assumed, I had the impression that he wasn't exactly a

· · · · ·

novice at the art. Though of course that's silly, anybody can learn to knife-fight; hadn't I myself spent countless hours studying books on surviving, and winning, knife fights? I did study, I told myself, so dammit, *remember!*

With the knife in his right hand, he was slightly crouched, his left hand up and out to his side. His face seemed set in a permanent snarl.

It didn't really require much knife-fighting skill for him to go after me, with my hands no use at all. And it was pretty evident that running wouldn't help me; he was considerably taller than I, and despite his age, it was evident that he had plenty of running left in him. With the condition of my left leg, I didn't have much more running in me than I did fighting.

But I had better do something fast. I have worked enough knife murders to know that I'd a heap rather fall from a trapeze and break my neck than be killed with a knife. I've seen the defense wounds on the side of the hands, from the end of the little finger to up above the wrist, where people had tried to ward off knife attacks.

It would hurt—maybe paralyzingly—if I tried to grab anything. But anything I did was going to hurt, and considering what Beppo had in mind, if I didn't do anything I was going to hurt even more. If I could just persuade my hands to *work*—

I could. I picked up a chair, holding it by the back, thrusting all four feet of it at Beppo the way a lion tamer (not the one in the circus last night, who didn't use a chair at all, but a fictional lion tamer one might see on television) thrusts a chair at a lion.

We circled around, Beppo and I, he with a knife and I with a chair, he blind with rage that couldn't possibly have originally been for me, I on the verge of going into shock. He feinted one way with the knife; I feinted the other way with the chair; and then we were right back in the same relative positions we had started out.

Yes, in one part of my mind I was quite aware that there were two cooks in the kitchen. Why didn't I scream? Why didn't I yell for help?

I do not know. All I can say is that I didn't think of it.

·　·　·　·　·

I was far enough into shock by now that I wasn't feeling my hands and leg so much, as I tried repeatedly to keep Beppo away from me and he tried repeatedly to move around first to my left side and then to my right and I turned repeatedly in a small circle like a bullfighter with too many bulls and no sword. Beppo was mumbling something but I couldn't understand him; it wasn't in any language that I spoke or even recognized.

It was pretty obvious that we were at an impasse, but it was even more obvious that we weren't going to stay in one. I was already slipping in my own blood on the slick concrete floor, recovering my balance with slightly more difficulty each time, and my bleeding wasn't getting any less and wasn't going to, until I got bandages on my hands and leg. On top of that I was increasingly cold, increasingly nauseated. I was heading into shock. I didn't have time to stay on the defense. I had to go on the attack.

I moved toward him. I think that surprised him.

I couldn't see his face very well—most of the overhead lights were out; I should have noticed that earlier, but I didn't, maybe because when I came in here the only thing I was interested in was the trapeze, and lights up there were on—how stupid I had been, the lights were on up there and I'd never seen them on there unless somebody was working there, and I knew Luisa and Jan—and hopefully Arlo— would be at the funeral so the only person who could possibly have been up there was Beppo. He must have gone down to get something, or maybe even to turn out the lights, just before I went into the dining room and started climbing. If I'd just paid attention, if I hadn't been so full of myself, I'd have known Beppo was here, and I should have realized that since I couldn't see any alternative killer, Beppo had to be the killer even if it didn't quite make sense yet.

He had sidestepped my first charge, and I charged again. I couldn't see his face that well, but I could see the knife. Even if it was that wonderful high-carbon steel Gene had spoken of, it probably wasn't as sharp as it had started out to be, as sharp as Beppo thought it still was, after he'd used it to saw through that tough rope. But it still glinted in the light coming in from the kitchen, and it was still plenty sharp enough to accomplish his purpose.

He sidestepped my second charge and then came in fast, under the chair, which I was holding rather high. If he'd had a sword instead of a knife he'd have had me then, but he had only a knife, and I slapped the chair down on the knife and Beppo's wrist, and heard the knife clatter on the floor.

He turned and ran.

I thought I couldn't run, but I could, for my life and Luisa's life and the lives of everybody else he'd determined to kill. I dropped the chair and went after him. He ran into the kitchen and snatched a cleaver from a cook's hand and turned around to come back at me, and this time I didn't have a chair to fight him with.

He swung the cleaver at me once, hard enough that if he'd connected he'd have split my head in two, and then backed up a step to recover his balance and hit at me again. I tried to kick him, but I had on sneakers and I couldn't kick hard enough and anyway I couldn't kick high enough to do any good, and I was still bleeding, and I slid again in my blood on the kitchen's vinyl flooring and fell, sprawling, with Beppo Sarana above me, an evil grin on his face and the cleaver in his hand.

By now the chefs had figured out what was going on, and one had run past us and was yelling in a high, frightened voice, presumably into the telephone in the dining room, while the other headed for Beppo's back with a frying pan held high and brandished as a weapon, but then he paused, puzzled. If he brained Beppo, the cleaver would fall on me.

I tried to roll out of the way, to my left because a cooking range was in my way to the right, but I had to roll fast, because Beppo was diving toward me, and although I couldn't defend my front very well in this situation I could defend it a heck of a lot better than I could defend my back, so I had to roll all the way over, not just halfway.

. . . . .

Beppo tried to move faster than I could.

He nearly made it. The cleaver struck down, hard, in the vinyl flooring where my head had been about a second earlier, close enough that it trimmed a little of my hair, and there it stuck.

I rolled on over again, out of the way, and looked back up at the chef, but the chef was gone. I could hear him yelling into the phone, now; seemingly he'd snatched it from the other chef.

I managed to scramble to my feet, leaving what felt like more of my hair than it probably was, before Beppo could get the cleaver loose from the flooring, but he was already turning around toward me again by the time I grabbed the frying pan the chef had dropped and slammed it toward him. Cleaver and frying pan crashed together, clanking eerily like a blacksmith's hammer making a horseshoe, with so much force that both of us went down again, though this time we were sliding in the blood of both of us because Beppo had cut his hand forcing the cleaver out of the flooring, and then somehow Beppo was on top of me again.

I'd like to think I could have won. But it was Harry, with both hands clasped together, who brought a double fist down hard on Beppo's neck and then hurled him one way and the cleaver the other. I heard the cleaver hit the concrete floor in the dining room after I heard Beppo hit one of the metal kitchen appliances.

"What are you doing here?" I asked, when I was able to talk again.

"I skimmed through the rest of the Internet stuff," he said, kneeling beside me to examine my hands, and his face was pasty white. Behind him, looking very unshaven and rumpled, more green than white, was Mark Brody, struggling now with Beppo. "Then I started trying to get you some backups, but I couldn't find anybody I knew at the police station, and that dumb-ass dispatcher at nine-one-one kept telling me that you weren't on duty and anyway if you needed any help you'd ask for it. Then I tried to call here and nobody answered. So I woke Brody up and told him to come with me, and I came over here." He turned angrily on the chefs. "Why didn't one of you an-swer the phone?"

"No listed phone in here, boss," one of them said, his voice delib-erately bland but his face shocked. "Phone rings at the front desk. We got orders, don't answer the phone. People call for reservations, they get the answering machine. I called the cops, I called nine-one-one. They're coming."

"What did the Internet stuff tell you?" I asked Harry, and then yelled, "Ouch!" This latter was not addressed at Harry, but rather at the other chef, who had knelt beside me and begun carefully wrapping around my hands gauze, which the emergency medical technicians would undoubtedly shortly unwrap. The general idea apparently was to stop me from bleeding, though I very much doubted I had bled nearly as much as it looked like. Even a small amount of blood can look like somebody bled dry.

"It told me he's dangerous," Harry said, his voice cracking. "Some-body in the Sarana family managed to keep it all quiet, but this guy on the Internet knew about it. He—Beppo, I mean, not the guy on In-ternet—was in the Yugoslavian Resistance during World War Two, and he's an explosives expert. He was in a mental hospital in Florida about seven years, after he tried to set fire to Barthold Gluck's house in Sarasota, and he spent the whole time swearing revenge on Jan Pender and Barthold Gluck. He—got a little specific in what he said. They shouldn't ever have let him go, and they didn't until Barthold Gluck was dead. When they did let him go, they damn sure should have warned Pender. And Arlo, because Arlo is Barthold's son." Yes . . . I'd heard most of that this morning, from Gene or Mario. Why hadn't I realized then that that was the missing piece of the puzzle?

Because I had my mind on the fact that Arlo was still missing, that was all I could think of.

By now Beppo was sitting in a chair—not the one I had attacked him with, which seemed at some point to have lost a leg, but another

. . . . .

one. Brody had found my purse, taken out my handcuffs, and hand-cuffed him with his hands behind his back. "Of course they let me go," he said, in a kind of vocal strutting. "Jan and Barthold, they take away my Pamela. A father has the right to avenge."

"Why did you want to kill *me?*" I asked him.

"Miranda warning," Harry said, half under his breath.

"Doesn't matter," I muttered to him. It didn't. Even I could see this man was legally, as well as morally, insane.

"You try to stop me from avenge," Beppo said. "And you steal man's job. Women aren't supposed to do man's jobs. I never let woman do man's jobs. Even in Resistance—if a woman try to do a man's job, I stop her. I stop her good." His voice was gloating.

I could hardly believe what I was hearing. The Resistance—that antedated Pamela's death, probably even antedated Margaret's death. Even the most rabid keep-the-women-barefoot-and-pregnant jerk I'd ever met wasn't that bad; how many Resistance fighters had he killed for being women?

And he'd never believe the world could be otherwise. . . . I looked over at him. "Why did you kill Julia?" I asked. "Why were you trying to kill Luisa? Your own nieces—how can that avenge your daughter?"

"You don't understand," he said. I still wished I could figure out what accent that was. But as much as he'd undoubtedly traveled all his life, as many people from different places as he'd been around, it was probably an accent he'd picked up piecemeal from dozens of different sources.

"I certainly don't understand," I said. "That's why I'm asking you. It seems to me if you were going to try to kill anybody, after Barthold Gluck was dead, it would most likely be Jan Pender." The chef had finished bandaging my hands, and Harry was pushing me down when I tried to sit up. He still wanted me to lie down on the floor. I couldn't figure out why, but it did seem like a rather good idea, the way my head was swimming.

· · · · ·

"Jan is careful!" Beppo burst out. "Jan goes to confession every week! What I want to kill him for, when he goes to confession? Avenge my daughter by sending her murderer to heaven? You don't understand—him and Barthold between them, they kill my Pamela, they not just kill her body, they kill her soul! My Pamela—one of them talked her into fornication, then she don't go to confession, then they kill her! My poor baby, my Pamela—she not even go to purgatory, so no matter how many candles I burn, no good, Pamela in hell! So—I kill him and he go to heaven? That's not avenge Pamela. I take away everything he love, just like he take away Pamela and kill her soul. I take away his flying—"

"You caused that accident?" I interrupted.

"Accident? That was no accident; I make it happen. If I make it happen it's not accident. Easy enough. He trust me. He fool, kill my daughter and trust me. I wait a while. You say I was in hospital, yeah, sure I was in hospital. Rest. Rest and plan. Then they let me go, when Barthold was dead. And then—I follow Jan. He get the restaurant in Las Vegas—right place for sinner like Jan—everybody sin in Las Vegas, city full of lust, fornication, adultery, devil women tempting men, devil men seducing women, evil, evil, evil—but I find him, I convince him I need work, I old man, too old work in circus, and he give me work because he feel guilty about what he do to Pamela. And I go inna kitchen, make food not taste so good. He lose restaurant. He lose flying, he lose restaurant—then he come here, he get new restaurant, and he hire Arlo and Julia work for him. First I just think, take restaurant away, burn restaurant. But then—I see him, I see how he look at Julia, I see how he look at Luisa. I take from him Julia and Luisa. I know when Julia go to confession, she die next day—"

He was still talking as the door opened again, as Luisa walked in hand-in-hand with a young man, as Arlo walked in with an old man beside him, an old man wearing a clerical collar and a long black cassock.

The priest, Arlo, Luisa, and the man with her, all heard the rest of

．　．　．　．　．

what Beppo said. The best I could tell, he neither saw nor heard them enter. "I know when Luisa go to confession, she die next day. Julia and Luisa good girls, they go to Blessed Virgin, they be happy, but Jan, he suffer like I suffer. His restaurant—The Bird Cage! I make it the Cooked Bird. And Arlo too—Barthold take Pamela away from me, Arlo his son, I take Julia away from Arlo. You think I'm through, now you catch? Not through. Avenge not enough. Holy Virgin, she let me go free again, I finish avenge!"

"Why Arlo?" I asked. "Arlo didn't do anything to you; do you think it was right to kill Arlo's wife, and the baby she was going to have?"

"Arlo?" Beppo yelled. "I tell you, Arlo is Barthold's son! Barthold kill my daughter, my unborn grandbaby, I kill Barthold's daughter-in-law, his unborn grandbaby! My grandbaby in limbo, he got Barthold's grandbaby to play with!"

Arlo turned, his face contorted with tears, and ran out the kitchen door; the priest ran out after him as Luisa turned to weep in the arms of her companion; and Jan entered before the door swung shut again.

"What about the money you got from Jan?" I asked Beppo. "Were you trying to get money from anybody else?"

It is hard to shrug with your hands bound behind you. But Beppo managed. "Jan love money, I take his money. I don't want anybody else's money. Anything Jan love, I take away. I don't need money. I use his money, pay cost of taking away other things Jan loves."

I closed my eyes, briefly, thinking of the awful waste this man had created to avenge an accidental death, the waste he'd created to maintain a world he thought was necessary for his masculinity—and what a pitiful, weak, sense of manhood he must have had, to feel that way.

Harry was squeezing my wrist; normally he'd have been squeezing my hand, but obviously he wasn't going to now. "Guy's squirrel bait," he muttered to me.

"Uh-huh," I breathed, wondering what that odd sound I was hearing was. Then I realized and thought, instant—sort of instant—re-

. . . . .

222

play. This wasn't the first time this week I had only half-heard sirens outside until I noticed the silence when one of the sirens stopped. The EMTs, and the emergency room, were going to get tired of me.

I must have been a little crazy myself by then, because I think I looked at Mark and said, "What do you think you're doing here?"

"Hi, Deb," Mark Brody said sheepishly, when it appeared that Beppo was through talking. "Sorry you got hurt." He hiccuped, breathing stale whiskey toward me. "Sorry—I—uh—you know. Sorry . . ."

"I wish you'd go away and sober up," I told him. (Harry looked slightly shocked at that. He considers that apologies should be accepted. I wasn't ready to accept that one quite yet.) "But first go see who that siren is," I said more gently.

The first siren was Captain Millner, who entered fast, walking past Jan and Luisa and the young man, with Brody now tailing behind him, and said, "Ralston, what is it going to take to get you to ask for backups? What in the hell is it going to take?"

"Next time I will," I mumbled.

"You better, because I swear I'm going to put you on suspension next time you get hurt because you didn't ask for backups. Congrats on clearing the case, anyway. What led you to the right answer?"

"Internet," Harry said succinctly, and I sort of nodded, as well as I could lying on the floor on my back.

"Well!" Captain Millner sounded highly pleased. "I knew all that computer stuff would be worth it! You can get back to that next week, since things have quieted some."

"Uh-huh," I said, and then sat straight up until Harry pushed me back down. "Are you nuts?" I demanded. "Work on the computer next week? You haven't seen my hands yet, have you?"

"It's obvious you're the worse for wear, but I haven't looked closely, why?"

Harry told him, just as the second siren cut off, and Captain Millner said, "It'll be something good you can work on while you're recuperating, then, so you don't have to use up all your sick time but you won't have to come in to the office to work."

"Tell me who that siren was," I mumbled, having decided I absolutely, positively, was not going to discuss computers anymore right now.

This time it was the EMTs. I was very glad to see them. But if the truth be told, I didn't see them long. Harry says I passed out, but I didn't, I just went to sleep. The last half hour I'd been working pretty hard, and I was really tired. I woke up—briefly—in the emergency room, and then I went back to sleep again, sleeping all night Saturday night and on into Sunday. I even slept through the time I should have been in church.

I think Harry was with me a lot of the time, though, because every time I started dreaming about Beppo Sarana's face and started trying to fight him off again, Harry started talking to me, and I went back to sleep again.

But now my hands are out of the bandages, and I'm afraid that means that now I've *got* to learn to use the computers.

. . . . .

Epilogue

I COULD THINK of just about any number of things I would rather do Tuesday night than go out to dinner at the Bird Cage, especially when I was still pretty doped up and so thickly swathed in bandages that I could eat only if someone—usually Harry—cut all my food into bite sizes for me. But how could I refuse an invitation from the management, especially when the management wanted to treat the whole family, including grown daughters, sons-in-laws, grandchildren, and everybody else? Our table also included Jan Pender; Arlo and Luisa, who left long enough to do each show and then came right back; one Terry Robinson, who'd been introduced to me as Luisa's fiancé and the son of the best woman snake-trainer in the business; and one Father Flanigan, the circus's Catholic chaplain. That was where Arlo had gone on Friday night, to find and spend the night with Father Flanigan, and it hadn't even crossed his mind that Luisa would worry.

And the knife wasn't his at all. It was his father's. Beppo had stolen it the night he set fire to Barthold Gluck's house, and the Sarasota Police Department still had it listed as stolen property.

Of all of us, I think Father Flanigan was the most shocked by the entire situation, because he was an old man who had known every one of the people involved with the tragedy. "Of course that sort of desire for revenge is massively evil," he said, "and—if he'd just talked to me, if he'd just talked to me—" He stopped for a moment, tears rolling down his face, and then said, "Pamela had been to confession just two

· · · · ·
225

days before she fell. I had told her I would work with her, to try to decide what the right thing was for her to do. She was truly repentant and I believe God, not I, had absolved her. As to the babies—I don't know. There are different opinions. I don't know. But whatever happened to their souls—'Vengeance is Mine,' says the Lord. Beppo—had no right—he let it drive him mad. I knew him before Pamela died, before Margaret died. The man you met—Mrs. Ralston, all I can tell you is, you never met Beppo Sarana." He was weeping openly now. "I'm sorry—I can't eat dinner—please excuse me—"

I didn't know what to say. Perhaps I hadn't ever met Beppo Sarana. But I had heard what Beppo said about women in the Resistance, and I couldn't help wondering as Father Flanigan stumbled toward the door whether he himself had ever met Beppo Sarana.

Jan Pender left with him, to take him back to the home of the priests with whom he was staying the night before flying out in the morning to rejoin the circus. Arlo left too, after the last show, and the only people remaining were my own family, Luisa, and Terry.

When he was first introduced Terry had started to shake my hand, looked startled, apologized, and shook hands with Harry instead. But he was looking at me, at the end of dinner, when he said, "I can never thank you enough for saving Luisa's life. And don't say you were just doing your job, because it's pretty obvious that you went a long way beyond doing your job. I thought—my mom's boa constrictor is pregnant now—I thought I'd send you one of the babies as soon as they're big enough."

Harry slightly choked and put his hand over his mouth, probably to keep himself from yelling in protest. Misunderstanding the objection, Terry said, "They're really good pets. And when it's bigger, maybe if you wanted to you could use it to scare somebody like Beppo. They ought to be ready to go in a couple of months. I'll bring it out next time I come to visit Luisa."

With two dogs, two cats, four children (even if three of them were grown and gone), two sons-in-law who didn't live with me, and a daughter-in-law-to-be who did, to say nothing of six grandchildren, I could hardly wait for the snake to arrive. At least Harry couldn't complain that it was my fault we got *this* pet. But he'd probably do it anyway.

At least, he would if we got the snake. But did I *really* want a snake?

I had a pet grass snake when I was sixteen, until my mother found out about it. It was beautiful, green on top and yellow beneath, with lovely ruby eyes. But—then I was sixteen. Now I was pushing fifty. If I had really wanted a snake I could have kept one of the snakes the cats kept bringing in last year, when they found a garter-snake nest.

I cleared my throat and said, "Terry, that's really generous of you, and I know snakes are good pets, but we just don't have an appropriate place to keep a boa constrictor, and I don't think the cats and dogs would like it. So—uh—why don't you, if you don't mind, keep the snake and just name it for me?"

Harry choked again. But then he grinned. "Yeah," he said, "that sounds like a good idea. Just name the snake for Deb. And try—if you can—just as an experiment, you understand—to see if you can keep it out of trouble."